MARGARET MCNELLIS

The Red Fletch

Silver Arrow Books

First published by Silver Arrow Books 2021

Library of Congress Control Number: 2021911400

Cover art designed with image(s) from © 1001Slide via Canva.com. Cover art designed with image(s) from ©FelixStrummer via Canva.com. Cover art designed with image(s) from ©David De Lossy via Canva.com. Cover art designed with image(s) from ©carlyartdaily via Canva.com.

First edition

ISBN: 978-1-7372579-1-2

This book was professionally typeset on Reedsy.
Find out more at reedsy.com

For my beloved parents, Rachel & James McNellis

Your unending support and love has always meant more than any words could ever convey.

Contents

1

Eavesdroppers

And much I thank thee of your comfort,
And of your courtesy,
And of your great kindness,
Under the green wood tree.
-Translated from *A Lytell Geste of Robyn Hode*

Betrayal.

Guy of Gisborne—*Sir* Guy of Gisborne now—had not visited Locksley in years. Not since Alys and Hob Fletcher were children. Now their cousin had returned on the eve of Hob and Robin of Locksley leaving for the Holy War to reclaim Jerusalem. Guy was there to talk to Alys's parents about her future. Hob and Alys craned their necks to listen under the sill, their foreheads aglow from the glimmering fire light in the midst of the room. She'd been booted from the kitchen to let the adults speak, and only the fact that her older brother had been sent from the house as well calmed

1

her indignation. Behind them stretched a carpet of green grasses leading up to acres of shorn sheaves of rye, streaked with highlights from the silver moon.

The cool grass pressed against her ankles in the waning glow of dusk. Alys plucked a few strands and strung them between her thumb and forefinger: one side raspy, the other smooth.

When she was a young girl, Da had snatched two verdant blades and positioned them between his hands before raising them to his lips. He'd blown and made a buzzing noise. Alys and Hob had rolled back, laughing. Da had called it playing the reeds. Though he had to tend the rye, manage the other villagers who farmed the Fletcher fields, and craft arrows, he always found time for Alys and Hob.

Now sixteen, Alys endured the sting of being barred from a conversation that concerned her fate. The rough side of the grass blade chafed her palm, and she grimaced.

"But without Alys," Da's voice, warm as the hearthstone on a winter's day, drifted outside, "we won't have enough hands for the fields, with Robert leaving on the morrow."

Her parents, grandda, and Guy sat around the table in the middle of the kitchen. Their four shadows danced on the mud-brick wall; they looked ghoulish, darting with the flutter of the white-orange flames.

"I can talk with the sheriff," Guy said. "Perhaps he will send her back to help with the harvest."

Alys mouthed: I don't want to leave, Hob. She knew Ma hated that she still called her brother that. When Alys was little though, she never called him Robert, and she didn't plan to start now.

Hob shook his head and pressed a calloused finger to his

mouth.

Alys rolled her eyes. She hadn't made a sound.

"It's not a job for Alys we need," Da said.

"She needs a husband," Ma said. Normally, her voice made Alys think of the stream that cut between their land and the rest of Locksley village: cool, crisp, and refreshing. Tonight, however, her words sounded clipped and harsh, like ice floes cracking as winter gave way to spring.

Neither Da nor Grandda argued in Alys's favor. Not this time.

"She'll have a better chance," Guy said with authority, "in the castle than in Locksley. My parents will not aid you if matters become difficult. My father would—" Guy's voice dipped to a murmur, and Alys was unable to hear the end of his sentence. He picked up again, "—if he learned I'd even come here. The castle is her best chance for a future. Serving Maid Marian will place her before worthy suitors."

Alys didn't want to live in Nottingham Town; it was filthy and noisy, and there was no way she'd be able to continue practicing archery, playing soldier, and running through the fields of Locksley. How could Guy do this to her? He was the one who had trained her to fire a bow. He showed her and Hob how to ride a horse.

The day after Guy's father had bought him his own pony, he'd ridden out to Locksley to visit. Guy called the pony Merlin, though Hob had suggested Barnaby. Merlin was brown with a white starburst on his face, and a white-gold mane and tail. When Alys asked if she could ride, Guy made a cradle with his hands, his fingers threaded together, and she'd put her foot in his palms to be hoisted onto the pony's bare back. Her heart had almost ceased at the thrill. Never had she been so tall! Guy showed her how to weave her hands into his mane and promised next time there'd be a saddle, but Alys preferred the pony's bare back. She had felt the soft, yet tickling, itching hair of the creature. Merlin's breaths expanded his rib cage between her knees. The pony wore a rope for a bridle, and Guy walked ahead, leading the animal with Alys atop it. Hob tagged along, awaiting his turn and trying to convince Alys to dismount. It hadn't taken many more visits before Alys rode on her own.

How could Guy try to rip her from freedom after he'd been the one to teach her what it was? How could he expect her to enclose herself in stone walls, courtly customs, and a maidservant's life?

"We're eternally grateful for you and your kindness, Sir Guy," Ma said.

"I'll come for Alys the day after tomorrow." A chair scraped against the wooden floor. The other chairs echoed Guy's.

Alys reached for her brother's hand and squeezed hard. She glanced around at the cleared rye fields that abutted her family's three-room farmhouse and drew in a slow, deep breath. The Locksley air smelled sweet, and Alys needed to trap the aroma of a sunbaked harvest forever.

A tug on her arm. Hob was on his feet. "Move away from the window," he hissed.

Alys stood and followed. They ran to the middle of the field where they wouldn't be overheard or have to meet Guy again that night.

I don't want to see Guy again, ever. Alys sat next to Hob and crisscrossed her legs, creating a valley with her skirt. She plucked a few fallen rye stalks and dropped them in. "Can I march with you tomorrow?"

4

Hob scoffed. "Alys, you're a decent shot, but I don't think Robin or the king would welcome me bringing my sister to war."

Alys gave Hob a playful shove. "I could follow the army to help cook and clean."

Hob scowled and rubbed his shoulder. "You're a dreadful cook. Wouldn't do to poison Robin."

"I am not a dreadful cook. I'm… a fair cook who has never poisoned anyone on purpose or by accident. And what would Ma say if she heard you refer to him as Robin instead of his lordship?"

"Robin says to call him Robin."

"That doesn't mean you should. He acts like your friend, and you follow him to take up arms. Do you… do you even believe in it? That you need to crush the infidel Turks?"

Hob picked at a broken stalk. "No. Do you?" He tossed the stalk in with the ones Alys had gathered. "But I don't want to be a peasant, either."

"I don't get to go to war, so it doesn't matter whether I believe in it. But why don't you want to be a farmer? Few rye stalks have ever stabbed a man."

Hob shook his head. "Hunger will kill a man. If I go to the Holy Land, to battle for God and country in Jerusalem, Alys, I can come back distinguished. Honored. You've seen me with a bow. You've watched me with a sword. A spear."

"Take care, brother. You sound prideful, and that's a sin." She shoved his shoulder again, lighter this time, and he rolled back onto the broken stalks, chuckling. "I loathe that you can leave for war and find your honor, and I must marry a man to get mine. And even then, mine would be mostly reliant on a husband's."

"We cannot play heroes together forever. Life isn't like that."

Alys looked back at the house. The door opened and Guy stepped out like he owned not merely the farmhouse, but the entire village. Soon he would. The new sheriff had already appointed Guy to run Locksley in Robin's absence. Alys watched him stride over to his gelding, ease the reins from a tree, and mount the horse. He was taller than the last time she'd seen him, but it'd been years. His shoulders were broader, too, and Alys wondered if she could still out-shoot him with a bow and arrow.

Guy is only trying to help. Alys pushed aside the thought, along with the knowledge that her cousin was a decent sort of man. At least if Hob had to go to the Holy Land, and Alys had to go to Nottingham Town, their parents and Grandda would be all right. Guy would look after them.

At least she hoped Guy would watch after her family. Trying to help or not, she didn't think he was doing a great job of looking after her, taking her away from home like this. But if both Alys's parents and Grandda wanted to send her away to the castle, Alys knew there was little she might do to protest.

Hob and Alys stretched out on their backs and stared at the stars as they peeked out.

I wonder if they'll look the same in the Holy Land. It would take Hob almost six months to get there. Alys looked over at her brother; he had the Fletcher nose: long, pointed, and too large for his head. His eyes were close together, like hers, and both of them had slim, long faces. When they were little, sometimes they would go with Grandda to the market in Town. People who didn't know them mistook Alys for a lad because she looked so much like Hob. Once, Ma had shorn her hair short because Alys kept getting it tangled and refused to let Ma comb out the knots—at first glimpse, even the villagers in Locksley confused her for her brother.

"Maybe I should disguise myself," Alys said.

"No," Hob said right away. "That's a worse plan than coming with me as you are. You'd be arrested. You know what falls upon girls who dress as youths."

"It'd be worth it."

"Why? At least if you're in Town, you can return for each harvest. Besides, it's war, not a game."

"You know I can shoot as well as—or better—than you." Alys turned and braced herself up on one elbow.

"And what happens if the line breaks? And the Saracens run at you brandishing swords? It's not enough, Alys. Besides, if the king's men discovered you, you'd be hanged… if you were lucky."

Alys dropped back onto the ground with a groan. "That's the worst law ever. Who cares what I wear?"

Hob sighed. "I don't. You know I'd let you do whatever you choose. But I'm not in charge."

They observed the skies in silence until the late summer night chilled their faces. When they were certain Guy had left, they rose and made their way back home. Alys kicked stubborn rye stalks, so they broke and buckled to the earth, like subjects bowing before their liege lord.

2

A Vow to Thee

Hastily I will prepare, said the knight,
Over the salty sea,
And see where Christ was quick and dead,
On the mount of Calvary.
-Translated from *A Lytell Geste of Robyn Hode*

Inside, Da and Grandda had already retired to bed;
Grandda snored in the adjacent chamber, and Hob
shuffled off to join them. The men bedded down in one
room, and Alys and Ma shared the room on the other side of
the kitchen. Ma was still cleaning the kitchen, which smelled
of pottage and sun-warmed herbs: rosemary, sage, and thyme.
She was a slim but strong woman. She pushed the rag over
the bench like she was trying to bore through the wood. Alys
was the image of her ma, only younger. Taking up another
tattered remnant to help wash, Alys dipped it in a pail of water
on the floor.

"I don't want to go to Town, Ma." No point in being timid as Guy was coming for her in two days' time.

"Alys, not tonight. Please." Ma scoured the kettle since Alys was tending to the table. She gathered scraps for the hogs at Robin's manor house. Robin always shared pork with his peasants, so they shared scraps when they were able to spare them.

"But Ma." Alys stood up straight, scrubbing abandoned. "You need me here."

"You should be someone's bride by now."

Alys wrinkled her nose.

"Why do you not wish to wed?"

"Why don't I desire a husband? A man to order me where to go, what to do, how to think?"

"It is not always like that. Look at your Da and me."

Alys started to clean again.

"It is a girl's best chance, a suitable marriage."

Alys scrubbed harder.

There must be some speck of dirt I haven't discovered yet.

"And Maid Marian cannot be bride to all the eligible suitors in Nottingham."

"That doesn't mean they will favor me instead, Ma. We aren't the only two women of marriageable age." Alys dropped the rag in the bucket, wrung it out, and pushed it over the board with greater force. She wondered how to explain to her ma that she'd never noticed a man except to wonder at his prowess with a bow or his seat on a horse as measured against herself.

"But you will be there—your life will be exciting, Alys. You should be in the castle. It is what is due to our family."

"Your family forgot who we were when you married Da."

9

Alys knew as soon as she heard those words in her own voice, she shouldn't have said it. Even in the disappearing light of the fading fire, Ma looked like someone had smacked her. Alys wanted to atone, but the words withered on her tongue, replaced by a sour taste.

Ma rinsed her rag and returned to cleaning the kettle. "Sir Guy hasn't neglected us. He's not yet married…"

"I am not marrying Guy." Guy, who wished to take Alys away from her family. From the farm. From Locksley. Guy, who would rather have a bride who preferred to be married. Who wanted to be a lady. Someone who would boss around the servants who kept house. Alys learned how to manage the house but she'd rather do anything else. No, not anything else—be a warrior, like Hob, fight for honor and truth and justice.

"If he proposes, you will. You can't afford to reject a man like Guy."

Alys chucked the rag into the wash bucket and tore out of the kitchen. She heard Ma call after her, but let her name roll off her back. That night, Alys wished they didn't share a room. She wished there was space around the hearth for the wool blanket and mass of hay that formed her bed.

Sleep was as unwelcome as the next dawn. Alys prayed to God to suspend time, to stop the war or send her instead, to stop Hob from leaving, to stop Guy from delivering her to the castle. Alys closed her eyes and knew God would answer none of her pleas.

* * *

The sun had no right to shine the day Alys said her farewell to

Hob. It had no right to glint off the point of his spear, or on the lighter strands of his hair. Or on the blades of the other men lined up to march with Robin south to Portsmouth and onto a ship bound for places Alys could only imagine. Coal-black clouds should have coated the sky. Better still if the heavens had opened, and torrents fell to the earth; storms might have prevented Hob's departure.

Although Hob was older than Alys, they had never perceived that difference. Alys wasn't sure if that meant Hob was too childish or she wasn't childish enough, but it'd never mattered. They'd found joy playing hide and seek on the farm or in the village, sitting with Da as he fashioned arrows, and recounting tales that dated all the way back to before William of Normandy claimed the throne.

Alys pulled Hob close and held fast. "Don't you dare perish or forget your way home."

He gave her a one-armed hug since he perched his spear on the opposite shoulder. Hob had already said farewell to their parents and Grandda, but they had to go to Nottingham Town today for the market. Hob lifted her with his free arm, and Alys could feel his smile against the side of her head. "I don't aim to." He set Alys back down on the ground.

The village green was full of peasants-turned-soldiers. They seemed out of place, surrounded by the kirk, smithy, bakehouse, and wisewoman's cottage. In the distance, sparrow song lilted on the breeze.

"And bring me something back."

"What would you have me bring?"

"Saracen arrows. Or a bow, if you can manage." They'd heard from Da that the arrow tips were different—narrower but still able to pierce armor—and that the bows were shorter

11

and lighter, but still powerful. Alys always thought her da's arrows were both graceful and powerful, but that didn't stem her curiosity to learn how archery worked elsewhere in the world.

"Any other demands?" Hob adjusted his spear, so the point caught the sunlight again.

Alys's smile dimmed. "Yes. One more. Don't kill anybody unless you have to."

He shuffled his weight from one foot to the other. "Robin said the Pope himself absolves us of slaughtering any Saracens in order to recover Jerusalem."

Alys tried not to imagine her brother on the battleground. She struggled not to see Saracen soldiers surrounding him with their curved sabers, slender-barbed arrows, and shortened bows. Hob pushing his spear through them. Or blood—anyone's blood—splattered on golden sand. Alys pictured herself in Hob's place and believed she'd always had more soldier in her than he did. "It should be me going. You know I'm a better shot than you."

"Alys…" Hob put distance between them.

Alys almost swooned under a swell of panic.

Don't leave. Not yet. She stepped closer to her brother and hugged him again. "Try to stay out of the worst of it then."

"I'm marching to war, not a fair." Hob sounded agitated. He almost never became impatient with her. "I don't doubt I'll have to fight." He tightened his grasp on the spear, and the point rotated out of the sun's rays.

Around them, other men said goodbye to kinfolk, friends, and animals. Their voices were like the flutter of rustling leaves. The sour aroma of yeast was in the air, wafting from the chimneys and windows of the alehouse and bakehouse.

"War is going to transform you, and I demand my brother back, not someone else."

"Everything changes, Alys."

"No, it doesn't. Our family has lived here for generations. We've farmed this land for generations. Were it not for the king, were it not for our lord's crusade for honor and prestige—"

"A minute ago, you declared you would rather go than me. And do not speak of Robin in that disparaging way. I'm proud to fight for our family, for Nottingham, for England, for... for Christendom." He sounded like he was struggling to recite a speech. Alys figured these were Robin's words, regurgitated like bile.

She sucked her teeth. "I would declare anything to keep you in England. Besides, you know I'm right. As for Robin..."

"Come on, you always admired him."

"Not anymore. Not after taking you away."

Hob rested a hand on her shoulder. "Would you rather I served another? At least he'll look out for us. He's my best chance of coming back home."

Alys didn't want to admit that Hob spoke true. Robin of Locksley was honorable and had always treated everyone in the village better than most lords treated their peasants. But he was still taking her brother away from all he knew and loved to travel thousands of miles and fight. And for what? "You could remain home. Farm the land."

"I can't leave with you angry at me for it."

"Fine, then I won't forgive you and you'll have to remain."

Hob dropped his chin and pressed his lips together. Alys knew it was no good; she'd never been able to hold a grudge against him for two days, let alone the months it would take for him to reach the Holy Land. The years, perhaps, to fight and win and return. Hob was correct; if he didn't answer Robin's call, he might have to fight for some other lord. Alys's breath shuddered.

"Wait here," she said, and turned away. Alys glanced over her shoulder and planted him to the earth with her gaze, like he might disappear at any moment. She ran to the head of the line, in the shadow of the kirk's bell tower. There were about fifty men standing by to become soldiers, to follow Robin out of Locksley, out of England, out of Europe. Right now, they milled around like trees in a wood, standing in random clumps. But soon they would stand shoulder to shoulder, and eventually they would brace against the onslaught of another army. When she spotted Robin, she bowed and caught her breath. "My lord."

"Alys Fletcher," Robin said, a smile warming his tone. "Hob told me you requested to join our ranks. I'd welcome you if I could. Unless you want to follow, cook, and clean for us?" Robin wasn't taller than most men, nor stronger than most, but his bearing made him stand out, somehow made him seem larger than all the others. Part of Alys wanted to cower, to show the deference she knew was due to him.

Instead, she straightened. "I request to go instead of my brother. To fight." Despite what she'd said to Hob the night before, she had no desire to play maid to a company of soldiers—she didn't even want to do so for Maid Marian. But she wasn't ready to give up on Hob.

He'd flay me if he knew what I just said. Alys eyed Robin. He always looked fit to pounce, but with a grin that might mask a joke or a trick. Like a fox. "We need him here."

"Your brother already made a commitment. I've made a

commitment. To the king. To bring fifty men from Locksley to the Holy Land."

Alys clenched her jaw. "Then you owe me a pledge, too." Robin didn't owe her anything. He could banish her from Locksley if he wished, or he could have her shut up in the bowels of Nottingham Castle. But Hob was worth the risk.

Robin crossed his arms. Some men around them oohed and snickered and hailed her as a firebrand.

"Promise you'll bring him back. Alive."

What a preposterous promise to demand of men marching to war. But Alys needed it, all the same. She trampled the truth down until it was so small that the thought seemed naught but a murky memory. "Hob isn't just another field hand." Alys took a deep breath. "My lord, he mended your hound's leg when that cart struck the poor creature. He fished the river with you. He has been as perfect a companion as he has been a subject." She followed each heavy breath in and out of her lungs while she waited for Robin to answer no. To call her impertinent. To banish her. To issue some unimagined punishment.

"We're headed into war," Robin said. "Such guarantees are not—"

Alys tightened her fists at her sides until her nails cut into the creases of her palms. "Promise me, my lord. Promise me that and I promise—I promise Maid Marian will wait for your return." Alys knew Robin loved Maid Marian because Guy had told her once that the pair had pretended to marry when they were young. Marian, a couple of years older than Alys, was no doubt under pressure from her guardian, the crown, to wed.

Alys knew offering this oath to Robin was a risk. That youthful romance might not extend into the practicality of adulthood. Maybe Robin was like her and had no wish to marry anyone. After all, he'd not yet asked for Maid Marian's hand. Maybe he was ruminating on an appropriate punishment for Alys's boldness.

Then the slightest flicker of his expression told Alys that she had him. She'd been right: Robin pined for Marian. Robin asked, "And how would you keep your word?"

"Sir Guy comes tomorrow to bring me to the castle to serve as her handmaiden. I could... I'm clever enough to see that either she rejects her other suitors while you're gone or that they reject her." Alys felt like Robin's heart was beating so loud and so hard that the pulse was tangible in the air, and as loud as the measured, heavy, grinding turn of the millstone. Could she stop Marian from marrying another? Alys was not certain. What else did she have that Robin would ever want? Da already supplied him with arrows, and the rye her family grew already fed the entire village. Alys owned nothing except her wits and her skill with a bow. If he would not lead her to the Holy Land as a warrior, she had no other currency with which to bargain.

God forgive me for making a promise I might be unable to keep.

For a moment, Robin scratched at his chin where a short beard outlined his jaw. It seemed like the others had all disappeared, and it was just Robin and her in this field, bartering for Hob's safety and Marian's hand. The bleating sheep and singing birds were muted. The bell in the tower was still. Even the river had stopped running behind the kirkyard and orchard. What was Robin's heart's desire worth to him?

He thrust his hand out so fast that Alys jumped a little, fearful he might strike her for her presumptions. She heard the laughter of the villagers-turned-soldiers around her; the world moved and sounded and smelled again. Robin wasn't trying to hit her; he was offering his agreement. Alys reached forward and shook. His grip was firm, but he didn't crush her fingers.

"You have my word, Alys Fletcher. I will do all in my power to see Hob home safe."

"And you have mine, my lord. I will do all in my power to unite you and Maid Marian upon your return."

Robin released her hand and turned back to the men.

Alys ran the length of the line to Hob and threw her arms around him. "Be careful."

Hob's face split into a smile. "Don't fret, Alys. I'll do my best to come home. I don't think this war will take long anyway, with King Richard the Lionheart leading the charge."

"It had better not."

They hugged again.

"What was that about, anyway?" he asked.

Alys shook her head. "I wanted to find out how long it would take for word to reach us. You better write to me, Hob Fletcher." Their Ma, having learned her letters, had taught them. In all of Locksley, aside from Robin and her ma, Hob and Alys were the only ones who had learned how to read and write, though the innkeeper knew his numbers.

"I could have told you that."

One last hug, then Alys stepped back to watch him leave. She kept her eyes fixed to the back of her brother's head until he mixed and melded with the others.

Alys would have stood under the morning sun until it warmed to midday and beyond if there weren't chores to do at home. She longed to see the men leave the village, march toward Sherwood and the road that wove between its trees.

Alys knew if she did that, she'd collapse in the nearby meadow and the whole day would go to her tears.

Her path home, past the mill, was slow and dogged, each step dragging in the dirt and over the bridge, and then through the rushes on the floor once she reached home. Through the window, Alys spotted the villagers who helped work their fields, their heads bobbing as they collected the remnants of the year's crop.

Standing before the fire that warmed the room and the belly of the kettle, Alys would have thought the cold in her stomach would have dissipated. But she couldn't shake the fear that if Hob returned to England, she wouldn't recognize him.

3

Change of Scenery

And when they came to Nottingham,
They walked in the street,
And with the proud sheriff, it was,
Soon again they [did] meet.
-Translated from *A Lytell Geste of Robyn Hode*

T he morning after Hob left, Guy came to retrieve Alys from her family's farm. She made no commotion about leaving this time, but packed her one spare dress and apron—wrapped around a fletched arrow—in a satchel, and met him in the kitchen. The air smelled of pottage, and it hooked into her like she was a fish in a barrel. There was no choice but to go with Guy, to keep her pledge to Robin, so he would uphold his vow to her.

"Go ahead and say your farewells; I shall wait outside." Guy avoided looking her in the eye. "There will be the chance to see your family each month if you please, when you have a day off from your duties."

Alys nodded. To see her family more often would fill her heart, but she did this for Hob. A promise to Robin kept should yield a promise from him held aloft as well. After Guy stepped out of the farmhouse, she could see his silhouette against the early sun through the open window. Guy patted the nose of one of two horses. Alys crossed the kitchen, closed the shudders, and hugged her grandda first. Grandda had once been a brawny fellow, but age and decades of work had twisted his back.

"Don't fret, Grandda, I will be here on occasion to help plant and reap."

For a minute, Alys wished she could shelter in her grandda's protective embrace forever. Ma may have shown her how to read and write, but every ounce of wit and sense she had came from Grandda. In this moment, she relived every evening by the hearth, listening to stories of his youth. Listening to how the world had changed, how the village had changed—and the ways it had remained the same over so many decades. A favorite of these tales was when he told her about his first wheelbarrow. Not because of the wheelbarrow itself. The story appealed to Alys because that had been a time of bountiful harvest that led to a village festival. "The wheelbarrow," he'd say, "overflowed with so much rye I could have lost a house in it."

"I don't worry about you, Alys." Grandda's voice was grizzled and gruff. "There's no doubt in my mind you'll manage." He released her.

Alys wanted nothing more than to crawl back into another hug. But she had to say goodbye to her parents, too—and Guy was waiting. She hugged Da next. Da was a copy of his own father, but his hugs had not yet softened with time. He had hair like thatch: what remained on his head was golden with streaks of brown and stick straight. Deep-set, discerning eyes were warmed by the crinkles at the corners when he grinned. Alys waited until he let go so she could draw a whole breath again. "Save some arrows for me to fletch."

Da chortled. "Alys, how many hours do you think there are in a day that you'll be able to help harvest and craft arrows? Will you tell your ma that you'll help her cook and clean, too?"

Alys smiled. "If I could, I would shoot the sun and pin it to the sky to give us many days in one."

But Alys didn't pledge to help with chores when she embraced Ma. She'd never liked them the way she'd enjoyed farming or crafting arrows. If asked, she would help, but she perceived her role as Maid Marian's handmaiden would be chores all day long. Was it unjust to crave something different on her one day with her kin each month?

"Maybe when you return, it will be with word of a suitor," Ma said.

Alys sighed. "I would not anticipate such tidings."

"I love you. I will always hope for you. Write to me, Alys. Through your letters, I wish to experience the castle."

With a smile, Alys pulled away and dragged her feet to the door. There, she turned. The light in the kitchen was gloomy and dusty. Alys knew that though she could return in a month, unlike Hob, she—and everything—would be different. Childhood had lived its days in this house and the neighboring fields, and now that was over. Her years of sporting and practicing archery with Hob and Guy were over. They were over before moving to the castle, but Alys didn't realize it until it was time to leave behind the place that had nurtured those fond recollections.

On a shaky sigh, Alys stepped out into the blinding light. "I'm ready, Guy." Ready as she'd ever be to leave behind her home. Ready as she'd ever be to leave behind Locksley.

Guy nodded and mounted his gelding. Alys mounted the mare; they steered the horses toward the road heading to Town.

"What's the castle like, Guy?"

"Tall," he said. "Cold in some places, warm in those rooms with a fire."

"Many people live and work there? You live there, right?"

"I did. I'll be dividing my days between the castle and Locksley now, while Robin is in Jerusalem."

"So you're my liege lord now?"

Not bad being a cousin of the lord.

Guy shook his head and snapped the reins. His horse nickered and trotted forward. Alys's horse followed. "The sheriff will be your liege now. But we'll see one another. I am at the castle most days. I'll look in on you." A curious smile—one Alys had not noticed before—stretched across his face. He wasn't teasing her. Alys couldn't guess what thoughts Guy entertained, but decided perhaps the sun was in his eyes.

"Thank you. I welcome your good will. Especially considering—well, you don't have to."

"I am my own man, Alys. My father's will no longer dictates my actions."

Alys smiled and laughed aloud. "They never did. You started visiting us since as far back as I can recall."

"Yes, well, I had to practice bossing someone around."

Alys spent the remainder of the ride to Town reliving her childhood once more, to commit it to memory, as though the castle might seize her earliest memories from her.

* * *

She'd never ridden through Town. People jumped out of their way, pulled children out of the street. Some dipped their heads in deference to Guy. He became aloof, his face like a statue, frozen in stoic gravity. Alys couldn't help but notice the poverty that plagued the townspeople. Children with no shoes. Beggars with palms open to the heavens. A one-legged man using the wall of a derelict building for support, daub crumbling between his fingers.

The closer they got to the castle, the more serious Guy became, the more Alys realized that even the memories of her youth didn't have a place here. This place was severe. This was where edicts were issued, where justice was carried out, and though she'd never met the sheriff, she thought he'd be like the castle itself: imposing and immovable.

They passed beneath a portcullis that reminded Alys of the teeth of some enormous beast, ready to snap down on those who tried to breach the gate without approval. After they dismounted, a squire received their horses. Alys tried to watch where he led them, but Guy told her not to dawdle. He guided her up the steps into the keep, the part of the castle where the wheels of authority turned. Alys was certain some invisible spirit had tightened a cinch around her breast, like she'd never be able to draw a deep breath in this place.

Torches in iron brackets along the walls replaced daylight. Between them alternated weapons, shields, and tapestries depicting battle. It felt like the castle might wage war. Alys wanted to rip one of those shields down and shelter under it. Her shoulders slouched as she followed Guy, eyes wide to take it all in. A pair of guards passed them, their chain-mail rattling like coins with each stride. They each gave Guy a nod, but ignored Alys; she spun to watch their retreat.

"Come on, Alys," Guy said. "We haven't all morning."

She scurried to catch up behind him. Guy led her through what seemed like a maze of corridors and up a vast set of stone steps to a pair of doors. Oak studded with iron. Guy raised his arm and pounded on the door with the meat of his fist. From beyond the doors, a deep voice bid them to enter.

Guy opened the doors and stepped through. Alys couldn't see around him.

"My lord." Guy bowed his head and shuffled to the side. "My cousin, Alys Fletcher."

The sheriff was tall, with a ring of hair around his skull, the top bald as a monk's pate—except he didn't wear the humble vestments of a monk. Ermine-trimmed leather draped him. His eyes were hard, and his lips formed a grim line as he pressed them together.

Beside her, Guy said, his voice a clenched-teeth whisper, "Curtsy."

Alys felt her body obey, but her back was rigid, which made her anything but graceful. "M—my lord. I thank you for this position."

The sheriff picked at his teeth with the tip of his tongue, then turned to spit a morsel onto the stone floor. Tall, thin windows, paned with flattened horn, stretched from knee to eye-height behind him. Though they weren't shuttered, the light seemed unable to penetrate the severity of the chamber. It scarce touched him. Most of the light came from the fires burning in the grates at either end of the room. The sheriff leaned back against an immense table and studied Alys, then Guy. "Mouse of a thing, isn't she?" He waved a hand in dismissal. "No matter. I'm certain she'll learn to carry a few buckets of water up for Marian each morning."

Alys straightened. "My lord, I am strong."

When Guy swung his head around to glare at her, the whites of his eyes showed. He shushed her.

The sheriff chuckled. "Spirited too, to speak out of turn." He pushed away from the table and strutted right up to Alys, within arm's reach. He smelled of leather and wine. To Guy, he said, "Robin of Locksley has been too lenient with his peasants, it seems." The sheriff turned back to Alys. "Disrespect me again, girl, and you'll spend the night in the stocks."

Alys felt dizzy. She bowed her head and closed her eyes, slid one hand into her satchel and clutched her spare gown wrapped around the arrow. She swallowed bile.

What would he do if he knew I held an arrow? Few may bear arms in the castle. Guy was permitted because he was the master at arms. "Yes, my lord."

"Good girl. Obedience to authority will carry you far."

When Alys looked up, he had returned to his table to sit behind it and examine some parchments spread on its surface. One of them was a map. Of England? It looked like England. Guy had drawn it in the dirt for her once. She yearned to creep closer, to spy what else was on that table. She'd never seen so many parchments in one place before. But Guy moved in front of her and herded her into the corridor.

Then they were hurrying through another maze of weapon-lined passages. Alys wanted to ask Guy if the sheriff was always so curt. She wanted to ask Guy not to be cold with the families of Locksley like he was with her here. But she followed in silence. This was not a place to ask questions. The sheriff had made that clear. It was a place to work and follow orders. Guy opened a door to the tower steps; they curled up and up. After climbing so many of them, her legs throbbed.

"Every morning, you will fill buckets at the well," he said to Alys. "Bring them to the kitchen, heat them, and carry them up for Maid Marian to wash. Then you shall do whatever she asks for the rest of the day. You will go where she goes. Ensure she has all she needs throughout each day. And if you are fortuitous, you may find a husband before long." He stopped at the top of the staircase and looked her over. "You are well past the age you should marry; but so too is Maid Marian." That smile—the odd one—appeared on his face once more. Guy knocked at the door where the tower steps stopped.

Maid Marian was everything the sheriff was not. Her voice, when she told them to enter, was like a perfect note struck on a lyre. When Guy opened the door, it was like Marian herself lit the room. The scent of lavender wrapped around Alys, and she felt the tension melt out of her shoulders and back.

Alys had seen Maid Marian once before, when they were both much smaller. She'd come to Locksley with the King on his progress. It was just after her parents had died. She was King Richard's ward. When Prince John took on that guardianship, Marian came to live in Nottingham Castle. Then the prince passed along her care to the sheriff.

This time, Alys curtsied on her own. "My lady."

Guy bowed his head. "Allow me to present your new handmaiden, Alys Fletcher."

Marian smiled. Her smile was beauty and gentleness, and Alys couldn't help but think it didn't belong in this castle, this prison of severity and somberness.

"You are Sir Guy's cousin, are you not?" Marian asked.

"Yes, my lady."

Marian smiled at Guy. "Then I know I am in excellent hands."

Guy offered that strange smile again.

So it has something to do with Maid Marian.

"Alys will help you with anything you require. She also has her letters," Guy said.

Alys detected a hint of pride—as though Guy said even though her da might be a peasant, he didn't mind the connection. She felt a glimmer of the past, and all the dread and fear evoked by meeting the sheriff ebbed away.

"I will leave you both to get acquainted." Guy bowed his head to Marian again and told Alys he'd return to show her where she would sleep. He took her meager belongings and said they would be there, waiting for her. Alys feared he might notice the arrow and that she'd be punished, but if he noticed, he said nothing of it.

She let out a relieved sigh.

Marian walked around Alys, examining her. "I have some old gowns you may wear. It would not do for you to attend feasts and festivals in tattered dresses. You may keep them for any scullery work though, if you wish."

"Thank you, my lady."

"After my morning ablutions, I dress. I shall need your help with my wimple." She stepped around to stand in front of Alys again. "In the afternoons, it is lyre practice, archery practice," Alys's ears pricked at the word archery, but she let Marian continue, "embroidery… on pleasant days I like to ride. Do you ride, Alys?"

Alys nodded. "Sir Guy taught me."

Marian smiled. "Most excellent. Where I go, so too shall you. The only exception is on Saturdays, when I attend confession and I understand one Sunday a month you are to visit your family."

Alys nodded.

"Good. Family is important. I will not pretend it is easy for you to leave them."

Alys looked up and met Marian's eyes, her own hazel to Marian's sapphire blue. "Thank you, my lady."

Marian held her gaze for a moment. "Come. The archery master awaits."

Down the spiraling tower steps they went. Where Marian seemed to float, Alys trudged, her tired legs like trees, unused to so many steps. Down was easier at least, but Alys couldn't quiet the thought that she'd have to climb these stairs at least twice a day.

Marian must have the strongest legs of anyone in this entire castle. The thought made her smile. Maybe the noble lady wasn't as delicate as she seemed.

4

Archery Lessons

Their bows bent and forth they went,
Shooting all in fear,
Toward the town of Nottingham,
Outlawes as they were.
-Translated from *A Lytell Geste of Robyn Hode*

Out in the courtyard, a man in a black tunic embroidered with silver thread waited, a bow and quiver in hand. Not far away stood a ringed target on a stand. Alys stood by while the archery master handed Marian the bow and instructed that she fire. He held the quiver of arrows while she nocked one, her elegant fingers smoothing the fletching feathers.

Her shot sailed over the target. The second one passed beneath it. The third didn't come close.

"Well done, my lady!" the archery master said when the quiver was exhausted. Arrows lay on the flagstones like discarded chicken bones after a feast.

Alys saw nothing that was well done. Marian's form was sloppy. She closed one eye. When she drew, her elbow shook. She held her breath when she loosed. But the archery master filled the quiver again and echoed the exercise—and his praise. When his smile didn't reach his eyes, Alys decided he had tried to teach Marian, and she continued to miss the target.

He gave up. He must get paid to pretend to instruct her, the same as he would get paid to actually teach her. Did a noble maiden need to fire a bow? Alys did not think Marian hunted nor would she ever be in a battle. But archery was a sport for all, and Alys thought Marian should at least be able to hit the target.

It bothered Alys that the archery master praised Marian for her lack of skills. She opened her mouth to speak up, but closed it again, summoning the sheriff's threat of the stocks for voicing an opinion out-of-turn. The pillory and stocks stood across the courtyard, squared off like they were braced to confront her.

It wasn't until she and Marian were alone again—back in the tower, Marian seated with her needlepoint, that Alys felt it was safe to speak. Marian was too mild to threaten her with the stocks. She lacked the sheriff's hostility. First, Alys took a deep breath. The room smelled of rose oil, but it wasn't overwhelming. "My lady," she said, "Did my cousin tell you how fond I am of archery?"

Marian nodded. "Yes. I thought you would enjoy watching my lessons."

"How long have you been practicing, my lady?"

"Oh, I began studying with the archery master a few months ago. The sheriff thinks it will give me something to discuss with potential suitors."

"I... see. Do you often miss the target, my lady?"

"Well," Marian drew her embroidery needle through the fabric to complete a yellow blossom, "the sheriff doesn't think it that important I hit the mark."

"But would you like to?" No *my lady*. No waiting to be invited to speak.

Marian looked stunned, but no threat of discipline followed. "I—well, yes."

"Let me instruct you, my lady. Sir Guy taught me."

Marian smiled, but then shook her head, returning her attention to her embroidery. "But what would the archery master think? No... the sheriff would learn of such insolence. He would judge me ungrateful."

"Do you enjoy embroidery, my lady?"

"I do not dislike it."

"But do you enjoy it? You could still meet with the archery master. I will tutor you here."

"We have no target. No bow. No arrows."

"I have an arrow. My da made it. I took it to remind me of home. If you can get a bow... we can use a pillow for a target."

Marian pressed her lips together. Alys didn't realize she was holding her breath at first, not until Marian answered with a nod.

"I will get us a bow," she said. "But, Alys—not a word to anybody. I do not believe the sheriff would like it."

Alys smiled her first genuine smile since setting foot in this place. "I won't tell a soul."

* * *

The next eleven months were an endless cycle of helping

Marian bathe, dress and shoot arrows, accompanying the lady on a regular ride and to chapel, and visiting Alys's family on her monthly day off. Aside from returning home, Alys most enjoyed watching Marian improve in archery.

Every Saturday morning, they rode out and practiced at the boundary of Sherwood Forest. So long as they came back for Marian's three o'clock confession, no one asked questions. No one stopped Marian from going where she pleased. During the week, they practiced in her chambers. The archery master's praise had remained steady. Alys wondered if he even watched Marian shoot or if his head was in the clouds. So tremendous had been her transformation with the art of the bow.

They spent each meal in the great hall where three tables were arranged in a u-shape. The head table was on a dais, and Marian sat at one end. Alys had a stool beside her, but there wasn't space on the dais, so the table almost came up to her chin.

Alys slid onto her assigned stool beside Marian one afternoon and poured herself some wine. She leaned close and whispered, "You don't want to wed Sir Percival. He may strike a fine figure, but rumor is that he excused himself from the Holy War by feigning injury and that he is wicked. Even his barn cats fear him." She observed as Marian's smile flattened. Percival, a visiting knight from York, perched on a bench at the other side of the hall. He lifted his goblet toward Marian. For all Alys knew, he could be the kindest knight in Christendom, but she had a promise to keep.

Alys knew that while Marian seemed to care for Robin because of how often she spoke of him, her patience was waning. Marian was almost twenty, and Alys knew the rising tide of judgment against her, because Alys heard it every time she visited home. Ma would say Alys should be wed by now. She would say Alys should have her own children. Even Da had started to agree, much to Alys's consternation, for he'd always been on her side when she stated she just wished to farm and make arrows all day. Grandda didn't argue for either side.

Marian lifted her own goblet to her lips, then said, "Thank you, Alys. Where would I be without you?"

Alys grinned. "Married to a monster who snores, sweats through his tunic, and has a potbelly."

Marian looked scandalized, but her blue eyes flashed with a secret smile. "I admire your freedom to speak whatever is on your mind."

"I am but your fool. And I admire your freedom to choose a suitor. I think my Ma would sell me if she could at this point." Alys folded her hands in her lap, though she squirmed in her seat.

"Very well, Alys, I should like to practice my archery."

A grin stretched across Alys's face and she stood, waited for Marian to do the same, and accompanied her from the hall. In their wake, Alys heard dozens of chair legs scraping against stone as all the men stood out of courtesy. She knew that tribute was for Marian, not for her. But to Alys, all that mattered was entering the refuge of Marian's tower, where she didn't have to bother with keeping eager suitors at bay, where she didn't have to worry about encountering the sheriff, where she didn't have to fret about someone catching her training Marian in archery. The best way to protect her agreement to Robin was to keep Marian away from potential suitors.

The pair of them ran giggling like children up to the tower. There, Marian retrieved the bow and arrow from under her

33

bed. She'd secured the bow by claiming she wished to practice her form on own—and what mischief would arise from a woman with a bow but no arrow? The arrow was, after daily practice for almost a year, looking a little worn out.

"Do you suppose next time you go home," Marian asked as she passed her fingertips over the frayed fletching, "you might procure a new arrow?"

"I can try," Alys said. "But the last few times I've gone home, the guards checked me at the gate." Alys chewed her lip for a moment. "I'll try to sneak one back in my boot. Maybe I can get the pieces into my boots and fletch the arrow here." Though, she didn't have the tar to bind the gut string to the arrow shaft. Perhaps if she tied it tight enough, the point and the fletching would stay on. If they could find pitch at the castle, that would be best.

With a plan in place, they whiled away the rest of the afternoon, practicing shooting the arrow they had into one of Marian's pillows. Whenever Alys demonstrated, the tip of the arrow would thud into the headboard.

"Lucky then," Alys said, "that I'm the one who tidies your chambers. If anyone else came up here, they'd wonder about all those holes." She reclaimed the arrow from the wood and offered it fletching-first to Marian. "Now, don't rush this next shot. Remember to draw it to your jaw, hold it, let your breath out, and for God's sake keep both your eyes open."

"You should not blaspheme, Alys," Marian said, her tone gentle as ever.

"Sorry." Alys crossed herself. "For St. George's sake—"

Marian perched one hand upon her hip.

"What? St. George isn't God." Alys sighed. "Just don't close your eyes, my lady."

Marian laughed. Then she sobered and did as Alys instructed and, for the first time in all the months of private practice, she shot the arrow through the down pillow. Like Alys's, it thudded into the headboard. Alys smiled so much her face hurt, and she cheered and applauded.

A knock sounded at the door. Alys froze. She snatched the bow from Marian and stashed it under the bed, then struggled to fetch the arrow while Marian answered the door. Alys yanked on the arrow and almost tumbled off the edge of the mattress—but the arrow remained burrowed in the wood. Wide-eyed, she spun toward Marian and shook her head. Alys tried to arrange the pillows to cover the arrow and stationed herself in front of the bed.

Marian opened the door. Guy stood on the threshold, eyebrows raised.

"Why isn't Alys answering your door for you?" Before Marian could respond, Guy waved off his own query. "No matter. How do you fare today, my lady?"

Marian replied, "Well, thank you, Sir Guy. To what do we owe this pleasure?"

"I'm here to speak to Alys. About her family."

Alys stepped forward, her face ashen. "Who's hurt?"

"No one is injured or ill," Guy said, the words rushed to allay her worst fears. "We best speak in private."

Alys started toward the door, but curtsied first to Marian. She saw Guy's gaze dart to the arrow buried in the headboard. He said nothing. She followed him down the winding steps of the tower to her own chamber, which was small enough to fit several times over in Marian's.

Alys's room had no windows. She suspected it was once a storage cupboard. It had a small bed—but an actual bed, off the ground—and a chest. Alys didn't mind that it was dark or cold because she'd never had her own quarters before coming to the castle.

Guy followed. He grabbed the stub of a candle off the chest and reached out of the room to light it on a bracketed torch. Then he returned and closed the door. "It's about the farm."

"Were the crops ruined?" It'd been a dry year. Whenever Alys was home, she'd spent half the day hauling water from the river to irrigate the fields.

"The last storm... there was a fire. Half the field is lost."

Alys dropped onto the side of her bed. "What will the village do? Everyone relies on that rye."

"That's not all. Because of that... your da came to me to say he wouldn't be able to pay his taxes."

Alys felt like some demon had hollowed out her chest. Like someone had carved her heart out. No money for taxes meant imprisonment or eviction. She clutched her chest.

"I cannot cover it; the sheriff would grow suspicious. Your family owes back taxes. He always paid enough to keep the farm, but... Alys, I've done what I could to keep him free of the gaol. But your family will lose the farm."

Alys wiped her eyes. "I have to see them."

"You're not cleared to leave the castle for another fortnight."

She stood and walked right up to him. Alys put her finger in his chest. "This is because of you. You took me away from the farm. If I'd been there, I could have helped save more of the crop."

"Alys, I—the opportunity you have here—It isn't my fault, you know, there was a storm. I did not conjure the lightning."

"You're going to make this right."

"I've done all I can. The sheriff will not arrest your father.

I've even found them a home here in Nottingham Town. Your father can keep your family from starvation with his arrows."

Alys felt a swell of relief before her anger boiled over again.

Why is it all right for Guy to place my family elsewhere but not to supply the coin they need to remain in Locksley? "You took me from my family, Guy. You owe me. I want to see them, and I want to see them today." There was an edge in her voice that was never there, least of all when she spoke to someone of Sir Guy's status.

"I can talk to the sheriff but can't make any promises."

After Guy left, Alys didn't return to Marian right away. She sat on her bed and stared at the candle until it sputtered out, leaving the room in darkness except for the impression of the flame on the inside of Alys's eyelids. Hob was gone, in the Holy Land, fighting some unknown foe for the king and the pope. Now her family's farm and home were gone, too. Or would be soon. What else would this war take from her?

5

Cost of Living

Full fast came to the high sheriff,
The country up to rout,
And they beset the knight's castle,
The walls all about.
-Translated from *A Lytell Geste of Robyn Hode*

For the following two days, Alys performed her tasks in a haze. By sundown each day, she held a faint vision of filling Marian's basin. Helping her dress. Dining with her. Shooting their one arrow in secret into the headboard—though Alys did not know how Marian had wrested it from the wood. She didn't ask, either. The only memories she seemed able to live in were the ones when she saw Guy and pestered him about obtaining her permit to visit home. Most of the time, Guy avoided her or excused himself before she could ask if he'd secured her passage out of the castle. Not even Marian's polite questions about what had happened could coax Alys out of her resentment, sorrow, and reticence.

On the third morning after learning about the loss of the farm, Guy caught her on her way up to Marian's chambers, a pail of steaming water in each hand. "Let me help with that," he said.

Alys narrowed her eyes. "Now you want to be helpful? As though you expect it will make me forgive you for not bringing me home? Or do you need a reason to meet with Maid Marian? She won't wed you, you know."

Guy backed into the wall like Alys had shoved him. His eyes grew round and then became cold and hard. He tore a bucket out of her hand, splashing some of the water. "And here I've come to invite you to accompany me to Locksley this afternoon." Guy stomped up the steps.

"Guy! Wait," Alys called after him. When he didn't respond, she tried again. "Sir Guy!"

He stopped, but his shoulders were stiff and almost up to his ears.

Alys needed Guy's kindness, and besides that—they'd never quarreled. "I'm sorry. I shouldn't have said that. I want to visit Locksley with you. Thank you."

Guy didn't look at her, but after a moment's hesitation he said, "You're welcome," and then he proceeded up the steps, Alys in tow.

She accepted the bucket at the door and agreed to find Guy in the courtyard after the midday meal. It would mean skipping archery practice with Marian, but she thought Marian would understand. Guy left and Alys filled Marian's basin, helped her dress, and told her about going to Locksley while she fixed Marian's wimple.

"How much coin does your family owe the sheriff in taxes?"

Marian asked.

"I don't know."

"I do not have much money. Most of what my parents left me is maintained by the prince and sheriff, but I have a few shillings…"

Alys's stomach churned. She didn't think her da would want Maid Marian to pay his taxes. She would be someone else he owed. "Thank you, my lady, but please keep your coin. I'm sure if it was just a few shillings, Sir Guy would have taken care of it." Alys had to believe that Guy cared enough for her ma, for her and Hob, that he would help her family keep the farm if he could.

"Very well. The offer stands should your family decide it would help."

* * *

After the midday meal and another round of warning Marian away from potential suitors, Alys met Guy in the courtyard. He held out a knife for her.

"What's this for?"

"There have been some reports of banditry. You don't look like you have any wealth on you, but just in case."

The knife was heavier than Alys thought it'd be. Leather and gold filigree wrapped around the hilt. On the handle was a blue sapphire. If Guy had sold this, he could have helped her family with the taxes, she was certain. "I don't know how to wield this."

"You hold the handle and push the sharp part into anyone who tries to hurt you."

Alys sighed. "I know that much."

Guy laughed. "Sometimes just showing that you're armed can be enough. I don't intend on burying my cousin this week, so don't fret over it too much. You could always throw it. You have a trained eye."

Alys smiled and together they mounted horses—Guy on his black gelding and Alys on a chestnut bay—and walked through the gate. She watched the portcullis lower to the ground after they passed. No one checked Guy. No one checked her when she was with him. "I should get you to escort me to Locksley each month... or I guess to Town now that my family won't be in Locksley anymore. I'd save time getting in and out of the castle."

"Oh, the checkpoint? Why does it take so long?"

"Because the guards don't read well. Some of us need a pass to come and go from the castle."

Guy's neck turned red. "I can talk to the sheriff about that. I don't think you're likely to smuggle any weapons out to the peasantry. Though that arrow in Maid Marian's room..."

"Don't tell anyone. I've been teaching her."

"She needs a husband, Alys, not a bow and arrow. Same as you."

Alys pulled the reins up short. "Don't. I get that plenty from my parents."

Guy turned. "How do you expect to survive in the world? Will you be a handmaiden forever?"

"If I must." Alys waved off the conversation and started forward again. The sooner they were away from the castle and Town, the better. Though she'd only been to the farm a couple of weeks ago, Alys ached for that place. For the smell of strewing herbs on the kitchen floor. Root vegetables stewing in the kettle. The rye fields warmed by the sun. "How much of the field was destroyed?"

"You'll... see. Soon enough and for yourself." Guy stopped in the middle of the high street and faced her. "Listen, Alys... about today. The sheriff will serve the eviction this afternoon."

"What?" Her heart quickened. It jumped into her throat. "Why didn't we go sooner to Locksley?"

"He declined my request for you to go at all until now."

"Can't he delay the eviction? Tell the bailiff to wait?"

"Does the sheriff strike you as the type of man to delay?"

Alys made no reply, save to drive her heels in a little harder than necessary. The mare gave a startled whinny and bolted forward, and people leapt out of her path. Alys rode hard the rest of the way to Locksley without another word.

* * *

Guy seemed fine with her silence. They did not encounter any bandits either, and the tension in her shoulders and arms eased. She had no desire to use the knife he'd insisted she hold. Maybe some bandits saw them, saw they carried weapons, and decided not to rob them. Either way, Alys was glad to reach Locksley without a fight.

At least, she was glad until she saw the damage. Half the crop—gone. Burned. Charred. Remnants of rye stalk and banks of ash covered the soil. Alys stood before what was once a field full of golden grass and let the knife slip from her hand. It hit the ground, and she had the vague sense of Guy dismounting and stooping to collect it. He disappeared to the fog of her periphery as her parents and Grandda poured out of the cottage.

"Alys," Ma said, "what—how are you here today?"

Guy answered. "I thought Alys should see the farm one more time before... you know."

Alys slumped from the saddle and felt her parents and Grandda wrap their arms around her, and she leaned into their embrace, saying how sorry she was again and again. If she'd only been here, if Hob had only been here. She cursed Robin for taking Hob away, and she cursed herself for allowing it. For striking a bargain with Robin that made it all right to lead Hob so far from home.

A few moments later, alone in her family's farmhouse—Guy did not follow inside, even though he was kin—Ma showed her a letter from Hob.

Dear Ma, Da, Grandda, and Alys,

This letter will not reach you for almost half a year. It might be harvest time when you read these words. I am alive and well. Through my service to our king, I serve the Lord. I have had the honor of meeting King Richard four times now. Once he has even invited me to dine with him, Lord Robin, and several other noblemen and high-ranking soldiers. He said it was permissible because of my actions on the field and because I have some noble blood in me.

When first we arrived, the Holy Land seemed strange to me. The language, the food, even the sight of the desert—all were beyond imagination. I miss you all, and the farm, and long to say more than can fit in a letter.

Perhaps after we reclaim Jerusalem, I will return and tell you all of my tales of this crusade.

Yours ever in duty and love,
Robert Fletcher

Alys read over the letter, grateful for all the lessons Ma had given her and Hob in their youth. All that time poring over their Ma's Book of Hours paid off. The warmth of relief, like a hug or a bowl of pottage in the depths of winter, washed away in the chilling tide of the impending eviction. Would Hob's next letter find them in Town? Would he one day return to Locksley to find the fields fallow or another family under this roof? Alys clutched the parchment and wept.

She felt Ma's arms wrap around her, soft and warm. "Will you tell him what has happened when you write him back?" Alys asked her ma.

"No," Da said. "We would rather he think the farm flourishing. Something to return to."

Alys nodded and wiped her eyes, though more tears assailed them, an unrelenting army of anguish. But avoiding upset to Hob made sense. She imagined she was in her brother's boots, fighting a battle, her mind thousands of miles away from Nottinghamshire, with the family forced to abandon the farm they'd lived on for generations. "Can I add a line or two to the reply?"

Ma looked from Da to Grandda and back again. "We—we already sent it."

"Without my response?" Alys felt hollow, like her family had left her for dead and carrion birds had eaten out her heart. "Hob will think I have abandoned hope for him."

"No," Grandda said. "Your Ma wrote to say you were at the castle and we were sure you missed him."

"But—" Alys said.

"We thought," Da said, "you would not visit for another two weeks, and the courier was ready."

Alys stifled her rage. How could she argue against that? It

wasn't as though there were regular couriers between Locksley and Jerusalem. Or even the continent, where a letter might travel on from there. Parchment was expensive enough—it wasn't as though they could afford to hire a courier of their own, especially with the taxes owed on the farm.

Curse Robin for taking Hob so very far away. Alys blew out a slow breath. "Very well. But if he writes again, tell him for me: He best return in one piece."

Someone pounded on the door. Expecting Guy, Alys opened it, only to find the sheriff. Her breath caught, and she wanted nothing more than to scurry and hide, even though he'd given his permission for her to leave the castle and see her home. Her next instinct was to slam the door in his face, but she knew that would anger him and do nothing to delay the eviction. So she stood and stared. Behind the sheriff were the bailiff, Guy, a handful of castle guards, and two of Guy's servants.

Her parents and Grandda gathered around her while the sheriff unfurled a scroll of parchment and read, his voice monotone.

"By the order of the sheriff of Nottingham, this property is hereby seized until such time that you remit taxes in arrears and current to the shire in the amount of one pound silver."

Alys balked. Her numbers were never as good as her letters, but that sounded like years' worth of taxes. How was her family ever going to earn that back by making arrows? No wonder Guy couldn't do anything to help—to do so would contradict the sheriff. Everyone would wonder how the Fletcher family came up with such a sum. Marian didn't have a spare pound of silver or even half. Alys wondered how the farm could be in such trouble for so long.

"That's four times what we owe!" Grandda said.

"Times of war," the sheriff said. "The king requires more from each shire."

"How will we repay such a debt?" Da said.

The sheriff rolled the scroll up. "I suggest you gather your belongings. Sir Guy informed me he has found adequate lodging for you in Town. If you hurry, you can make the walk before sundown." The sheriff turned toward Guy, dropped the scroll in his hands, and said, "Deal with this." Then he mounted his horse and rode away, his guards in tow.

"Guy," Alys whispered, "how can we owe this much?"

"It's as the sheriff said." He sighed. "I have a cart ready for your family's belongings, and they can borrow a draught horse to pull it."

"Thank you, Sir Guy," Ma said. "You have always shown us kindness and generosity."

Guy nodded and handed the scroll to Da. "My men will see that you've what you need to settle in your new home. I best escort Alys back to the castle now. You can bring the cart and horse back on the morrow."

"I don't want to go," Alys said. "I need to help my family."

"There isn't time, Alys. The sheriff wants you back for the evening meal so you can tend to Maid Marian."

Alys wondered what would happen if she refused. But she realized that might only cause Guy trouble. Or her family. The sheriff could have taken her da or grandda to gaol. With a shuddering breath, she turned to bid them farewell. "I will come and see you as soon as I can. And I will keep sending any coin I earn."

Her family embraced her. Alys tried not to look back as she and Guy mounted the horses and trotted out of Locksley but she couldn't help it. Hot tears streaked down her cheeks. Alys thanked Guy in her thoughts for not commanding her not to cry. It would have been worse if he'd tried to cheer her up. Maybe he didn't know she wept; he just continued on.

Soon, Nottingham Town and the castle came into view again, only to grow larger and larger on the horizon. More than ever, Alys felt the place was a prison, even with Marian's friendship and Guy's care. They were her friendly wardens.

That evening, Alys sat beside Marian in silence, save for when she asked for a cup bearer to pour her more mead. She had not overindulged before, but she preferred her head to be fuzzy. Alys needed to forget the sting of the sheriff's words and of being unable to respond to Hob's letter with the rest of her family. If she dove into her cup's depths, perhaps her memories would pull her back into her childhood, when she played in the rye grass with her brother under a midsummer sun.

6

Suitors

Gramercy, lord, then said Robin,
And set him on his knee;
He took his leave full courteously,
To green wood then went he.
-Translated from *A Lytell Geste of Robyn Hode*

T hree months after her family lost their farm, Alys scanned the hall at Nottingham Castle. Enough food to feed all of Locksley for an entire winter was heaped in silver bowls upon the tables. On each side of the long tables, the benches were crowded with nobles and merchants and those wishing for the sheriff's ear. He relaxed in the middle of the dais, surrounded by his favorites, including Guy.

Alys cradled her goblet, but did not sample the burgundy within. She knew it would taste sour, even though it smelled of fresh fruit. None of the food here had seemed the same since the sheriff forced her family to leave Locksley. A shiver skipped down her spine. Not even the fires and tapestries drove out the chill.

"What do you think of him?" Marian's melodic voice cracked through Alys's focus on the cold. She leaned close so they could confer without being overheard, though the lyre and flute players, and voices, would have drowned out all but shouting.

"Hm?"

"Sir Edward." Marian's gaze flickered toward the man who sat halfway down at one of the long tables, conversing with a man next to him, twisted away from them. "He is here to seek my hand."

Alys wasn't in the mood for gossip, legitimate or otherwise. Besides, she didn't recall which one Sir Edward was. Had he lost his first wife to her childbed, or was he the one who had slaughtered innocents during some campaign or another? Perhaps he was the knight unhorsing his peers at tournament.

It doesn't matter which one he is. "What of Robin?"

"What?"

"Robin of Locksley. Did you not agree to be his wife?"

Marian turned her own goblet in her hand. The cup grated against the wooden table.

Alys wanted to smack Marian's cup onto the floor. Stain the linens and Marian's dress with the red wine. Stain this entire world. Ruin it for everyone here. Alys clenched her jaw.

"He is at war. Who knows if he will return? I will be twenty in two months, Alys."

"You gave him your word. Yet you give these other men an audience. Don't you have any faith that he will return? You must have foreseen you would have to wait a long time. The Holy Land is two thousand miles away."

Marian drank from her goblet. "You have been acting

strange of late, Alys. Why do we not shoot some arrows?"

"No thank you, my lady." She downed the contents of her own goblet, clutching the stem until her knuckles whitened.

"I can command you."

Alys turned toward Marian, meeting her gaze for perhaps the first time in months. "You could, my lady. And I would obey, but for my wages, not out of friendship. Marry—or do not. But you should wait for Robin. You gave him your word."

Marian stood. Her eyes hardened. "I did not. He never formally proposed. Our parents had wished we would someday wed, but…" She shook her head and stormed out of the hall.

Alys wasn't certain if Marian meant for her to follow. She held her goblet aloft, and the cupbearer filled it to the brim with more wine. Alys drank. She drank until the hall and its occupants—the sheriff, Guy, Sir Edward, soldiers, lords, lyre, flute, and drum players, as well as servants—were all blurs of movement, their conversations hovering at the edge of her awareness. Only when the sensation in her lips vanished did Alys abandon her goblet—and the hall. She went to her room, her windowless stone box with a bed, a chest, and the stub of a candle. A remnant of one of Marian's candles.

Alys plopped onto the edge of her bed, the flicker of the flame in her peripheral vision. She tried to conjure an image of Hob. Would he look different now? Over a year had passed. Would he wear a full beard? Would he look just like their da, but without the wrinkles or silver hair? Or perhaps Hob's face was lined from the heat of the desert or the heat of battle. Was he fighting right now? Was Robin with him? Did Robin sense that she'd been unable to keep her promise in ensuring Marian's focus did not wane? If Robin knew, would he withdraw his promise to Alys? Was Hob safe? When would he return? Alys wondered what it would be like when Hob came back. She wept in the near darkness of her cloistered cell, alone with the naked stones.

* * *

The next day dawned gray. Alys thought back to the morning Hob left almost fifteen months ago, the way the sun shone even though she'd wished for a drenching rain. While she tended to her duties, she and Marian spoke only when necessary. Was the water warm enough? Which dress did her lady want to wear? Was she pleased with this wimple or that?

Sir Edward called on Marian while she practiced her embroidery. He brought her a bouquet. He asked to court her. Marian agreed with a shy smile that sparkled in her eyes and hinted of something more beyond courtship. Alys knew she had to prevent Marian from marrying him or anyone else but Robin, but her tongue refused to conjure any wicked rumors.

At the midday meal, Alys approached Guy—who had ignored her most days since her family's expulsion from Locksley. "Sir Guy, we need to speak," she said over his shoulder.

Guy had been laughing, playing dice with some guard. "Alys, I am busy."

"Later then."

Guy nodded. Alys watched the dice game for a moment until Guy asked her what else she needed. With a shake of her head, Alys returned to sit beside Marian.

The day passed in a haze for Alys. Marian took out the bow and suggested they fire the arrow a few times, but Alys refused. She'd been unable to get a new arrow, and theirs was much worse for the wear: the tip was blunted, the shaft splintered, and the fletching feathers, while still intact, looked like they'd been shredded by a cat.

Once Alys completed her chores for the day, she waited outside her door for Guy. Alys heard him before she saw him—the sound of his spurs ringing on the flagstone. She straightened and opened her door. "In here, Guy." Calling her cousin *sir* felt strange when it wasn't necessitated by the presence of others. She'd known him before he even became a squire. Once inside her room, she shut the door and said, "Marian feels the pressure to marry."

"I know," Guy said. "The sheriff told her that her keep is a burden he doesn't plan to pay for past her twentieth birthday."

"So why don't you ask for her hand?" If Guy became one of Marian's suitors, perhaps competition between him and Sir Edward would stall Marian deciding on either of them. Then Alys would have more time to convince Marian that Robin was the correct choice.

Guy turned away. "You can tell? That I care for Marian, I mean?" He ran his hands through his hair. "Alys, don't misinterpret this. I like your family. I do what I can for them, for you. But Maid Marian deserves better than a connection with peasants. She is the King's cousin."

Alys felt like he'd punched her in the ribs. She couldn't get air. She grabbed for the wall, her fingertips scraping on the edge of a stone. "But she is not a princess herself. You would let her marry Sir Edward?"

"You lack an understanding of nobility, Alys. Your mother severed those roots when she married your father, I am afraid, and you were not raised to understand the importance of purity in a royal line. Besides, life isn't always about what we want. You must know this by now—what happened to your family—and once Marian marries, you will need to find a husband."

Alys pushed aside the insult of Guy's remarks about her own family's roots. His mention of a husband for herself stopped Alys cold. "No."

"Alys. Sir Edward will provide his wife with a servant. I'd hoped you might have found someone in the time you've been here."

"I don't want to marry."

Guy turned. "Too bad, Alys. Your parents cannot take care of you forever. I cannot take care of you forever. Worry not about who your lady marries and start looking for yourself." Guy brushed past her and left the room, closing the door between them. The ring of his spurs quieted as he marched down the corridor.

Alys collapsed to her knees. If only Robin had let her go to the Holy Land. She could have been with her brother, could have helped protect him, could have fought for the king—even if she thought the war itself was foolish. Why should Richard care who the Saracens worshipped? Were there not enough holy sites between England and Jerusalem for pilgrims? Why did the king and Robin have to take Hob away? Her brother had always championed her wish to avoid marriage.

Squeezing the fabric of her skirt between her fists, Alys felt like the Holy War was at her doorstep, without the benefit of her brother being nearby. She sat back on her heels and traced the line of the mortar between the stones with her gaze. Alys knew staying in Nottingham Castle made her feel helpless. She might have to leave Nottinghamshire altogether. Robin and Hob left to find glory at the edge of a sword... why could she not do the same? Why should being a girl stop her?

Marian would marry. Alys didn't know how else to keep her word to Robin.

She had never imagined her wedding day or seen herself in an amorous embrace with a man. She'd never imagined herself with children or her own house to keep. Alys had pictured herself as a soldier, even though none but her brother and Guy, in their youth, had encouraged the notion.

But all there was for her in England was marriage. Being forced to bear a man's children. To keep house for him. Alys would not do that.

The idea came to her when her hair slipped over her shoulders as she bowed her head to the floor, intent at first to seek God's guidance. Her hair. When Ma had cut it in her youth, passersby had confused her for a boy. She could pass for a boy again.

Alys would cut her own hair and go to the Holy Land as a youth. From Portsmouth, she might book passage to… well, she did not know which port yet, but Alys would find some way to map her journey to Jerusalem. She would find her brother and fight alongside him. There was no harvest in Locksley that needed her help. She wouldn't have to marry. She would impress Robin so that maybe he would forgive her for breaking her word. Maybe he would make her a member of his own private guard.

Two months until Marian had to wed. Two months to prepare. While Marian readied to meet the sheriff's deadline, Alys would use her own chamber as a place to gather provisions and weapons—and a plan. But before that, she needed to apologize to Marian. Resolved to make her peace with her ladyship the next morning, Alys went to bed. Visions of the desert sands stretched out before her. Hob stood there, a lone figure, a red cross on his white tunic, chain mail glinting in the sun, waiting for her.

* * *

The next morning started the same as any other, but Alys knew that her life had changed. What would Marian say if Alys said war was preferable to marriage? She smiled at the notion as she carried kettles of boiling water up the steps for Marian's morning washing.

Upon seeing Marian, Alys offered a contrite smile. "My lady, I apologize for my churlish behavior of late." Alys poured the kettles of water into the basin. "I have been angry since the sheriff forced my family to leave Locksley. And I did not know about the sheriff's ultimatum that you must marry before your twentieth birthday."

Marian received all of Alys's apologies like a relic receiving prayers.

Alys breathed deep again. She wondered: Had Marian been nervous to see her this morning?

"Oh Alys, I am sorry too. I knew not what to say to you about your family. And… I am guessing it was Sir Guy who told you of the sheriff's ultimatum?" She sighed. "I may choose or he will choose for me, and I should rather marry a man who brings me flowers than one who brings the sheriff political gain with no care for my person."

Alys smiled. "I understand. If marriage is your only path. I just thought you loved Robin." She helped Marian out of her nightclothes so she could bathe.

"I do. But Robin may not return for years. He may not

return at all. Sir Edward serves the prince. I do not want to spend my life wondering if my husband will ever return to England's shores. If he has perished in some war in faraway lands. Lands I will never see. If Sir Edward leaves, it will be to London. I may accompany him." She slid down in the bath to wet her hair. When she came up, she asked, "What of you, Alys? I should like to find you a husband in our remaining time together."

Alys readied Marian's gown and wimple. "I do not plan to marry."

Nodding, Marian asked, "You plan to join a convent, then?"

Alys didn't disabuse Marian of that idea. To fight in the Holy Land was to fight for the Church. Whether she did so as an archer or a nun was her own business.

"I thought of the same, but I want children," Marian said while she washed.

"By God's will, you will have them, my lady." Alys helped Marian out of the tub and to dry her skin. Next came dressing and fixing her hair, even though the wimple would hide much of Alys's efforts all day. She dabbed some lavender oil on Marian's wrists. "There," Alys said. "Ready for courtship."

Sir Edward called on Marian again that morning, and Alys did nothing to discourage his or Marian's attentions. Instead, she made silent vows to Hob and to God that she would help her brother get home alive. Over and over, she made this vow, hoping it would supersede her promise to Robin over a year ago.

I cannot control the sheriff. Or Marian. But she could find her brother and get her family back.

7

Clemency

Make good cheer, said Robin Hood,
Sheriff, for charity,
And for the love of Little John,
Thy life is granted to thee.
-Translated from *A Lytell Geste of Robyn Hode*

T he midday meal started with announcements from the sheriff, which included a new tax on farmers and mills, as well as tomorrow's scheduled execution of a man referred to as Little John. Alys had never heard of him, but then she only left the castle once a month and did not always pay attention to the sheriff's announcements. But on this day, the name Little John stuck with her. It made her think of someone helpless. Even though the sheriff charged the man with banditry and assaulting the guards, Alys didn't believe he deserved to die for it.

So lost was she in her own thoughts, she didn't notice at first a voice of dissent. It was a familiar voice, but she couldn't place it. Alys searched the room until she found its owner. He wasn't the biggest man in the room, but he exuded confidence. Robin of Locksley. Alys froze, a piece of bread halfway to her mouth. Even the surrounding air seemed frozen, and that was when she realized Marian had stilled, too.

Whispers scurried around the room, rolling over the benches and tables that, positioned at an angle to the dais, created a U-shape. The sheriff sat on the dais, and men filled the space between the two long tables. Their hats, hair, and scalps bobbed like rocks tumbling in a current. Robin of Locksley was back. Did this mean the king had won the war? Or lost? Why was he back so soon? Travel to the Holy Land should take five to six months. Robin had been gone fifteen months. Alys heard all the surrounding whispers, the questions, but the only one burning in her mind was: Where was Hob?

Abandoning Marian's side, Alys wove her way through the room. She had to walk all the way around one of the long tables to get to Robin. Her heart was frantic. Her brother was not present. Was he here at the castle? Was he at home with their parents? Was he standing in an empty field, peering into an empty cottage? Or was he still thousands of miles away, home but a dream?

"Your request for clemency is duly noted, Locksley," the sheriff said, "but you have not been here. The Holy War has crippled the English people. Impoverished them. They are desperate, and those who turn to banditry for personal gain must be punished."

"Not by losing their lives," Robin said. "If you think I will let you take a man's life just because he was unable to feed his family—"

"Let me? I am the sheriff. You owe all deference to me, boy. I will have order in Nottinghamshire. If you wish to show him solidarity, you can join him on the gallows, Locksley. Your opposition has been registered. Now you will be silent on the subject, or I will send you from here."

The crowd seemed to thicken as more people pressed forward to make their pleas and catch the sheriff's ear. Guy stepped up to bring order. By the time Alys nudged her way to where Robin had stood, he was gone. She craned her neck to see over those around her. No Robin. No Hob. She gripped the edge of the table, fingers digging into the wood. She met and held Guy's annoyed gaze, like a storm rolled in right over his head. Then she looked for Marian. Her lady's face was white as a cloud on a sunny day.

Alys pushed her way through the crowd and out of the hall. She cried out. "Robin! Robin of Locksley!" She ran toward the courtyard but he wasn't there either. Had she imagined him? Had she wished so hard for his return—and her brother's—that she'd imagined the whole thing? The preparation of the gallows in the middle of the courtyard for tomorrow's execution felt too real, as though the punishment for Little John the outlaw promised Robin really had returned.

Alys ran for the gate, but one soldier stopped her, his gauntleted hands closing around her upper arms.

"Where're you going, mouse?"

Alys struggled. "Let me go! I have to see my family." Maybe Hob was home. Maybe he was with their parents and Grandda. The notion that a month since her last visit hadn't passed didn't occur to Alys. She was too desperate to get home, too desperate to see her brother back on English soil, too desperate to find him in one piece.

"You don't have permission to leave today," the guard said. His voice was gruff and harsh.

Tears stung at the corners of Alys's eyes. "I have to go!"

The guard wouldn't release her, though. He called to another that he was going to escort her back into the castle. He all but dragged her. At the iron-studded doors to the keep, he pushed her back against them. "None leave without the sheriff's say so. You'll stay in the castle or you'll stay in the gaol beneath it."

The threat of the dungeon sobered Alys's attempts at escape. She stilled. The iron studs pressed into her spine, and the steel of the guard's gauntlets pressed into her arms.

"Fine," she said. She wanted to spit it at him, but treating the guards with disrespect wouldn't help her, even if she procured the sheriff's permission to leave early again.

The guard released her. "Tend to her ladyship." He dismissed her with a nod.

Alys wrenched open the door and stomped into the keep.

These walls may trap my body today, but not forever. She didn't go to Marian, but to her own chamber. She needed to think.

Robin must have seen Marian in the hall, so he must have seen Alys, too. Why, if Hob was not with him, did he not bring her news of her brother? Had he already been to see her parents? Was the news so dreadful he could not bear to face her? If so, then Alys would declare Robin a coward. Had he been unable to keep his promise? If he'd failed, she'd declare him a liar.

It's war. Of course he couldn't keep his promise. Alys dove her fingers into her hair and pulled hard. She wanted to scream, but didn't want to alert the guards. Alys threw herself on her bed instead and let loose her rage and fear in a bloodcurdling cry, muffled by her mattress. Tears slipped from the corners of her eyes, dampening two circles on the linen.

Robin, but no Hob. Is he home? Is he in Jerusalem? Is he... will I never see him? As she sobbed, it became harder and harder to believe she'd allowed herself to think Robin could have ever promised to bring Hob home. Now he was back, Robin would get to marry Marian. He'd live in luxury and the afterglow of his crusading glory. What did Alys have? A knot of cold, hard hatred began to tie itself in her stomach. If Hob was not home, Robin would suffer for it.

* * *

An hour or two later, Alys found Marian in her chambers. "My lady," Alys said, "I pray you forgive my absence. I had to know if—if Robin was really back in Nottingham."

"He is," Marian said. A smile split across her face—the biggest smile Alys had seen her wear in all her time in Marian's service. "Look." She held out her hand. On her fourth finger was a simple ring of intertwining silver ivy.

"Sir Edward asked for your hand?"

"No, Alys—Robin did. He sought me out after he left the hall. Tomorrow, after the execution, your cousin will return Locksley to him, and then—we can marry, Robin and I."

Alys felt empty. Robin would get his bride, but where was Hob? Robin would get his Locksley back, but her family's home remained out of reach. "Wait—you saw him after he left the hall? I thought he left the castle. So he might still be here somewhere?" Alys started toward the door.

"You will not find him in the castle again today, Alys."

"But—he can't have gotten far."

"He has angered the sheriff. He will keep his distance for the rest of the day."

"Then Town—or Locksley even." Alys grabbed the door handle.

Marian crossed the room and covered Alys's hand with her own. "I tell you he will not be found today. Trust me. You would do better to wait. Besides, there are more glad tidings. He will restore your family to their farm in Locksley. As a wedding gift at my request."

"What? My—we can go back to Locksley?" Disbelief and joy dimmed Alys's dread about Hob for a moment. She also felt flushed at having entertained feelings of envy and jealousy toward Robin. But then, despair over her brother's wellbeing settled back in, its icy grip closing around her heart and making it difficult to draw a deep breath. "That's a lot of money to pay the sheriff. You and Robin will need it, for your future. And the sheriff will not take kindly to such favor bestowed upon peasants. I—thank you, my lady, but you should not. I just—I want to see my brother. How long ago did Robin leave the castle? Can you get him to come back?"

Marian worried her bottom lip. "Alys… do not be so quick to refuse a gift. And Robin will return on the morrow. He is going to try once more to prevent the outlaw's execution." Her eyes shone with a worshipful light, but the notion that something was wrong lingered for Alys. That it wasn't for Marian's sake Robin offered to restore her family to Locksley.

She couldn't shake the feeling that something was wrong with Hob, and Robin's generosity was to lessen the blow.

I would sense it though, if Hob was gone from this world. Wouldn't I? Alys plastered a fake smile, one that she hoped looked like gratitude on her face—for Marian's sake.

At least Alys hadn't broken her word after all, and on the morrow she would find out if Robin had kept his.

* * *

The courtyard was full of noblemen and women and peasants alike by the time Alys trailed Marian down to that stone enclosure. A line of soldiers with drums stood before the gallows; their instruments were quiet for now. Alys eyed the crowd. Robin's face was easy to spot, but he wasn't looking her way. He, like many others, watched the throne-like chair at the top of the courtyard, where the sheriff would observe the execution.

The sheriff came out with Sir Guy at his side and a handful of his best guards. Alys presumed they were his best, anyway—they were the half-dozen that always seemed to be around him whenever he walked through the castle. Guy carried a scroll of parchment. A fanfare blasted from the battlements above. When it ended, the sheriff stood before his chair, and Guy handed him the scroll.

From another side of the courtyard, guards tugged the arms of largest man Alys had ever seen. He was at least a head and a half taller than his captors, and a single sweep of his arm could have knocked them all off their feet. He was middle-aged, with moon-silver and sun-yellow hair and a beard. Leg irons and chains between his wrists clattered and rang out in the absence of the completed fanfare. *That man might be named John, but he certainly isn't little.* She wondered how she got caught and captured. How many guards had it taken to subdue him?

"On this, the eleventh day of November, in the year 1192

63

of our Lord, I, the Sheriff of Nottingham, do hereby pass sentence on the outlaw John Nailor of Nottingham, known otherwise as Little John. For the crimes of theft and assault of the sheriff's guards, he shall be hanged by the neck until dead."

The drummers raised their drumsticks, but before they tapped a tattoo on the drumheads, Robin's voice rang out.

"Sheriff! You know this is wrong! Good people of Nottingham, let not this man's life be forfeit for such crimes. He does not deserve death. This is unjust!"

Alys glanced at Marian, not the sheriff. Marian's face filled with the light of hope and love. She turned her ring on her hand. Around and around. Alys was mesmerized.

"All the evidence has already been considered," the sheriff said. He waved his hand in dismissal. "Proceed with the execution. The people of Nottingham will have swift justice for criminals."

The drummers beat their drums. Guards dragged Little John toward the scaffold. The black-hooded executioner slipped the noose over John's head and tightened the knot, and the fight went out of him, dissipated like a storm pushed out by calmer skies. He stood there, stoic. Like he didn't know this was his last morning on Earth, or like it no longer mattered. The executioner spoke to Little John, but Alys couldn't hear his words. She saw the outlaw nod. Little John did not seem angry at the executioner. The executioner covered Little John's head with a black hood. He moved over to the lever and closed a leather-gloved hand around it. The drums beat again. And again. And a third time. The executioner pulled the lever, and Little John dropped as the planks beneath him opened on a hinge.

Alys caught the glint of sunlight on something metallic—a

dagger. She followed its arc back to Robin. He'd thrown it. The rope sliced in twain. The blade lodged in the wood of the gallows. Little John emerged from beneath the stage of his own execution, pulled the rope off of his neck and slipped it around a guard's.

The sheriff was on his feet. He yelled and spewed and spat for his guards to "arrest those men!"

Alys missed the rest of what happened because Guy steered her and Marian back into the keep. Marian took Alys's hand and ran. Up and up. Their breath huffed. Alys's heart slammed against her ribs. Her legs pumped. Boots stomped all the way to Marian's room, which looked out on the courtyard. Alys pushed the window open. From up here, they spotted flashes of swords and helmets. They watched the guards surround Robin and Little John. Alys expected both men to be executed on the spot. Marian trembled beside her, elbow to elbow as they were, to peer at the scene below. Alys put an arm around Marian.

Marian sobbed, but neither of them tore their gazes away from the window long enough to console or be consoled. The aroma of lavender blossoms wafted around Alys, but the scent failed to relax her. Little John and Robin stood back-to-back. Robin held a sword in both hands, and Little John had a spear. He must have disarmed a guard while Alys and Marian ran up to her chambers.

The guards closed the circle and attacked. Alys glanced up at the battlements over the gatehouse to see archers readying to fire. Without thinking, Alys cupped her hands around her mouth and yelled out of Marian's window, "Archers!" She saw Robin look up.

He said something to Little John, and then they attacked

the circle of guards with the ferocity of bears. At market fairs, when bears were set upon by starved dogs, the bears never survived. This time, though, Robin and Little John broke through the line of guards. Little John ran under the portcullis. Arrows flew toward Robin and bounced off the flagstones. A bell rang. The portcullis rattled toward the ground.

Alys leaned out the window to watch, but Marian dragged her back through the casement into the room.

Robin jumped and rolled on his shoulder, sliding under the portcullis before it lowered to the ground.

The courtyard was like an anthill, guards swarming to and fro.

The peasants chanted Robin's name. Little John's too.

Alys turned and sank to the floor. She drew shallow breaths. "Do you think—do you think the sheriff heard me warn them about the archers?"

Marian sat on the edge of her bed. "Perhaps. If the sheriff questions you, say… oh, what could you say?"

"Would the sheriff buy that I exclaimed in surprise?"

Marian gave her a look.

"Right. Of course not. I could say I did not want anyone to die."

"That is more believable. The gentility of our sex would support such a wish."

Alys had her doubts. She knew she had to be the least gentle of any female who had ever set foot in the castle. But she'd have to cling to the hope that such an answer would suffice. *Even better if the sheriff never asks.* There was little else to hope for.

Robin of Locksley was now a hero. But he was also an outlaw. Anger and hatred simmered in Alys's gut—Robin had thrown away so much to save Little John. Marian's marriage, Alys's family returning to Locksley, and learning what became of Hob seemed more out of reach than ever before.

8

In Name Only

I shall you tell of a good yeoman,
His name was Robin Hood.
Robin was a proud outlaw,
Whilst he walked on ground,
So courteous an outlaw as he was one
Was never any found.
-Translated from *A Lytell Geste of Robyn Hode*

Groggy from several fitful nights of attempting to sleep, Alys trudged up to Marian's chamber. That Robin should be home without Hob seemed surreal. The sheriff had declared that morning that Robin of Locksley was an outlaw, and it was the duty of every man, woman, and child to do Robin harm. Beyond that, there had been no gossip on the matter. Recent events had arisen so fast, and Robin had not returned. Guards at the castle were more alert, and the sheriff had denied Alys's request to call on her family.

Alys's relief that Little John had not been hanged plagued her mind because while she was not eager to witness a hanging, she still bore raw anger at Robin for dashing her hopes.

When Alys reached Marian, she discovered her already dressed. "My lady?"

"Good morrow, Alys. I have news."

Alys hoped it would be news about her brother, but doubted it. She'd told Marian nothing about Robin's promise—or her own. Marian still wore Robin's ring. "I'm listening."

"I spoke with Sir Guy. Robin has not come back to Locksley. The sheriff has guessed that he took up with Little John in Sherwood."

"Oh. So… will you have to wed Sir Edward?"

Marian shook her head. "I know not. I hope not. The sheriff is plotting to lure Robin here with an archery contest. There is a silver arrow on offer to the winner, and a pound for whomsoever takes second place."

Alys knew Robin for an educated, canny man. "Will Robin will take the bait?"

"Robin has never avoided a competition, especially one which concerns archery. I doubt the sheriff will arrest Robin, though. Even you thought he had left the castle after pleading for Little John's life, and you are smarter than many of the guards here." Marian stared at some spot over Alys's shoulder and exhaled a dreamy sigh.

When Alys cleared her throat, Marian recalled herself.

"But Alys," she said, "you should enter the archery tournament. We cannot know what the future will hold, whether Robin will be master of Locksley again…but your family might make use of a pound."

"And females can compete?"

"Sir Guy suggested you shoot in the contest, so I do not

believe the sheriff has forbidden it."

"Shouldn't we be trying... you know... to warn Robin?" Maybe he wouldn't show. Maybe he would reclaim Locksley somehow. Maybe her family could still have their farm back. Or if not that, then at least without Robin present, first place—and the arrow—would be Alys's. After settling the taxes owed to the sheriff, her family would have extra coin. And if Marian could get in touch with Robin, then perhaps Alys could find out what became of her brother.

"Leave that to me."

"But how? My lady, you should permit me to attend you. To leave the castle alone—it—it isn't safe."

This should be a plan we concoct together. Alys felt a sting at the idea of Marian venturing beyond these walls without her. *If she desires a private word with Robin, I can offer her that.*

"I can get word to him. Without setting foot outside the castle. And I shall—but he will enter the contest, regardless."

So she knows some way to summon him. He probably visited her under cover of darkness, which means I can't meet with him. It might arouse suspicion, my being up in the tower so late. Even though I doubt anyone would watch my movements or care about them. The notion that Robin would risk his freedom to compete perplexed Alys. She cocked her head. "Even if he knows it's a trap?"

Marian nodded. Her expression shifted from urgent to worried for a moment before her focus returned to Alys. "No matter what transpires, you and I only have two months left together. I can give you some money, but that pound will help."

"I don't doubt I can win the pound," Alys said. Realizing how prideful that might sound, she flashed Marian a sheepish smile. Then she hesitated. Marian seemed unwilling to acknowledge the risk Robin would assume if he showed up for the tournament. "But what if the sheriff succeeds in capturing Robin?"

"He will escape, and if he cannot, Little John will help him. I am certain of it. And there are others. Outlaws who have long lived with Little John in the green wood."

If Alys competed in the archery competition, regardless of whether it was a ploy to catch Robin of Locksley, she might gain back some of what she'd lost.

Alys spent the rest of the day focused on her chores and Marian's needs; she tried to dismiss all the deficits of life that dogged her.

* * *

On Alys's day off, she wondered what her lady did without her, but perhaps Marian didn't require Alys's service after all. Perhaps Alys was more of an appointed companion than a servant. *That's probably why she can't bring me with her once she marries.* Despite wanting to stay with her parents, Alys took pride in her work. The idea that it wasn't necessary bothered her like a splinter in her palm, while at the same time, she was warmed to have Marian's friendship.

Today, she left the confines of the keep. She presented her pass, issued by the sheriff, at the portcullis. The guard inspected the pass, then Alys, with suspicion.

"Arms out," he said. His voice reverberated from behind his helmet. Alys complied. He patted along her forearms, her upper arms, her sides. He reached into her pockets.

Alys had attempted to sneak food out of the castle two

months ago, and this same guard had confiscated it. The sheriff didn't like anyone taking food or money—least of all weapons—out of the castle without his permission. The guard had cautioned her that if she were caught again, she'd waste a day in the castle's bowels, in the gaol, with criminals. She wasn't afraid of the criminals in the sheriff's dungeons. Most were those who were unable to afford their taxes, but she refused to spend her only day off a month locked up.

"Learned your lesson, eh, girl?" The guard laughed at her expense.

"I still hold," Alys said, "that I should be able to redistribute my own rations to my family."

He placed his palm on his sword. "Redis—dist—what you said? What does that mean? You threatening me?"

Alys blew out a breath. "No. Can I be on my way?" It wasn't her fault she knew words he didn't. She couldn't help that Ma came from learned stock, that she taught Alys her letters. *It's not on me that this guard's head is as hard as his helmet.*

He scrutinized her like she might hex him and backed away, hand still on the pommel of his sword.

No one should allow oafs like him to handle something so sharp. He hailed another guard in the gatehouse, and the portcullis rattled up to set Alys free on the road.

The town of Nottingham possessed none of the castle's grandeur. Buildings there weren't built of stone. When she first arrived with Guy over a year ago, the castle had seemed even more foreboding and startling, like a mountain in the middle of a forest clearing. The buildings in Town had deteriorated since then. Sometimes, on her walk to see her parents and Grandda, she would notice a new hole in a wall or almost trip over a loose cobble. Other days, like today, Town seemed to have suffered years of dereliction in the last month.

Walls of wattle and daub caked and crumbled under thatched roofs, which reminded Alys of hair on the scalps of balding men. A river of human waste ran into the ditches alongside the road, and where there were no ditches, it pooled in wagon tracks or else lay in fetid puddles alongside—and sometimes mixed with—mounds of horse dung.

Alys remembered visiting Town with her grandda years ago, when the farm produced more than their village could consume. There hadn't been piss in the middle of the street and the houses hadn't been falling apart. It might be a symptom of time, but Alys was unable to shake the feeling that Town withered under the rule of this sheriff. Years ago, it'd been a different man in power, King Richard's man.

Alys circled around a stinking puddle and wished she had a horse, even though her family's hovel was in Town and not far at all. As she side-stepped and hopped through Nottingham's streets, she yearned for the honeyed air of home.

The Fletcher house was like all the rest in Town, save for one difference: racks of arrows, all in different stages of completion, sat between the building and street. No one dared touch them. No one dared steal them from her da because his arrows supplied the sheriff's men, and to filch them was a theft from the sheriff himself. The minimum punishment for theft was the loss of a hand.

Alys lifted one arrow-to-be and cradled it along her arm at eye level. The shaft was true, and the fletches aligned at perfect angles.

Da opened the crooked door of the house. "What do you think, Alys? Reckon she'll fly to her mark?"

Even though she perceived it would, Alys smirked. "That

depends on the archer's skill." This was always her answer. Alys replaced the arrow on the rack and hurried to her da.

He folded his arms around Alys and squeezed a little too tight, but she let him.

"Welcome home, daughter." But this wasn't home. Home was in Locksley. This was a two-room cottage under a saggy, patchy roof on a street overflowed with muck and dung and urine.

Da released her, told her how fine and well she looked. The only differences were she washed more often, and she ate three times a day instead of two. Da's smile stretched, broad like his shoulders, like his back. A dark, square gap caught her eye.

"Another tooth gone?"

He dismissed the loss with a wave of his hand. "Still got plenty of teeth. And my arrows. And a daughter who visits every month. By God, it's good to look on you." The smile slid from his face. "Go on inside and greet your ma."

Alys noticed. She always noticed. Her parents had been quarreling again. The flint that sparked that fire was almost always coin and their lack of it. Sometimes it was position and stature, too. "Where's Grandda? And Hob? Is he home?"

"Your brother is still in the Holy Land, as far as we know. We heard Robin came back, but haven't heard from your brother. Your grandda's walked to Locksley to see if anyone's found out anything from him or the other men who left with Robin for the war." He fidgeted. Da almost never fidgeted. "Your ma will be glad of seeing you."

Maybe Hob is in Locksley, helping Robin get his lands back. A moment after the hopeful thought crossed her mind, she rejected it. Guy would have said something. Swallowing the lump that formed in her throat, and the idea of Hob still fighting for the king, or worse, Alys offered a dutiful nod and crossed the threshold.

Her skirt swept the strewing herbs into a little maelstrom of dust and shriveled leaves; more dried herbs hung from one beam in the kitchen. Ma stooped over the hearth, poked and prodded at food while flames tickled the bottom of the pot.

"Alfred," Ma said, "if you make it to the market this week, we are out of eggs."

"Da's outside. It's me," Alys said. She coughed on the smoke that curled toward the ceiling. Before living in the castle, the kitchen smoke never bothered her, but most of her time at the castle was spent out of the kitchens.

Ma stood and whirled so fast she had to steady herself with fingertips perched on the table in the middle of the room. She abandoned her spoon on it, and bits of carrot and drops of broth splattered onto the scrubbed oak. Ma rounded the table and hauled Alys into a tighter hug than Da had.

"Can't… breathe." Alys hugged her back though, a little tighter when Ma relaxed her hold enough to let Alys draw air.

The older woman framed Alys's face in calloused hands; her once dainty fingers swept up against Alys's hairline. "A month is too long," Ma said, and she pulled Alys again to her bosom. "With your brother away and you at the castle… we heard about what happened with Robin."

"I'm safe, I promise," Alys said when Ma released her. "Guy was quick to usher both Maid Marian and myself inside." The kitchen smelled like dried sage and rosemary, cooked carrots, and body odor. Ma had a few dirt smudges on her forehead and cheek. "I would have brought food but—"

"I remember. They will not let you. That sheriff is evil."

Alys pulled away. "Shh… You know the cost of such talk. Besides, he's just doing his job. He's just doing what the prince commands."

Ma waved her hand through the air and spit on the floor. "The prince. Don't get me started on him. Or the king. I don't see how you can give the sheriff any leeway at all after what he did to our family."

"Ma!"

"I suppose as you live in *his* castle, you're accustomed to his depravities."

Alys rolled her eyes. "You know I spend all my time with Maid Marian. If I see anyone else, it's Sir Guy."

The lines on Ma's face softened, and she smiled. "Now there is a proper man. Looks after his family. Pity he has not turned his head your way."

"Ma." Alys stretched the word out into as many syllables as possible.

"It is time you think of your future, of a husband."

"I have no wish to marry him and I assure you, he has no wish to marry me." If Sir Guy wished to marry Alys, he would have asked. Besides, the idea of becoming his wife twisted her stomach. Not that he was unkind to her, because he wasn't. And she supposed many might consider him pleasing to look at. But Alys had never once thought to swoon over a man, kiss him, or worse—marry him.

"Oh, my own sweetheart, you are not an unhandsome girl. Why should he not want to marry you?" She kissed Alys's forehead.

Alys leaned away. "How are you, Da, and Grandda?"

Ma sighed and took up her spoon again, stirred her carrot stew—with more vigor than carrots merited—and neglected the broth and carrot pieces on the table. Those scraps held Alys's attention. There should be meat there, too. Not chicken, because chicken was too expensive, but pork at the least. If only the sheriff had allowed her to bring food from the castle.

"We're fine." Ma's words sounded quiet and clipped.

Alys knew it was a lie. Just as she didn't want to discuss marriage, Ma scorned talk of coin. Alys hated the uncomfortable silence between them. "I'm going to enter the sheriff's archery competition." She offered what she hoped was an enthusiastic smile.

"And that will help fetch you a husband? Or do you plan to be a maid-in-waiting forever?"

"I do not want a husband."

Ma pointed the wooden spoon at Alys. "Your cousin brought you to the castle to find one."

"Well, he didn't ask what mattered to me first." Alys's cheeks flushed like it was her hunched over the kettle, like it was her face the flames warmed. Sharing her plans of tracking down Hob in the Holy Land, if he was still there, was impossible. Alys didn't have a plan so much as an idea. No matter what, she had to find Robin and ask him. "The tournament isn't about finding a husband. I stand to win a pound. We'd be able to go back to Locksley."

"And when that is spent? We best stay here. We can afford this."

Alys felt like some demon had sucked all the air out of the house. How could Ma say such a thing? "Th-then you would be able to fix the thatch. With increased production of Da's arrows—"

"No. We cannot rely on that any longer."

"Why not? England is at war. There's plenty of need for

arrows. The sheriff goes out hunting every Saturday. More arrows. People fire them for sport—more arrows."

Ma threw the spoon against the far edge of the pot. Tears stained the smudges on her cheeks. Her shoulders shook, and her underslung chin—which Alys had inherited—wobbled.

"What's wrong?"

"His eyes. They're not—they can't—he will soon be a fletcher in name and name only."

Alys didn't believe her. She couldn't. Da's eyes had seemed fine. The arrows had seemed fine. Alys wondered if Ma only said these things to entice her to hunt for a husband. *Ma's wrong; it's a ploy*. Alys didn't know if she spoke because while she felt her mouth move, all she heard was a rushing thump between her ears, again and again, like a drumbeat carried on the wind.

No arrows meant no income. No income meant no hope of ever paying the sheriff back and getting home to Locksley—especially since Robin was an outlaw now. Alys had no choice but to win that silver arrow—the pound was no longer enough.

9

A Fletcher's Future

He purveyed him a hundred bows,
The strings were well tight,
A hundred sheaf of arrows good,
The heads burnished full bright.
-Translated from *A Lytell Geste of Robyn Hode*

Her skirt snagged some strewing herbs on her way out and dredged them from the house. They left a trail behind her. The toe of her boot hooked on a stand of arrows, and both she and the stand crashed to the ground. Arrow shafts clattered. One of them rolled away into a puddle of piss; the fletching got soaked. The acrid smell clawed its way into Alys's nostrils and made her eyes water. Da's hand closed around her elbow, and he lifted her from the ground.

She opened her mouth to apologize, but all that came out was a strangled groan. He said nothing, but bent to pick up the rack. Alys collected the in-process arrows—all except the one in the puddle. She peered at it. Two white fletching feathers and one gray—this was a target arrow, a practice arrow, one like Marian would use, but not now that it was in a piss puddle. Her da always chose the color of the indicator fletch based on the arrow's purpose. A gray feather? Target practice and often traded to nobles. Brown meant the arrows were for hunting, and he sold those to anyone and all. But arrows fletched with two white feathers and a single red one were for war. Da sold those to the sheriff and other lords. The color fletching system, he'd explained years ago, assured he always had enough arrows for his wealthiest buyers.

"I'm sorry, Da." Something about those fletching feathers, wet and clumped together, helped Alys find her voice. She focused on her da's eyes, to discover for herself if they were milky or otherwise impaired. They looked as they always had.

Alys couldn't ask him. Not about his sight. What if asking upset him? What if his eyes were worse than imagined? Instead, she inquired if he would allow her to craft one of the arrows. She allowed him to believe she pleaded out of guilt for tipping them. The truth was, making arrows was one of Alys's favorite activities, and it'd been something for them to do together since she was first old enough to work.

"I have a few you can fletch."

He passed her three feathers from a box on a bench against the outer wall of the house: two white, one red. Alys sat beside him and started binding them to the arrow's shaft.

She twisted the gut string around the arrow, coiling it like a snake on a branch. With a thin line of pitch, she positioned each of the three feathers. Placement of the red one was crucial; it would inform the archer which way to nock the arrow on a bow. She blew on the pitch until it dried.

Alys recalled Da's advice: "Be patient with each feather, child. Arrows need both patience and skill in their first and final moments."

The fletching feathers were stiff but yielding. When she dragged her fingertip over their edges, the vanes separated. They were reluctant, but they bent to her will and the barbs released so the feather vanes fanned out. Alys fit the gut string above one vane and stretched it tight to the arrow's shaft.

She arrived at the red feather and stayed her hand. "Da?"

"Yes, child?"

Child. Like she was still a little girl. The word from him felt like a hug. Alys wanted to ask about when he and Ma had last argued. She longed to know about his eyes. But arrows required patience, and sometimes fletchers did, too. "Will you convince Ma that it would be a wretched mistake for me to wed her cousin, Sir Guy?"

Da's eyes crinkled again. "I shall say what I can to dissuade her. But be gentler with your ma. She only wants what's best for you."

"Sir Guy is *not* what's best for me. And I'm not what's best for him."

"She scaled down several rungs of the ladder when she married me, Alys. Sometimes... sometimes it's difficult for her to recall why she did so."

"Not if she loves you."

He let out a sad laugh. "Life has a way of quieting love sometimes."

"I would never marry Sir Guy."

"It won't come to that. He would have wed you by now if he aimed to. He doesn't want a wife who can outshine him with a bow." He leaned so his shoulder gave a gentle push against hers.

Alys didn't have to say thank you. She just had to fletch the arrow. Da always appreciated actions more than words. He always said promises were easy to make—it was holding them that was hard. Keeping her promise to Robin was proving to be almost impossible, unless he could clear his name within two months. And his promise to her? Had he kept it? Was Hob somewhere safe, on his way home, or perhaps running some errand in England for Robin?

Around and around Alys wound, holding gut string in one hand, spinning the arrow and fanning the feathers with the other.

She fletched two more arrows. The light was fading, and her pass from the sheriff only pardoned her absence until sundown.

Before she returned to the castle, she hugged her da again—and gave a short, light hug to Ma.

"Tell Grandda I love him, and send me word at the castle when you hear about Hob." She kissed Da's cheek, then his hands. Fealty. Filial fealty. She feared his eyes might look different next month.

* * *

Alys returned to Nottingham castle, to its portcullis, to its guards, to its stones. The same guard who checked her for food before she left examined her pass again. He offered it an indignant eye, like he didn't investigate it earlier in the day. Same pass. Same words. Same signet seal.

By the time they let her through the gate, Alys was amazed she still made it back to comb and brush her lady's hair. Alys could feel Maid Marian watching her in the looking glass on the vanity, but Alys avoided her gaze. Instead, she focused on Marian's hair, and the way the glow from the firelight, from the seven candles—seven expensive candles!—glinted off the strands so they shone like the rays of the sun.

"Alys?" Marian said. Her hair knotted. Alys had been away for one day and Marian's hair tangled.

How did that even happen? Maybe she needs me after all. Alys's hair was once that fine, when she was a child. But as she'd grown, the texture had altered. Her hair was thicker now. It didn't knit as easily. Alys wondered if God gifted Marian with the perfection of eternal youth. No one who has survived to adulthood should be so delicate. That there was someone in the world with no scars, fine hair, and lips that never seemed chapped even in a chilly wind seemed preposterous.

The chasm between the two of them hadn't felt so vast since they first met. Both of them faced substantial changes in the coming months, but all Alys could muster was bitterness. Marian had to marry, yes. Alys doubted Marian would love her husband, since the sheriff seemed disinclined to grant Robin clemency. Nevertheless, Sir Edward wasn't a cruel man. Marian would be all right. It didn't hurt that Sir Edward wasn't poor, either.

In contrast, Alys's family was on the brink of even worse penury than before. If she failed to win the silver, the only other way she could look after them would be marriage. Even then, it wasn't likely Alys could meet a kind, rich husband. If Alys were to wed, the benefit would be adding another worker to the family. Alys knew that if she marched to the Holy Land and deserted her parents and Grandda that they would suffer for it. They would starve for it. As much as she yearned to bring Hob home, the journey alone would take about a year to travel there and back. Could her family live off her da's arrows when his vision was fading?

Marian reached up to lay a gentle hand upon Alys's wrist and called out to her again, her voice soft.

Alys stopped brushing. The bed of boar bristles rested on top of Marian's head. Alys pulled her gaze up to find Marian's perfect reflection. "Yes, my lady?"

"I've secured your place in the archery contest."

Was it charity that led Marian to help Alys? Before today, it might have looked like friendship. Alys glanced away. "My lady should not have done. But I—" She swallowed. The words were so hard to form. Her tongue pushed against her front teeth and glided under them. "Thank you."

Maid Marian sat up straighter. It shouldn't be possible to improve already perfect posture, but somehow, she managed. She pulled her shoulders back, so it looked like her collarbone might crack or bend and never straighten again. Her eyelids, with their too many lashes, swept down. She dipped her ladylike chin. "I am glad to be of help to you. But Alys, are you quite well? You are speaking with uncommon formality tonight."

"I'm just sleepy."

"Oh, then you must not fuss over me any longer. Get some rest. With the tournament coming up, you will need to be in your best form."

Alys curtsied and set the brush on Marian's vanity before excusing herself from the room.

10

Entrance Fee

The sheriff swore a full great oath,
By Him that died on a tree,
This man is the best archer
That yet saw I me.
-Translated from *A Lytell Geste of Robyn Hode*

On her way to her chamber, Alys made an alternative plan. Not for marriage, not for war. She would win the silver arrow, not the pound, and her family would pay the sheriff back. They would return to Locksley—and then she would send for Hob herself if he wasn't already on his way back to England. She'd be able to afford to write him.

Alys didn't fear most of her competition. She practiced archery more than the average peasant, and she harbored more desperation for silver than the average nobleman. But if Robin of Locksley showed up, she didn't know if she could best him. Robin had always enjoyed renown for his skill with a bow, even before he rose to the rank of leader of the king's guard.

Alys knew she had to try. Even with the likelihood Robin would compete, she had to try. Maybe, at the least, she could ask why he didn't keep his word and discover where Hob was. Was he still with Richard the Lionhearted?

Lionhearted when he has an army at his beck and call.

Alys slowed when she noticed a tall figure with broad shoulders in front of her door.

"Cousin," Guy said with the smallest dip of his head.

Alys placed a hand over her heart. "You startled me."

"I'm afraid it's too early for you to turn in."

"But Maid Marian is settled for tonight."

His breath quickened at her name. "Sheriff sent me to fetch you."

He plans to interrogate me about warning Robin. Or accuse me of trying to smuggle food out of the castle. Her stomach knotted. "I didn't bring food out of the castle, no matter what that guard says, I swear."

"Not about that. Come." Guy turned and started down the corridor.

Alys followed, three steps to his two, a steady tempo throughout the castle. She wiped her hands on her skirt, but she could not dry her clammy skin. Torchlight bounced off suits of armor and mounted shields and swords and spears and bows and axes and maces. How many men died and took lives in those suits, with those shields and endless weapons? Alys tried to imagine a time before this castle, before the sheriff. Her heart thrummed with every step.

The sheriff was a man who had seen battle, though which battle Alys knew not. He was a man who had donned a suit of armor. He was a man who made Alys feel like she should rip one of those shields off the wall if she was going to meet with him.

"Make sure you curtsy without almost toppling over," Guy said. He paused before the double doors.

She narrowed her eyes and said, "I can curtsy."

"Well, that is good. I trained you to fire an arrow. I didn't think I needed to teach you poise as well." He was teasing her. Alys could tell by the small smile that hid in the corner of her cousin's mouth, where the light from the nearest torch almost couldn't reach.

She tried to breathe in deep, but felt like bands of iron wrapped around her chest. Her breaths came fast and shallow. Guy pulled one of the iron-armored doors open; there the sheriff stood, behind his table. The man responsible for her misery and well-being. He speared her with a dead-eye stare.

Guy cleared his throat and Alys dropped into a stiff and shallow curtsy.

"Alys Fletcher," the sheriff said. Her name was oil on his tongue, until the last syllable when it hardened, like an arrowhead beaten into a point between the blacksmith's hammer and the anvil.

"How may I be of service, my lord?" It relieved Alys that her voice didn't quiver or break.

The sheriff walked around the table, dragging a fingertip along the edge. He propped his other hand upon the pommel of a sword sheathed at his hip. "I know you wish to compete for the silver arrow. I am inclined to consider allowing you to enter."

Thank the good Lord. Alys swallowed. *One step closer to Locksley.* "I thank your lordship for permission to participate in the archery contest and—"

The sheriff held up one hand, palm facing Alys. "Keep your gratitude—that isn't what I want from you."

So it is a favor. Alys looked from the sheriff to Guy. She waited, breath held, for him to speak his demands.

The sheriff gripped the pommel of his sword and the sheath creaked. His other hand grabbed Alys's chin. "I have plans for you, Alys Fletcher." He leaned close. The sheriff had onion breath, and Alys felt a wave of relief when he drew away again. "I want to allow you to take part in the archery competition," he said. "I shall guarantee you the pound. You shall be permitted to bring food to your family." The sheriff released her chin and stroked her cheek with his knuckles before patting the side of her face and neck.

Alys focused on the ermine fur on his shoulder. What she wouldn't give for a fur right now. Her hands and feet and lips and nose felt like ice. A cold stone settled in her stomach. For all that, what would he demand? Free arrows from her da when her family already had so little? Alys knew if he called for as much, she couldn't refuse.

Everyone in the castle was at the sheriff's limited mercy. Everyone in Town, in the villages beyond, was at his mercy.

"Both Maid Marian and Sir Guy have told me of your remarkable talent with a bow. I have heard it may even surpass the skill of Robin of Locksley, your former lord and master." The sheriff dropped a heavy hand upon Alys's shoulder, and her torso tilted under its weight. "What I require from you is to use that skill."

Alys forced herself to look into those dark, dead eyes of his. She imagined that not even the light of a thousand torches could touch their depths to add feeling to his face. His eyes were so different from Da's. She wished the sheriff could go blind instead.

"I want you, Alys Fletcher, to shoot and kill Robin of Locksley. He is a stain upon our good shire, upon England. He returned from the war alone, with a story of the king sending him back due to an injury and to bring a message to the prince... but the king has other emissaries, and the prince has never countenanced Robin's game at caring so much for peasants. I believe Robin of Locksley deserted. I believe he is a coward. More than that, I know him to be a criminal. He squeezes the wealth out of our town, our shire, our livelihood."

A rush of heat filled her head. "My lord, why do you seek my help? Surely there is one just as capable—"

"You know Robin well. He is likely to compete in disguise. With your skill and knowledge of him, you stand the best chance of getting close enough the fastest. Can you imagine," he said with a mirthless laugh, "if I had guards fire arrows at one of the contestants amid the nobility? It would be chaos." Turning his attention to Guy, he said, "It can hardly be one of us. I have tedious hosting duties and Guy is to see to the protection of the nobility."

Robin of Locksley deserted. Not only had he abandoned the king and her brother, but he'd also abandoned his promise to Alys. She clenched her hands into fists at her sides. For over a year she besmirched other men to keep Marian from marrying them. She forced her friend to consider accepting the offer on hand because she had no other choice now. Alys kept her side of her bargain with Robin. *What sort of man doesn't keep his word?* A coward. A liar. A thief.

What if the sheriff lies? "As you say, my lord, I know Robin well. He never seemed the type to desert. Perhaps there was some misunderstanding…"

"He may not have seemed so, but war changes a man."

I pray it does not change Hob.

"If Robin did not desert, then it is strange he did not bring back a single man with him. A travel companion. A manservant. The journey is perilous; it is never wise to travel so far alone. He would have brought another man back with him." The sheriff picked at a toggle on his jerkin, and then his gaze seemed to go right through Alys. "I hear he was close with your brother. If Robin did not desert, then why is not Robert Fletcher returned to you? Hm?"

Robin promised to bring Hob home safe. But he came back alone. The sheriff must be telling the truth. What do I know of men in war? Alys pushed the thought that the sheriff might be lying aside. If he had no honor, someone would have spoken up. Guy would not serve him. The sheriff might not be likeable, but that, she decided, did not mean he was wicked.

But Alys wasn't sure she could take a life unless in defense of her own. She could fire an arrow and hit any target she aimed for. However, if Robin did not attack her first, Alys wasn't certain she could kill him. She braced to keep her knees from buckling under the weight of the sheriff's hand, driven down by his dead eyes, under the magnitude of what he asked her to do. Murder wasn't the sort of sin one could erase with prayer and penance.

"I am trained in archery, as you say, my lord sheriff," she said. The hesitation at the end of her confirmation stirred danger in the air. She could feel both the sheriff and Guy hanging on it, ready to spring, to attack, to demand. "But I don't believe I can kill a man."

The sheriff leaned back against the table and lifted a goblet to his lips. He turned it in his hand as though this was the first one he'd ever seen. "Why can you not?"

"It is a mortal sin, lord, to kill."

"Are you saying I will go to Hell, Alys Fletcher? And what of your cousin," he waved at Guy, "who has also killed? I tell you this, worry not for your immortal soul. You will be absolved. Before you kill, if you wish."

Alys clamped her lips together and swallowed back a wave of panic. The room, the sheriff, Guy—all spun around her. "I am not you, my lord, nor am I my cousin. The absolution you speak of is beyond my grasp."

"I would summon a confessor of your choosing, and your absolution would be at hand."

Alys felt both men staring at her. Were they breathing? Was she? Her hands cramped, so she released them from fists.

The sheriff pushed away from the table. "I would be willing to... sweeten the pot. After all, everything has a price, my dear, and we are but hagglers. I can see you hate Robin of Locksley. Formerly of Locksley." He grinned at Guy like it was a private joke they shared.

Somewhere to her side, Alys heard Guy chuckle. *Does my cousin condone this?*

"I could," the sheriff said, "send for your brother. Bring him home. Forgive your family's owed taxes and restore you to Locksley."

Everything I want on the table, and all it would take is one arrow. One arrow to Robin's heart. Alys chewed the inside of her lip. Robin betrayed her... was it then an act of justice to betray him in return? But to murder him would be the ultimate betrayal. "How would you get my brother home?"

He stood straight. "Have you forgotten how to address me,

91

girl?"

Alys bowed her head. "My apologies, lord sheriff. You... you stun me, lord."

"That is better." He leaned back against the table. "The prince is my patron. And if I gifted him the outlaw, he would bestow upon me more power. The power to restore your family. What do you say?" The sheriff put down his goblet and ticked off his fingers. "You have absolution, your brother back, and your family shall have their home and farm once more."

Alys didn't imagine the sheriff wanted all of this just to knit her family back together. It was no secret Prince John liked this sheriff, perhaps even trusted him. What had the prince offered to sweeten the deal for the sheriff? "What if I assisted you in arresting him, my lord? If I left the execution up to your fine office." *Was it still murder, then?* Would she damn her soul for helping the sheriff catch an outlaw, even if she knew the noose awaited Robin's neck?

"I would bring your brother home. I will not forgive your family's debt to me—to this shire—if you merely help me arrest him." He paused. "Perhaps I might bend on that if you maimed Robin, so he could not escape the law..."

Guy spoke up. "Robin is an outlaw, Alys. He must be stopped."

The sheriff held up a hand and silenced Guy. "It must be her choice, Gisborne."

Guy's face was unreadable, like he'd put on a mask for this meeting.

"My patience wears thin, girl," the sheriff said. He feigned a yawn.

"Can I give you my answer in the morning, my lord sheriff?"

The sheriff sucked his teeth and looked her over then glanced at Guy. "Dawn. Give me your answer by dawn."

Alys curtsied low until her thighs burned from holding the position. "For your generous proposition, you have my deepest and humblest gratitude, my lord."

The sheriff smiled, stood, and patted the top of her head like she was a hound who'd learned to sit on command. Then, his hand buried in her hair, and he yanked her head back so she had to look up at him. Alys heard the scuffle of Guy's boots on the floor next to her. "Do not disappoint me, girl." The sheriff released her hair and dismissed her.

Alys staggered back, massaged her scalp, and scurried from the room.

11

Prayers & Promises

The one in worship of the father,
The other of the holy ghost,
the third was of our dear lady,
that he loved of all other most.
-Translated from *A Lytell Geste of Robyn Hode*

lys did not return to her chamber; instead, she shuffled to the chapel. The room was always open, though there wasn't always a clergyman. A priest or friar would arrive to offer forgiveness on Saturdays and a sermon on Sundays. A single pillar candle burned on the altar, the rest of the room and its benches cast into gloom, and she wished there were a clergyman here, now.

At the altar, Alys crossed herself, then lit a smaller candle and planted it beside the beeswax pillar. She knelt on the hard floor and peered into the two flames. Alys wished she'd prayed more over her seventeen years—if she tried now, would God hear her? Marian sometimes chided her for blasphemy.

Would God attend to one who so often took His name in vain?

She breathed out, and the flames flickered and gasped. "God, I beseech you, guide me. What road must I walk?" She observed the candles, as though God would grant her an answer via those flames. They burned calm and steady.

When her family first heard that King Richard would fight in the Holy Land, Alys had accompanied Ma to the kirk on the southern edge of Locksley. It had been late morning, sunlight streaming through the windows, drifting on dust mote dervishes. Ma had led Alys to the altar. There, she had prayed, then prostrated herself on the sun-soaked wooden floor, on her stomach, arms opened to the side and ankles crossed to mimic Christ's position in martyrdom. Above the altar, a carving of the savior looked down on them in benevolence and perpetual agony.

In the castle chapel, there was no carving of Christ. Only the altar, the candles, and six benches. The floor was stone—cold and dark in the night. Alys thought even if it were day, the floor would be cold. She walked back on her knees until there was space to stretch out on the floor. She crossed her ankles and put her arms out to the sides. She pressed the tip of her nose to the chilled flagstone, and she prayed again.

"Dear God. I know I have often sinned, even without seeking absolution for blasphemy or envy. I implore you, with all my heart, to forgive me and guide me."

She couldn't see the candles from the floor, but she saw the play of shadows their small lights produced. They waved over the stones, but in a slow, constant rhythm. Nothing to suggest any change. She remained there until her body throbbed from the hard floor. With a sigh, Alys stood. Perhaps God was too busy in the Holy Land, answering the prayers of his warriors.

Alys licked her thumb and forefinger and pinched out the flame of her own smaller candle. The flame was hot, but didn't singe her fingertips. The aroma of smoke curled off of the charred wick. She stared at the altar for a lingering moment, then left the chapel.

* * *

She still didn't return to her chambers, but sought Guy. Finding someone in the castle was no mean feat, especially since she didn't know where his chambers were. She climbed down the steps to the hall to seek a guard. Instead, she saw Guy, chatting with a group of off-duty guards who drank and rolled dice between them.

Alys wasn't sure what they'd make of her in the hall at this hour, for it was late, but she didn't care. She strode up to Guy, hoping she'd have an answer by the time she reached him.

When she was eight, Guy's father had promised to buy him a horse. Alys had wanted to ask if he would give them Merlin. What use would a knight have for a pony once he had a horse? By the time she'd opened her mouth to ask, the words wouldn't form. Alys had tried three times to ask Guy for Merlin, but couldn't find her voice. By the time she'd worked up the courage, Guy's father had sold the pony.

In the hall of Nottingham Castle, Alys clenched her fingers around the fabric of her skirt, and then released it to soften out the wrinkles. With each step, she ruminated on everything she and her family—and Marian—had lost because of Robin. Hob: Without Robin, he would still be home. The farm: Without Hob's absence, maybe her family could have afforded the sheriff's steep taxes. Marian's happiness: Without saving

Little John, Robin could have been her husband.

"Sir Guy," she said over the din of the guards and their game.

Guy glanced up, brows raised. "Alys. Should you not be asleep?"

"I came to make my answer, for the sheriff."

The smile left Guy's face, and he stepped away from the game and guards.

Her heart pounded in her chest, her ears, her throat. "I—" Her throat tightened around the next words, and all she expelled was a forced puff of air.

"Yes?"

Alys swallowed. Once again. It wasn't betrayal because Robin wasn't a lord anymore. He was an outlaw. He'd taken Hob. Because of him, her family was stuck in Town. Because of him, Marian would have to marry Sir Edward. Because of him, she might never see her family whole again. "I—I'll do it. I will identify Robin, disguise or no, so the sheriff can have him arrested." Her heart dropped cold into her stomach. "I want my brother back." Alys's heart rose into her chest again and warmed. The idea of Hob on English soil, safe, changed by battle or not—it wasn't everything. It wasn't returning home to Locksley. But it was something.

But what will Marian think? She will be there; she will witness me calling out her beloved. Her spine stiffened. Alys swallowed a few times to clear the lump in her throat. *Robin's arrest will avenge Marian. He deserted her. She must marry Sir Edward, a man she does not love, because Robin had to play the hero.* Alys swallowed once more. Marian would absolve her in time.

Guy's smile widened and lit his eyes. "I will inform the sheriff. No doubt he will be pleased, and if you succeed, you will reap the rewards, Alys."

"Robin has taken everything from me. He stole from me before he was ever an outlaw." Something in her hardened and cooled, like embers doused in water. Guidance from God or the devil, Alys knew her path. She knew what she craved, what she needed. Narrowing her eyes, Alys said, "I demand revenge."

Guy placed a gentle hand on her shoulder. "And it shall be yours, cousin." He squeezed. "I have never been prouder. Your loyalty lies on the right side." With a smile, he dismissed Alys.

She quit the hall and ascended the steps to her chamber. The stiffness in her shoulders softened, and she felt like she could float. Decision made: She would compete in the archery tournament. She would help the sheriff catch Robin. She would claim the pound—and the silver arrow. With those winnings, her family would return to Locksley. The sheriff would send for Hob.

Alys was determined to take back everything Robin had filched from her.

12

The Silver Arrow

A right good arrow he shall have,
The shaft of silver white,
The head and the feathers rich red gold,
In England is none like.
-Translated from *A Lytell Geste of Robyn Hode*

Betrayal.

Robin made a promise he did not keep. His need for glory took Alys's brother far from home, from family. His actions, intended or not, drove her family from their farm. By becoming an outlaw, he doused the last embers of hope for restoration of all her family had lost. Robin of Locksley was a traitor, and he would pay.

Alys had spent the last four days in a fog, with her thoughts moored to the silver arrow and Robin's arrest. How would she do it? Call out? Shoot an arrow at his ankle, so fleeing wasn't an option? She had to be ready for all eventualities—and all were more crucial than her work. Every one of those days,

Alys became more certain that helping the sheriff was the right thing to do. After all, Richard had left his brother John in charge, as regent. John had appointed this sheriff. And it was Robin breaking the law, not the sheriff.

It was Robin keeping her family separated, not the sheriff.

Despite her distracted state, Alys woke, carried buckets of steaming water to Maid Marian, helped her with her archery and embroidery, listened to her melodic airs, and brushed her hair. Alys slept and ate. But her heart wasn't in any of it and sometimes, she would step into the kitchens or her chamber and wonder how she'd gotten there. Maid Marian would ask her something and Alys's response would be a soft hum or nod, even if such responses made no sense to the questions posed.

On the day of the tournament, the hangman's platform had been moved to the side of the courtyard. Three nooses still wrapped around the top beam, like the sheriff was ready to hang someone if their performance was poor in the contest. *Perhaps the nooses are for those who perform too well.*

Trumpeters blasted a fanfare that cascaded down the steps from the keep. It filled the courtyard. Alys followed behind Marian, wearing a blue gown she'd given her. The neckline bore more fine embroidery than Alys could have produced or afforded. She ran her fingertips along it; Marian had embroidered it herself, she said. The dress no longer fit Marian, but on Alys it was loose around the bust and hips.

"I believe in you, Alys. You will win the pound and your family will not fear hunger this winter." Marian smiled and placed a hand on Alys's shoulder.

Alys nodded. "Thank you, my lady." Would Marian hate her soon? For helping to trap Robin? Or did Marian hold it against the outlaw for shattering her dreams, too? Something tickled Alys's mind—a consideration that had not weighed in her decision: Alys realized she didn't want to lose Marian's friendship.

But she'd given her word to the sheriff. And her anger was enough to fuel her actions against her former lord and master. Robin betrayed his vow. He would pay. He had to pay. Betrayal would not go unchecked.

Alys descended the steps to join the queue of archers waiting to collect their bows and arrows for the competition. The closer she got, the harder her heart pounded.

I am doing this for Hob. For my parents and Grandda. I am doing this because Robin has to pay for his betrayal. Because there must be justice.

Maid Marian took her place among the other gathered nobles, in their finery, in their jewels, shining in the sun. Sir Guy stood at the right hand of the sheriff like Christ to the Holy Father, only he was a messiah of ambition. Alys saw that in the way Guy stood, proud, a glint in his eye. But ambition was not wrong and evil. Guy could be decent and ambitious. Driven. So too could Alys. The sheriff had wrapped himself in chestnut leather and ermine and stood with his feet shoulder-width, one hand balanced on the hilt of his sheathed sword.

On a table before the sheriff's chair sat a purple pillow of velvet trimmed in gold, on which rested the silver arrow. The shaft shone and the silver fletching, engraved to look like real feathers, shimmered in the late-morning sun.

The prize was close enough to touch as Alys walked by. She flexed her hand and imagined the arrow belonged to her.

Another fanfare, and then the sheriff cleared his throat and spoke. His voice filled every crevice of the courtyard, every gap between every stone, every space between every set of shoulders. Alys even envisioned his words slipping between the fibers of the ropes tied into nooses on the gallows.

"Today, the best archers of Nottinghamshire come to compete for honor and silver," the sheriff said. "The tournament will be presented in three rounds, with eliminations following each round. All archers should present themselves to the master of revels." The sheriff swept a hand before him, indicating a man who stood at one side of the courtyard before two racks: one with bows and one with arrows. Guards flanked the racks. The master of revels waited with his nose turned up, facing the queue of contestants.

The man looked like God had squeezed him. Everything about him seemed stretched and skinny. To Alys, a master of revels should look more jovial, more well-fed.

Marian ushered her forward. Alys slid past the nobles and walked down the remaining stairs to the middle of the courtyard. The smell of bodies changed from sweet and light aromas to sharp and pungent odors. She watched her feet, certain that all others watched her, and wondered what she—a servant—was doing in this group of competitors.

"Name?" the master of revels said. It wasn't a question; it was a demand.

She'd pictured Robin's arrest, but not the moments afterward. She wondered what would happen; would the sheriff pretend she had naught to do with it? Alys wished she'd asked about these details. She glanced back up at Marian, who offered a nod and smile.

"Your name, girl. I haven't got all day," the master of revels said.

Alys hadn't realized she'd let her mind wander all the way

to the front of the line. "Alys Fletcher," she replied.

He scrawled down her name and studied her, then waved his hand at a young man behind him, who pulled a bow and three arrows off the racks. To bring a weapon into the castle without the sheriff's permission was a good way to get arrested. But Alys wondered how many of these archers owned their own bows. Practiced daily. She possessed skill with a bow, but even though she and Marian practiced almost every day, she hadn't regularly shot an arrow more than a half-dozen paces in over a year. With practice confined most days to Marian's bedchambers, Alys wondered if her arrow would hit a target, let alone a bull's eye.

She gripped the bow in one hand and the arrows in the other.

"Well?" the master of revels asked. "Move along. I've other archers to record. Mind that you return that bow in excellent form after the tournament, else it will come from your wages."

Alys moved to the side, where several other archers stood, like bears and dogs ready to fight. Their eyes darted, their hands tightened on their bows, and their feet shuffled and shifted in the dirt between flagstones. Alys searched the faces around her and those still in line to get their bows for the competition. She catalogued their brows, the bridges of their noses, the curve of their upper lips. Some of them didn't appear to have upper lips or she couldn't see their mouths through their thick beards. Alys dismissed those men; she'd never seen Robin of Locksley wear a beard like that.

No luck. None were familiar, none were obvious. Once all the competitors had their bows and arrows, the trumpets barraged Alys's ears with another fanfare. Twenty-one competitors, including herself. Pages unveiled half as many targets at the other end of the courtyard, fifty paces away.

A handful of servants Alys saw on occasion throughout the castle emerged from somewhere behind the nobles, carrying baskets filled with rocks. They lined all the rocks up as far from the targets as they could without upsetting the nobility. The master of revels commanded Alys and the other archers to take their places behind the line of stones.

"Two archers per target," he said. "Nock your first arrow."

Alys took her place between archers, both of whom were a head taller than her. They had broad shoulders and backs, like her da's, and Alys felt a fleeting desire that he should be among her competitors… though she knew he was not. He would be home, perhaps making an arrow. Maybe he struggled to see the fine work of his nimble fingers. Perhaps he argued with Ma about their lack of fortune or Alys's lack of suitors.

There was nowhere to stow her extra arrows. If she didn't have a quiver, she'd stick them into the soil but the courtyard was paved with flagstones. She and every other contestant on the line let extra arrows clatter to the ground.

As one, like an army, they all nocked an arrow. The master of revels called for them to draw. Bowstrings stretched and creaked, bows bent, and arrows pointed down range. Alys held her bowstring at her chin and breathed in and out. How was she supposed to help get Robin arrested when she didn't even know where he stood?

The master of revels bellowed. "Loose!" A twang reverberated down the line. Eight arrows embedded deep in bulls' eyes. Hers was one of them. Alys sighed in relief. She had another round to discover the outlaw. The others who succeeded included the fellow next to her, two on either end of the line, and four others yet too far away to see well. One of them had to be Robin. The master of revels dismissed everyone who didn't hit a bull's eye. The servants who placed the stones collected the fired arrows and the extra targets.

Alys rested the tip of her bow next to her foot. She eyed it up and down. A yew bow, she assessed.

"Not bad," said the man next to her. He wore a wide-brimmed hat, so she only saw his bearded chin. He'd draped a cloak of sage green around his shoulders; one cord that tied it closed had frayed.

"Wait until I win," Alys said with a broad grin.

The master of revels told them to prepare for the second round. Once more, two archers to a target. Four targets, eight arrows, all nocked in unison again at the call to do so. Both eyes open, Alys reminded herself. Both eyes on the target. Robin of Locksley was here somewhere, and she only had these two rounds to figure out who he was.

She turned to the left, to the right. The order to draw came, and Alys lifted her bow and pulled the bowstring taut. All the other remaining archers wore beards. Robin of Locksley must have grown one—or come in disguise.

"Loose!"

Once more, Alys released the bowstring and her arrow flew straight for her target, bit into its center and stayed there, a testament to her skill. The man next to her had similar success. The others did not. He had to be Robin of Locksley, and now the time had come for her to fulfill her side of the sheriff's bargain.

The pages removed the fired arrows and the extra targets. Alys wished she could hasten Robin's arrest. The nobles watched with breaths held; all was silent. Or, Alys thought, maybe her ears had failed her, since the sounds of the courtyard were drowned out by the hammer beat of her own heart. *Robin of Locksley is next to me. This is the moment.*

These facts repeated in her mind so she didn't hear the commands to nock, draw, and loose—the outlaw must have. He fired into his target with perfect aim, then turned toward her.

"Hurry, girl," he said. "Fire your arrow so I can take my prize."

Alys ground her teeth together and gripped her third arrow so hard the shaft bent a little in her hand. In an instant, she nocked, drew, and fired. Her arrow split his.

In her loudest voice, she turned toward him and, pointing, yelled. "Robin of Locksley! I will not let you claim this prize!"

She expected Robin to flee. Instead, he pulled off the hat and beard—now she saw it was a fake as she suspected—and his cloak. He bowed a courtier's bow.

There was just one problem.

She knew Robin of Locksley, and this man wasn't him.

"Good people of Nottingham," the man said. "I came for a silver arrow, but I will take a pound. I am Robin of Locksley, and by your leave, I welcome any donations."

You may resemble him somewhat, but you are not Robin. Alys glanced up at the sheriff and gave a subtle shake of her head.

A handful of men stepped forward and removed their guard uniforms. Underneath their helmets and armor and livery, they were dressed just like this man—in brown tunics and hose—they were the Merry Men, a band of outlaws who were rumored to follow Little John and now Robin. The real Robin had to be among them.

"Who are you?" Alys asked of the man whose arrow she'd split.

"Name's Wilmot Scarlet," he said. "Now run along."

Alys opened her mouth to tell him she had as much right to be here as he did, to remind him she'd split *his* arrow. He'd already left the center of the courtyard to join his companions. She thought about calling out that he wasn't Robin, but instead she watched them. What if she pointed out the wrong outlaw? The sheriff might give her nothing.

The courtyard erupted into cacophony and chaos. Guards—real guards—fought outlaws. Alys knew she had to get back up the steps. She might be talented with a bow, but she was out of arrows, and these men were fighting with blades. She had to get to the silver arrow. Or to Marian. She felt torn—but both were at the top of the steps.

That's when she spotted Robin of Locksley. Running for that violet pillow and the prize nestled atop it. The sheriff was busy shouting orders. Guy bustled Marian and other nobles into the safety of the keep. Alys raced for the steps. She took two at a time, but had to stop to duck as battle raged in the courtyard.

That silver arrow was hers. Not Robin's. He wouldn't take this, too.

13

Redemption

Bend your bows, said Little John,
Make all you pressed to stand,
The foremost monk, his life and his death
Is closed in my hand.
-Translated from *A Lytell Geste of Robyn Hode*

lys was almost at the top of the steps. Most of the
chaos raged behind her. She did not see the guard
running at her from the left. In one moment, her
boots were pushing off of a stone step, and in the next, her feet
were in the air as the guard lifted her away like she weighed
nothing. Alys screamed.

The sheriff's voice cut in. He ordered the guard to take Alys
away. Out of the courtyard. The guard complied and wound
a gauntleted arm around her waist to lug her into the keep.

Alys struggled to kick and punch but it was useless. She
couldn't get enough leverage to strike the guard hard enough.
Either he didn't feel it under his armor, or she missed. Alys

felt like her chest was being crushed.

Faith in Robin's promise had, once, swaddled all her hopes. While that faith was crushed, new hope had risen in the shape of that silver arrow. Now Robin was going to claim it and slip away. She felt it. In her heart, she knew the sheriff would fail to arrest Robin, like Marian had foreseen. It would be Alys who bore the weight of the sheriff's displeasure. He wouldn't send for Hob. He wouldn't forgive her family's tax debt.

"Stop struggling, mouse," the guard said. His voice was tumbling rocks in her ear. "I have duties. I ain't got all day to drag you around."

"Then let me go," Alys said through a clenched jaw.

"Orders." The arm around her tightened and pushed the air out of her body.

Something cold and hard curdled in her. Her anger toward Robin turned dark. Her friendship with Marian forgotten, Alys no longer wanted Robin arrested. She wanted him gone. Destroyed. All Robin did was steal from her. When would the chance come to take from him?

The guard deposited Alys in the sheriff's antechamber. She dashed to the window that watched out over the courtyard. The guards had restored order, and the outlaws were nowhere to be found. Guards and servants alike cleared up discarded bows, targets, and the rocks. It was as though the fight never transpired. The Merry Men had escaped. If they'd been arrested, the bells would be ringing.

Behind her, the door opened.

"I believe we had a deal." The sheriff's words were tight and terse.

Alys turned on her heel and bowed her head low. "My lord sheriff, I kept my end of our bargain. How could I have known—"

Two guards book-ended the sheriff, who interrupted her. His voice filled the room and Alys's ears. "I chose you because you know Robin of Locksley and could get close to him. You were meant to pick him out of the crowd. But you let your greed for the silver arrow distract you. You put yourself above all of Nottinghamshire, Alys Fletcher."

"No, my lord, I—"

"You dare to contradict me? We had a deal. A deal you did not honor. Had you kept your word, the nobles would not have been endangered so. You had three rounds to call Locksley out. Both of us would have benefited from his capture." He waved his hands forward; the guards marched into the room to seize Alys's arms.

"What are you—" Alys asked.

"Take her to the gaol," the sheriff said.

"My lord sheriff, I beg you."

The sheriff turned his back, and the guards tightened their hold on her upper arms and escorted her from the room. Alys wondered how long she would be abandoned in the gaol to rot before the sheriff ended her misery.

* * *

Alys struggled, but she wasn't strong enough to fight two men without a weapon. The guards led her down the corridor and turned down a twisted staircase wide enough for the three of them. The air from below, from their destination, smelled fetid. It reeked of unwashed bodies, vomit, and feces—all things that festered in the dank and the dark.

The sheriff's guards tossed her into an empty cell; Alys

landed in a meager pile of old and musty hay and heard the iron-barred door clang shut behind her. She scrambled to her hands and knees but the guard had already thrust a key into the lock. Alys pushed off of the hay-dust covered stone. The guard twisted the key and freed it from the lock. Alys crashed into the bars, one arm shooting through to clutch the key, like an owl that failed to cage a rodent in its talons.

The guard with the key laughed and dangled it in the air. "Look 'ee here," he said to the other guard, "a fox trapped in her little box." The rhyme conjured another bout of laughter from him, and his mate joined in.

"When I get out of here," Alys said through clenched teeth, "you'll be sorry!"

The guards roared again and turned from her. One of them shook his head before they started chatting about mead and the bosoms of their favorite tavern girls.

No silver arrow. No pound. No Hob. No Locksley... and where was Robin? *Gloating, probably. Crowing over his victory in Nottingham while he hoards both the arrow and the pound.* Alys's elbow and knee throbbed from being flung into this cell. Her armpit ached from her stretch through the bars. The odor made her head throb.

Alys kicked the stray straw into a thin pile and sat on it, bringing her knees to her chest. It was almost like Wilmot had known what she was about and goaded her into needing to best him at archery. He'd be sorry too, just like Robin, just like the guards, when she was free.

Alys's eyes burned. Her cheeks blazed, and pressure built behind her nose. She burrowed her face between her knees so no one in this place, this dungeon in the bowels of Nottingham Castle, could witness her sobs or tears.

Damp. *That's the word that best defines the dungeon.* There was always water dripping somewhere, like the dungeon cried itself to sleep at night and bemoaned its hunger by day. One prisoner was dead, Alys was certain. He slumped in the same slack-jawed pose when she lifted her head after her own tears ran dry. His eyes bored into the wall, like he expired without hope of release and couldn't have borne it to face the bars or the space beyond his cell.

So, when he shifted, she jumped an inch and hated herself for it. His movement was subtle: a dry swallow, a bob of his Adam's apple, accompanied by a rattle of air. *If he's not dead, then he's dying.* This was not how she envisioned her own demise.

But in those rare moments when she'd contemplated mortality before, speculated who might discover her old and frail form at peace, there were no iron bars involved. There was no dungeon. Sometimes it was her own bed here at the castle, in a warmer, drier part of the castle from this, where even the simplicity of a servant's chambers seemed the essence of comfort and decadence. Sometimes, she imagined herself in a tunic of mail, a bow in her hand, arrows strewn around her and one fixed in her neck or under her arm, those places of vulnerability, even in a suit of armor. In those musings, she was not old and frail but young and strong, and therefore her imagined demise was not restful, but glorious. Instead of bars there were trees, and instead of darkness, dappled sunlight glinted off her helmet.

Now, Alys wondered for the first time what it might be like to perish young and frail, in this cell of the damp, dark dungeon, gaze locked on the rough stone because she was too weak to hope for the miracle of escape or a swifter death.

112

Alys feared this was punishment from God for her greed. She'd coveted not only that pound, but also the silver arrow. And it should be hers—she was the best archer at the competition. She had more natural talent than Robin's man. Alys's breath snagged. It wasn't greed that prompted God to chastise her, for she wouldn't have kept the silver for her own aggrandizement. It was pride.

* * *

Heavy footsteps from four feet disrupted her thoughts of death and divine smiting, and she was glad for it. Two figures, both tall and one broad, one wrapped only in leather and the other with the softer outline of fur around his shoulders, stopped outside her cell. Sir Guy of Gisborne and the sheriff. Alys dipped her head and rubbed away the tear tracks and then rose. She forced her chin high into the air, mimicking Marian's stature.

"Have you come to amuse yourselves with my present state of wretchedness?"

The sheriff's laughter boiled and bled through the bars. Sir Guy was unmoved. "Girl, you were already wretched," the sheriff said, "but I am here about other business."

"You are to have a chance at redemption," Sir Guy said, but the sheriff held up a hand and the younger man clamped his mouth shut. Even in the low light, Alys saw Guy clench his jaw, that tiny muscle in his temple flexing.

"Your cousin speaks out of turn," the sheriff said. He stepped closer to her cell, though not close enough that she could reach through, dig her fingers into his ermine cloak, and smash his face against the bars until he was soft as bruised fruit.

113

"What business are you about then?" Alys asked. She flexed her fingers.

"He speaks out of turn, but not incorrectly. You have before you a second chance."

"Speak plain," Alys said. There was no point, she thought, in showing him such deference as their last meetings. What more could he do but hasten her death? She'd rather die with a noose around her neck in the courtyard, in the light, for all to see, than starve to death down here alone, forgotten, and moldering.

The sheriff raised both eyebrows. "You grow bolder. That's good. You will need boldness if you are to take on the task I have in mind." He cleared his throat and waited, like there would be a fanfare here to announce his next great idea. "We shall have an easier time catching the outlaw if we know what his movements will be ahead of time—a greater chance to stem his success. To stop him, to catch him is the prince's greatest desire."

Alys wanted to ask why the prince didn't come here himself then, if he wished it so much, but thought that would only earn the sheriff's ire—and now she was curious. "What will you give me?"

"Is the return of your brother, the return of your family's home, and silver no longer enough?"

Alys narrowed her eyes. "Spying on an outlaw is far more hazardous for me than identifying him. So, the reward should be greater as well. What's wrong, sheriff? Did you show your hand too soon?" She smirked.

The sheriff's voice came out in a growl. "How about your life, girl? And your parents' freedom? Is that worth it?"

Alys relented. She'd overstepped. A glance at Guy confirmed—his eyes were open so wide she could see the whites all around his dark irises.

"As good a bargain as any. In addition to all the rest." She didn't wait for the sheriff to counter. "How am I to spy on him?"

"By joining the Merry Men, as they're called… though they will not be so merry once I have them locked up down here."

Guy had schooled his face into an expressionless mask again, and she wondered how they could even be kin, linked through her ma, who showed her heart on her sleeve.

"And how do I know I can trust you?"

The sheriff's lips curled into an unnatural, mirthless smile. "I am not the one who went against their word. If you refuse, I shall execute you and imprison your family here for the rest of their natural lives. I shall have your brother banished so that even if he survives the war, he may never set foot on English soil again. Only a fool would turn down this opportunity of, as Sir Guy so eloquently put it, redemption."

Freedom from the dungeons and the gallows. Freedom for her parents. Freedom for Hob. The choice wasn't hard to make, but she still couldn't believe the sheriff did not have some duplicitous plan. "Double cross me," she said, "and I shall shoot an arrow through your heart."

Once again, the sheriff laughed, and Guy did not. "I will take my chances, girl. You may be a skilled archer, but you are a woman. I doubt you have the capacity to kill when you would not even agree to take Robin's life. After all he robbed you of, my dear." The sheriff turned on his heel, ermine cloak flowing around him like wings wrapped around a hawk, and left the dungeon.

Sir Guy of Gisborne remained, and though the dungeon

stunk more than the sheriff's breath, somehow the air Alys breathed in felt cleaner in his absence.

14

The Art of the Sword

There they fought sore together,
Two mile away and more,
Might neither other harm done,
The duration of an hour.
-Translated from *A Lytell Geste of Robyn Hode*

Sir Guy summoned one guard over and ordered him to unlock her cell. While he waited, he shifted his weight onto his back leg, sucked his teeth, and ran his tongue over them like he was hunting for crumbs that might try to hide in the spaces between. He waved the guard away when the door was open. For an instant, Alys thought of running past him to escape, but knew the castle housed too many guards between the dungeon and the gate, and she had no band of outlaws to assist her flight.

"Do you know how to fight with a blade?" He turned to lead her up and out of the dungeon.

The journey up the stairs and through the corridors differed from the trip down to the gaol. Since she walked of her own accord—though had to hurry to match Guy's longer stride—Alys noticed the shields and armor and weapons adorning these walls. They looked older. The higher up one went in the keep, the closer to the sheriff, the newer everything was, the more advanced, the more deadly. "I don't," Alys said.

Sir Guy sighed. "Very well. I will train you."

"But I won't be fighting—not up-close; I'm an archer."

"An archer you may be, but you still need to win your way into the Merry Men. Or did you not know? Rumor is that Robin requires his new recruits to best him with the sword. Probably doesn't want anyone showing him up with a bow." Guy smiled, a smile that said he still remembered their childhood games and lessons.

"That doesn't sound like Robin," Alys said.

"Being an outlaw changes a person."

Just like being a soldier. Will Hob and I recognize one another when this is over? Alys stopped. There wasn't enough time under the sun to train her to beat Robin with a blade. He was a soldier. A Crusader.

"Don't dawdle," Sir Guy said.

Alys forced herself forward and almost tripped over her own feet for the first few steps. When she caught up to her cousin, she heard him mutter something under his breath about a mistake, and her face heated. He led her to her chamber.

"Get some rest," he said. "We start at dawn." He turned and left before Alys could say anything to him without shouting it at his back.

She leaned against the wall. Her hands, smudged with grime from her brief sojourn in the gaol, trembled. They'd never done that, not from anger or fear.

118

Alys thought about the other rumors that followed Robin's name around the court. Tales of how he faced down an entire army. Tales of how he defended the life of the king, at great personal risk to his own—Alys had never doubted these. Here in England, in Nottingham, there would be tales of how he stood against the sheriff. Robin was too clever by half. Alys knew she'd have to become a convincing liar—as well as a somewhat decent fighter. If she failed, there would be songs and epic poems of how he bested his foes, though Alys doubted any of those tales would list one of his challengers as Alys Fletcher, one of his former peasants, killed by his own hand at seventeen.

Alys ducked into her room and shut the door, sat on her bed, and drew her knees to her chest. After a while, her eyes burned. She turned onto her side, her arms still around her knees, and closed her eyes.

* * *

The morning after the sheriff released her from the dungeon, Alys woke, clutched her chest, and panted. The nightmare flitted along the edge of her recollection, like mist slipping through her grasp. All that remained was the terror.

Her heart drummed a tattoo inside her body, in her throat, in her wrists, even in the soles of her feet. Breath shuddered out of her, and her body shook for another moment or two before the calm reassurance that it was just a dream settled over her. Alys touched her fingertips to her forehead: cold and clammy. She bunched up her bed linens and wiped her face and neck. Another deep breath, and her shoulders relaxed. Her neck and face softened.

Everything from the previous day seemed surreal. Alys should tend to Marian, but instead of arranging her wimple and helping her into her gown, Alys would spend her day learning the sword from Guy. She wasn't even sure Marian would speak with her.

The door swung open so fast it slammed into the stone wall. Guy filled the open frame, feet shoulder width apart.

"You look startled. You'll have to do better than that if you're going to fight Robin," he said.

Alys narrowed her eyes. She wanted to close them, lie down, and go back to sleep. "I only woke but a moment ago."

"I can't wait on you the whole morning."

Alys stood. "I'm coming, I'm coming."

Guy smirked and said, "Good. Let's go."

Alys's stomach ached, but she'd been hungry before. She didn't want to anger her cousin by telling him she hadn't eaten since breaking the night's fast the morning before.

Along the way to the courtyard, Alys asked, "Why did the sheriff ask this of me?" She hadn't asked the sheriff because she didn't want him to threaten her again. The sheriff didn't seem to like what he perceived as impertinence, and Alys knew she would have more luck asking her cousin.

From the sound of Guy's sigh, she could imagine he also rolled his eyes. "I should have thought that was plain. To catch Robin of Locksley. To prevent him robbing—"

"I know that part. But why me?"

"Robin thinks well of your family; his heart bleeds for all his peasants. Perhaps you haven't heard, but he's already distributed the silver he won among the villagers of Locksley. He is more likely to trust you than someone who wasn't one of his peasants."

"I don't think well of him!"

Guy stopped and turned toward her and took her forearm in his hand. His hold was gentle, but his hand encircled her arm. Alys didn't like that—she was proud of her strength, which helped her draw a bowstring and shoot with speed and accuracy.

"Alys, you've got to put that aside now. You must pretend to revere him, or at least not to loathe him."

"But if it weren't for him, Hob would be in England, safe. My family would still be home—"

"The sheriff would have levied taxes regardless of whether Robin stayed. So your family would have lost the farm, anyway, even if Hob stayed. The taxes are too great, Alys. And being in England is no guarantee of safety. Your best bet to bringing your family together, to returning home, is doing what the sheriff wants. And that means treating Robin like you don't hate him."

Alys screwed up her face. The last thing she wanted to do was grant reverence or even deference to the man she blamed for taking away all that mattered to her. "I—" She glanced away.

"If you cannot, he will suspect you. The sheriff will—Alys, even I could not protect you if you failed the sheriff in this. You must put your heart to the task. Please."

Guy had never begged her for anything. He'd often shown her kindness throughout their childhood, but he'd never used that word with her. There was no haughtiness to him now; he seemed as desperate as the word *please* suggested. But it wasn't just that which strengthened Alys's resolve—he was right. If she wanted to save her neck and her family, she had to do what the sheriff wanted. She had to pretend to like Robin.

* * *

Out in the courtyard, some guards turned their heads to watch. When Guy handed her a sword, she accepted it and flexed her fingers around the handle. It was lighter than she thought it would be, so she held on with one hand.

"That's a two-handed weapon," Guy said. "Grip it like so." He showed her on his own sword, the way his thumbs lined up. "Loosen your forefingers and the grip you have with your whole hand will be stronger."

Alys did as he said. Her heart beat a little harder, a little faster. Any minute he could strike at her; the last thing she wanted to do was drop her sword. She didn't think Guy would hurt her much, but it'd be embarrassing. One guard whistled at her. Alys fought the urge to issue a threat—even an empty one—in retort.

Guy showed her how to stand, one foot back and pointed on an angle, the other pointed at her opponent. He showed her how to strike with the sword, block with the sword, disarm her opponent's sword. Then he attacked.

The sound of the two swords clashing made Alys feel like Guy stabbed them into her ears. When she blocked his overhead blow, the force of his attack radiated in waves down her arms, through her shoulders, and around her chest to take away her breath.

"Breathe," Guy said. Then he jabbed her with the pommel of his sword.

The blow forced the air out of Alys's lungs so she had to drag in another breath. Then he swung again, this time from the side. She lifted her blade to block, but the force of his attack made her sidestep.

"Stand firm," Guy said.

"I'm *trying* to."

He turned his wrist and smacked her chest with the flat of his sword. Alys lost her footing and fell onto her rear.

"Never let an opponent get you on your heels. Get up. Get up fast or I will strike you where you sit."

Laughter trickled around the courtyard from the audience of guards.

She scrambled and brought her weapon up just in time to block again. "Why did you stop coming to visit us? Hob and me?"

Guy moved like water, yielding when he needed to adjust but powerful in each attack. "I was training to become a knight. My time was not my own."

Alys dodged. "And? You had no time in all those years for family?"

"What do you want me to say? My parents threatened to disown me, Alys. It wasn't until I came of age, until I was a man of means, that I could do as I wished, and even then—while my father yet lives, I must be careful. If he disowns me, I have nothing." He swung again. "Are you going to hit me?"

"You are a man. You can recover honor. Wealth. Respect."

"To a point. Now stop this useless prattle and strike!"

She thought she was doing better, at least until the sword left her sweat-slicked palms, and she saw it arc high into the air. It clattered onto a flagstone about a dozen feet away.

Guy put the point of his blade at her throat.

"Sloppy," he said. "That was sloppy. But at least you were trying to hit me." He lowered his sword and tipped his chin at hers. "Go pick it up. Attack me fast, or I'm coming after you."

* * *

Alys lost track of how many times she blocked, how many times Guy swung his sword down on her with enough force to make her bones rattle. That he would go easy on her had flown out of her head. The guards had gotten bored, or fearful of Guy's glare, and stopped watching her training at least. It was past noon when Guy sheathed his sword at his hip. Alys could have laughed with relief. They'd finished. Alys figured she'd be leaving Nottingham Castle today or tomorrow.

"Get some food," Guy said. "And some water. We go again in an hour."

Alys let her sword drop, and her stomach did the same. "I—I thought my training was completed." It hadn't taken her long to become comfortable with the bow, and Alys didn't expect to master the sword. She knew that took years. Competence was the goal.

He laughed. It wasn't a sneer or a snigger, but a genuine laugh from his belly. His eyes watered from it. "Robin of Locksley would flay you," he said between breaths of laughter, "if you tried to fight him like that. It will take days, maybe even weeks of training. It should take more, but the sheriff wants Robin caught as quickly as possible as a present to the prince." He patted her shoulder as he walked past her. "But thank you, cousin, for the jest."

Every muscle ached. Alys thought she could lie on the flagstone, next to her sword, for the rest of the day—and even that would be too taxing. She stooped to pick up the sword, and it almost pulled her down to the ground. It felt so much heavier than when she first clasped it. Her arms and back burned to lift it, and when she walked, the tip dragged on the ground.

Sir Guy spun on his heel, one finger pointed at the sword. "Pick that up. You'll ruin it, and you cannot afford to replace it."

Alys obeyed, but looked at Guy like she could summon a pack of wolves to tear him limb from limb.

"We could tell the sheriff you've changed your mind, of course, if you'd rather not learn the sword," he said.

"You shouldn't tease about that."

"A little gratitude would be nice."

Alys set the sword on a rack in the courtyard's corner. "Thank you, cousin, for teaching me."

"That's better." Guy disappeared into the darkness of the castle keep.

Alys rarely ate at midday. Servants only got food in the mornings before their charges were awake, and at night after they were asleep. Alys found her way to the kitchens, which were as deep in the bowels of the castle as the dungeon. The warmth of the hearths made the kitchens seem less desperate.

The cook spared her a bit of cheese, bread, and a quarter of an apple. Alys also downed a tankard of watered-down ale. When she finished, she ran back up to the courtyard; Alys didn't want to imagine what Guy would say if she didn't return before him.

When she got there, she was alone. Just her and the sword and the sun. Alys lifted it from the rack. Her arms and shoulders and torso tensed, but she practiced anyway. She practiced the blocks, the swings, the thrusts. She tried to imagine Robin here, in this courtyard, as her opponent. If she could best him in her imagination, maybe—with Guy's training—she'd be able to best him in the green wood, too.

Guy marched into the courtyard. "Put that down. In the afternoon, we train with staves."

"Why?"

"So I can hit you without killing you." He grabbed two sticks that were about three feet long and tossed one to Alys. She caught it and rolled her wrist, swinging the staff. It felt lighter than the sword, at least. Guy attacked.

"Have you fought Robin?" Alys asked between blows.

"I have not." Guy swung harder.

Before Alys could nurse her disappointment—Guy's insights into Robin's fighting style might be helpful—his staff hit her on the back of her leg, mid-thigh, and she felt her leg go numb. She tried to hop out of the way of his next strike but didn't hop far enough—she took a jab to the gut. Alys felt like she might throw up her lunch. She backed away and massaged her thigh with one hand until pins and needles filled her leg.

"What if this training isn't enough?"

"Don't worry, cousin," Guy said. "You'll be ready. We will train all day, every day, for as many days as we can. Because you either die or succeed. The sheriff's patience for failure wears thin because the prince's patience wears thin. Manure rolls downhill."

Alys managed to strike, though Guy's parry weakened the blow.

"Good," he said. "Faster though."

So Alys's training continued, until the evening hours and again the next day, and for many days after. After a month at this pace, the sword felt light in her hands no matter how many hours she wielded it. She was steady on her feet and faster than Guy. Being smaller than him in stature made it possible to outmaneuver and disarm him. Possible, but still

126

difficult.

Alys stood over him, where he sat in the courtyard, after she'd gotten him onto his heels. She rested her sword on one shoulder and smiled down at him. "What do you say, cousin?"

Guy got to his feet and sheathed his sword. "You're as ready as you'll be to challenge Robin—and we shouldn't ask the sheriff to wait any longer. You leave tomorrow." He grabbed the shoulder of her tunic and brought her close. "Don't lose, cousin. I don't like to waste my time."

Alys nodded and wriggled free of his grasp.

That night, she ate in her room. Her plate was full of cheese, bread, fresh fruits, hearty root vegetables, and beef. A servant gave her a goblet of wine. It was the most sumptuous meal Alys had ever enjoyed, but she couldn't help but think of the Last Supper, only in her case she played the role of both Christ and Judas, lamb and wolf. To spy on Robin for the sheriff might be to lead herself to her own slaughter.

15

Crossroads

Who is your master? said the monk
Little John said, Robin Hood.
He is a stronge thief, said the monk,
Of him heard I never good.
-Translated from *A Lytell Geste of Robyn Hode*

T he next morning, Alys sheathed her sword and
shouldered the bow supplied to her, as well as a quiver
of arrows. Arrows her da made. Arrows she might
have crafted. Two were fletched in white and red and the
other four in gray and brown. Alys ran her finger along one
of the red fletches and the vanes and barbs separated and fell
back together.

This was a soothing sensation of home. Of sitting next to
Da on the family's old farm in Locksley. Of the last rays of the
sun warming Alys's cheeks. Of the tickle in her nose whenever
the wind wafted across the rye stalks like God blowing on his
food to cool it.

She met Guy at the gatehouse under a blue sky. "Your pass is only valid today," he said. "The sheriff has never issued you a pass for a longer absence and thought to do so now might raise suspicion."

"Then how am I to bring you information?" Alys rested her now-calloused hand on her sword's pommel.

"You will have to ask for me or the sheriff at the gate. Or if you know I am at Locksley, you may seek an audience with me there. Either way, be discreet. Though I warn you: Do not sneak into the castle; the guards may seize you—or worse, shoot."

"Maybe mention to the guards I'm allowed in?"

One guard behind Guy slipped a glove onto the wrong hand, stared at it like he didn't recognize what a glove was, and took a full moment to realize it was on the wrong hand. He hiccuped.

Guy sighed. "Drunken fool."

"Erm, maybe not. I'll ask for you."

"Good."

Alys turned from him, but his voice halted her.

"Remember, don't perish, Alys Fletcher. I put a lot of time and effort into training you; do not you dare waste my investment."

Don't die, Alys Fletcher, because we're family would have been nicer, she thought. Alys cleared her throat. "I don't plan on it. If things look grim, I'll just flee," she said, relieved to hear the steadiness in her words. She wasn't certain at all. Last night she was. This morning, until now, she felt certain. But now, to consider of herself as Guy's investment and little else, a rung on his ladder of ambition, stripped her confidence and left her bare, a girl in an open desert under the scorching sun surrounded by an army she couldn't subdue.

Guy strode away, back to the keep, and left her at the gate. No fond farewell. She'd tried to talk to Marian once more the day before, but either the lady wasn't in her room when Alys had ascended that spiral tower, or Marian scorned her.

I hope Marian doesn't learn of my deal with the sheriff. If she tells Robin... I'm running straight into a trap. Was Marian still in contact with Robin? Alys couldn't be sure, but knowing how easily the outlaw got in and out of the castle, it wasn't impossible.

As she studied the expanse of stone before her, Alys told herself not to worry about Marian finding out and telling Robin. She could only control what she would do, what she had to do in order to safeguard her family and restore their home.

Alys knew she had to leave her castle life behind.

Life is a series of shorter lifetimes sewn together. She'd started out destined to work a farm. When that lifetime had run its course, Guy brought Alys into service at the castle. Once again, she had to leave all that she knew, all the comforts and grievances, and venture into Sherwood Forest.

Alys sighed and turned her back to the keep. Chin tipped high, she strolled toward the portcullis. With their instructions from Sir Guy to let her leave today without inspection, the guards raised it so she could go out into Nottingham Town.

She spared a brief thought about stopping at the chapel. It was as small as any of the hovels that clustered around like a pile of dogs on a frosty night. But the sheriff had promised a priest would absolve her of her sins since she would commit them in service to him, and to the crown. Alys decided it was best to wait until she committed sins and then confess. If she confessed ahead of time and the priest favored Robin, the outlaw might figure her for a spy before she could prove herself to the sheriff.

Can you be forgiven your sins, helping a man like the sheriff? And the prince? Alys scowled and stuffed these thoughts away to some dark corner of her mind. They were as unwelcome as the notion that it was foolish to hold Robin responsible for Hob's safety in the Holy Land.

If she took the main road straight ahead, she'd come to her parents' hovel. And though they wouldn't reveal her secret to Robin, Alys didn't judge it wise to go there. If they learned of her plans, their worry would be too much to stomach.

Besides, she was her own mistress for the first time in her life, at least as far as which path to take. When she was a girl, she had to go with her parents, grandda, or Hob. As Marian's lady's maid, Alys had followed her ladyship. She took a deep breath; even the Nottingham air smelled sweet for once. Warm tingles tickled her arms and legs; Alys closed her eyes to bask in the sensation that the sun shone on her, even when it hid behind a cloud.

Alys reached a crossroads: one path to the chapel, another to her parents' home, and a third that pointed north, toward Locksley. She stayed still and quiet, looking down each road. Then Alys chose. She turned north and wove and wended her way out of Nottingham Town toward her family's farm.

After all, the best place to start her search for Robin would be near Locksley. If she trusted rumors, he turned up near his old village most often.

The road she took would spit her out right on the borders of Locksley. Perhaps Robin would be in the village itself, delivering money and goods to his peasants. *Did he ever stop to see my parents in Nottingham Town? Did he care what happened to my family after he went to war and then took to the woods?*

She wondered if Robin ever felt guilty about leaving Hob behind to fight in the Holy Land with the king, or if he ever carried shame over breaking his word. With any luck, she'd soon find out.

16

To Throw a Gauntlet

Tell me truth, said Robin,
So God has part of thee.
I have no more but ten shillings, said the knight,
So God have part of me.
If you have no more, said Robin, I will not one penny:
And if you have need of any more,
More then shall I lend thee.
-Translated from *A Lytell Geste of Robyn Hode*

The town of Nottingham melted into a road spotted with cottages, spaced farther and farther apart, and Alys felt like she was walking back in time, so that when she reached the village of Locksley, it was years ago and she was a small girl, running up the street to show her da a feather she'd found for his arrows.

Peasants farmed their fields. Birds flitted over the lane, and a toad hopped alongside Alys, like it was trying to follow her. Alys walked through Locksley, and no one noticed her. Not the weathered woman who begged on the corner near the manor who had always told Alys stories of ghosts and goblins, nor the miller who had always helped Alys drag bound sheaves of rye into his mill to be ground by the millstone that was wider than she was tall. None of the children stopped to talk to her; they all dodged out of her way the same way she would have if a page carrying a sword and bow and arrows came walking down the lane. Everyone kept their heads down, focused on their chores, errands, or games.

Alys kept walking too, at least until she reached her family's old farm. Fields were fallow, but she couldn't see the dark mounds of rich soil because they were overgrown with long, thin grass blades that stretched across the ground like spider webs. The rye used to grow taller than her, taller than Hob.

Her family's old house looked sleepy. Not decrepit, but not in its prime either. A window sill sagged. The door hung ajar a few inches. The shutter over another window had fallen off, and now moss grew on it in the wall's shade.

Alys opened the door, and a rectangle of light pushed in before her. Something—or some things—scrambled deeper into the shadows. Each room was almost twice the size of the rooms at her parents' home in Town. There had been a dedicated kitchen, where her ma would take the grains from the mill and work magic to turn them into dough, then transform that into bread at the village bake house. The memory of sticky strings of dough and crisp crust made Alys's mouth water. Now, the kitchen rested under thick blankets of dust instead of a bed of rushes, and made Alys think of catacombs.

* * *

How long she stood in the doorway, Alys knew not, but when she left the house, she pushed the door closed, as far as it would go. It no longer fit snug into its frame. Alys walked past the fields toward the forest. Robin of Locksley had to be somewhere in there. The North Road ran right through the wood and there were always stories of outlaws robbing rich nobles on that road. She would start there.

Upon reaching the road, she pulled up the hood of her cloak and sang. Alys stepped on as many twigs as she could find and waited for an instant after each snap to see if outlaws would spring out from behind the tree trunks on either side of the road. Other than her own voice and stomping around, she heard only the scratches and skittering of small woodland creatures. Squirrels and rabbits, but no outlaws.

As the sun set, she weighed if she should venture deeper into the forest. But Guy had only taught her how to use a sword; she wasn't a tracker. She could fire an arrow at an animal and hit her target, but she didn't have a full set of hunting skills. Better, she thought, for the outlaws to come to her.

So she kept singing, stomping her way north, then south. The sun was halfway below the horizon when an arrow zipped through the air and burrowed into the earth at her feet. She stopped and stared at it. A straight, smooth shaft with two white fletching feathers and one brown. A hunting arrow—fletched by her da. Alys harvested the arrow and blew on the point. Soil and bits of moss flew off of it and flitted back to the ground. She twirled the arrow in one hand before dropping it into her quiver.

"Thank you," she called, "for the arrow. One can never have too many."

Leaves rustled to the east, and men—about a half

dozen—emerged onto the road. They wore tunics of green over brown hose—except for a monk whose brown robes stretched over a kettle-bowl stomach. She knew of Robin, Little John, and Wilmot—but there were a few others whose faces didn't come with names.

"Your purse, if you will," one of them said. He emerged from behind the others, cowl up.

"I have very little. A few pence at most." Guy had given them to her for this game—this game that Robin and his Merry Men liked to play.

"How little?" Robin asked.

"Five pence."

A wave of laughter moved around the Merry Men, who had arranged themselves in a horseshoe around her and Robin. One of them whispered something Alys couldn't make out to his fellow, and another elbowed the man next to him in the ribs—a light jab.

"If five is all you have," Robin said, "then we'll not take a single one. But if you lie, we take the lot."

For a moment, Alys didn't even want to show the five pence. She wanted to keep them, give them to her parents.

"If you've lied, I can understand your reticence," Robin said. He lifted his sword halfway out of its sheath.

Alys bristled. "I'm not lying. I only have five." Only. Alys didn't like when people said *only* with any amount of money, as though every farthing didn't help. As though a farthing was nothing to a peasant.

"Then be so kind as to show us," one of the Merry Men called.

Alys glanced at the speaker, a man with a rotund belly and a shaved pate. When she looked back at Robin, he'd moved closer. He was still out of reach, but Alys knew he could take her life if he wished.

She untied her purse, each movement deliberate. Guy had warned her—no sudden movements at this point in the game. They would read it as an attack. Alys loosened the strings and turned the purse upside down. Five pennies glinted in the dappled and retreating sunlight as they fell to the ground.

Robin dropped his sword back into the sheath. Wilmot counted to himself; Alys saw his mouth make the shapes of numbers, but she didn't hear his voice. "There are only five," Robin announced to the Merry Men. Their shoulders dropped, and it felt like their disappointment paved the road.

Alys wondered if outlaws reached a point where they no longer questioned the morals of their actions, but came to enjoy them. She thought they must, as eager as they were to rob her. Robin turned from her. Alys knew this was her chance.

"I know who you are, Robin of Locksley," she called at his back.

He stopped. "As do many in these parts. What of it?"

"I would join your Merry Men," Alys said. "It's—it's a travesty what the sheriff and Prince John are doing to Notting-hamshire, to England: robbing the poor with outrageous taxes, gaoling those who cannot pay, executing men for stealing bread to feed the starving. They take away farms and leave the fields to go fallow. They break apart families, take everything someone has. There was a time when I would have thought five pence a paltry sum, but now..." She stooped to collect the coins, blew some dead leaf bits away and brushed the dirt off one, and tipped them back into her purse. When she stood, she pushed her hood back.

"I know her," Wilmot said.

"Alys Fletcher," Robin said at the same time.

Alys ignored their recognition for now. "I would join your band of Merry Men and help bring succor to the poor. Food to the hungry. Hope to the peasantry of England. You are a beacon, a—"

Robin held up a hand. "Enough. I do not require flattery. But you are supposed to be in the castle. Serving Maid Marian."

Now it was time for it. The lie she and Guy had cooked up. "I can stomach working for the sheriff no longer. His abuses of the people..." Alys added to her story something not even Guy knew. She walked up to Robin and said in a harsh whisper, "Now we've both broken our vows." She stepped back and clutched the purse in her hand. The velvet pile tickled between her fingers. "What must I do to prove myself, so I may join you?"

"We will get to how you may prove yourself. I have questions."

So do I.

"How did you come by your weapons?"

"Filched them."

Robin scratched at his temple. "I wonder if you are so embittered toward the sheriff, and so wretched in your poverty, that you might have so merry a tune on your mind."

The heat of panic trickled down her neck. Guy had not rehearsed this with her. He had not warned her to attract their attention with a dirge. "I—I hoped to get your attention. My ma used to sing that song to me. It is difficult to think of all the wrongs the sheriff has committed without thinking of my family."

"Your family… why did you not go to them?"

"I love my family, and true, they would take me in. But I could hardly stand against the sheriff as the daughter of a fletcher."

"I see." Robin leaned closer, his hand on his sword, though he didn't level the weapon at her. He walked around her, examined her. "I doubt brute strength is your gift," he said. Laughter jumped around the men who surrounded them.

"No. Archery is my greatest skill, but I am trained with the blade."

"She was next to me at the tournament," Wilmot said. "She's a decent shot."

"Decent?" Alys said. "I split your arrow. And hit the bull's eye doing it."

Robin waved a hand at Wilmot. "This is not the time or place to argue who has greater skill with a bow. We could always use someone else to cover us."

"What if she's attacked?" This time, it was Little John who spoke. He leaned on a quarterstaff that sunk into the dirt.

Robin circled her again. "In order to join us, you must fight me. I need to be sure you can look after yourself. We try to take care of each other, but sometimes it's more important to escape."

"I've heard you like to challenge new members in this way. I am prepared."

"Are you?" Robin smirked. "And are you willing to do as I command, without question?"

"Yes."

"Are you willing to give money and food to the poor, even if your own belly is empty, and even if the only roof above your head is the sky?"

Alys grit her teeth. She wanted to start this fight—the sooner it would be over. "Yes."

Robin smiled down at her. "Then we shall fight. At dawn. It is getting nigh on dark now. Do you have a place to sleep?"

"I can shift for myself," she said.

"Then be here at dawn," Robin said. He and his Merry Men dispersed into the trees.

Alys didn't move at first, not until the last of their footsteps, soft on the forest floor like they knew where all the twigs hid under last year's leaves, dissipated. Only the sounds of the forest filled her ears: the staccato song of crickets, the low hoot of an owl, and the scurry of rodents.

A sliver of sun still lingered above the horizon, like the day itself didn't want to end. Alys returned to Locksley and the empty old farmhouse. The floors were bare save for a few old strands of hay and a carpet of dust. She curled up in a corner and tried to picture the house as it once was and might someday be again, full of life and warmth and family.

17

First Blood

Could you shoot as well in a bow,
To green wood you should with me.
-Translated from *A Lytell Geste of Robyn Hode*

Sleep didn't come until a hint of pre-dawn light glowed outside the windows. Alys spent the darkest hours of the night wondering if Robin would injure her, and what it would feel like to be wounded at his hand.

She didn't dream, or at least she didn't recall any dreams. A rooster crowed at dawn and woke her. Her eyes were full of grit, and her eyelids too heavy to lift without effort. It'd be so easy to close them again, sleep a full day, and sneak out of Nottinghamshire to start a life somewhere else. But for Alys, abandoning her family was not an option, not when their safety hung in the balance. Not when Hob's safety hung in the balance.

She pushed herself up from the floor and brushed away the dust and sparse hay. Alys stretched. She stood as high as she could and splayed her palms on a beam that spanned the ceiling; she ran her fingertips over the ridges of the wood grain. When she was small, she used to try to touch them, but even if she jumped, they were always beyond her outstretched fingers. Now that she stood tall enough to reach the beam, she trailed her nails along the grain. It seemed like a blade had cut those grooves into the wood.

Alys dropped her arms, unsheathed the sword Guy had given her, and swiped it through the air a few times. Parry, swing, thrust.

Don't think about the fight. It was time to leave her family's farmhouse, and as she did, Alys spared a bitter thought that if it was empty, it was even more cruel that her family was not permitted to live there and tend the lands. She turned to let the first rays of the sun warm her back and peered over Locksley. Doors were still closed, and no smoke curled from chimneys. No one was out of their homes yet, save her and the rooster—she spotted him on the roof of the house across the stream. Alys took a deep breath. Sweet hay, cow dung, and a sharpness in the air that often presaged a storm. Dark clouds draped the western half of the sky, and the sun illuminated their contours from the east. Beautiful but dangerous.

Kind of like God. If all men marched to God's plan, she wondered at the idea of a war waged in His name, families divided in His name.

She turned from Locksley, from the farmhouse, from the clouds, and from the rooster. She left the fallow fields behind and strode back toward the green wood, toward the road that cut through its trees. With each step, a sort of calm filled her. God's plan or the sheriff's—it mattered not. Alys was on the only path she knew to restore her family. *And it's not treachery*

142

to act against Robin. He is an outlaw, lord of nothing now.

But if she failed, everyone dear to her would suffer. Alys shook her head and swatted at the low, leafy growth. *Never let them get you on your heels.*

Alys steeled herself. A twig snapped over the ridge that led deeper into the wood but she didn't flinch. She didn't even turn. Alys closed her eyes. It felt so good to shut them, and she might have fallen asleep right where she stood, if not for the sound of people gathering around her. Alys opened her eyes. She wondered if they'd jump to Robin's aid if she held her own. She knew she could not fight a half-dozen men. She eyed the path that led her here and thought to always keep it in her sights—in case she needed to escape.

Robin stepped forward into the middle of the circle with her. "You're here."

"And you're late," Alys said. "You said dawn." *How rude to force someone to wait like this. I may also have been here past dawn, but I was here first.* He didn't need to know it gave her time to settle her nerves. Everything in her stilled. A soft breeze brushed the tips of her fingers. Her sword was within reach. If Robin attacked, she could block, parry, or dodge in the space of a breath. She wanted to ask him about Hob, but not in front of others. She didn't want bravado or reputation to stand in the way of an honest answer.

He smiled. *Smiled.* Like it wasn't important. Like this was part of the game to him. "Are you ready to fight? Only you look like you're not quite awake yet."

"Stop stalling." Alys drew her sword. The sun winked on the blade and reflected in Robin's eye; he turned away, and this made Alys smirk. "Draw." She gripped the handle with both hands the way Guy had taught her, her blade between them.

Robin stepped back. His sword rang as he unsheathed it, and he still clasped it in one hand. "The rules are as follows. First blood marks the victor."

Alys nodded. "Agreed. Let's get this over with."

One of the Merry Men behind her called out. "Are you so eager to lose, fledgling?"

She grated her teeth. Fledgling? She'd show them who was a fledgling. Yes, she was smaller than them. Maybe younger than all of them, too—though Wilmot and two others she didn't know looked close to her age. By defeating Robin, Alys would prove her worth with a sword. She had to best him. *I have no other choice.*

Robin gripped his sword with both hands and shifted his stance. Then he lunged and swung his weapon down at Alys; the blow might have killed her if she didn't hop out of the way. The Merry Men chuckled.

"I thought this was to first blood."

"You're fast," Robin said. "I'll give you that." He set up for another blow, but before he could strike, Alys attacked him with a side swing.

"That was to test my speed? You almost killed me."

He blocked. Their swords clanged, and a hush went around the circle of Merry Men so it felt like a bubble enclosed them, where the only sounds Alys could hear were the scuffle of their feet, their labored breaths, and the clash of their blades when they met. "I will not take your life, Alys Fletcher."

He came at her again. Parry, swing, thrust. Dodge, parry, swing.

Alys's shoulders and back throbbed as they traded blows. She blocked another of Robin's, but the force of his attack almost brought her own sword down onto her head. Everything ached. The sun sat above the horizon in its entirety now, and sometimes it burned her eyes. Sometimes Robin squinted. Alys tried to put the sun in his face as much as possible—but Robin tried to do the same to her.

She kept dodging and parrying, waiting for him to squint again. When he did, she kicked out, hard. Her foot connected with his gut, and he doubled over and dropped to one knee. The Merry Men shouted in protest, but she couldn't make out what they said. Everything sounded muffled except her own panting and her heartbeat echoing between her ears. Alys nicked the side of Robin's neck a moment before his blade sliced her skirt and bit into her calf.

She cried out and slumped to the ground. The surrounding men cheered, and the world found its voice again. Crows cawed and flapped away from the ruckus. The men stomped their feet, clapped their hands. Somewhere, from up high, a hawk's keening cry pierced through Alys's head. She dropped her sword and clamped a hand onto the gash in her leg.

Robin bellowed for his men to be quiet. "She cut me first." He touched the side of his neck and then held up his palm to present the blood. "Alys is the victor."

Robin smiled and clapped a hand on her shoulder. "Welcome to the Merry Many."

"You mean the Merry Men," Alys said. Her words were little more than a hiss. Even though she covered the scratch on her leg, the wound stung and pulsed. All she needed right now was to be anywhere but in the forest. *What comforts are there here?*

"I meant what I said. You are not the first female to join our ranks, and I hope you will not be the last. We are the Merry

Many, but the people will call us what they will. Come—we can patch up that cut." Robin nodded toward her leg and then retrieved his sword.

She put weight on her leg, but not all of her weight. Alys bit back a wince and collected her own weapon to sheath it at her hip. She limped along behind Robin and the rest of his followers.

"Where do you set camp?" *How far must I walk like this?*

"You'll see," said Little John. "Better than any hovel. Put your arm around me, lass."

Alys hesitated. "You were the one who was supposed to hang."

"That," Little John said with a smile, "was not my time. Come on then."

"I am glad of it, especially at this moment." She smiled and took another step but couldn't keep back the whimper of pain. Alys braced an arm on Little John's shoulder, and his arm wrapped around her back. He started forward, half carrying her.

Another man strolled up to her and matched their pace. He didn't look older than Hob, but had a lither frame. "You fought dirty, wee one," he said with an appreciative sideways grin. His Scottish brogue made it almost impossible for Alys to understand what he said at first. He dragged the word *dirty* out to sound like it had two extra syllables, and she thought he'd never stop rolling the r. The Scotsman was taller than Robin, but shorter than Little John. *Everyone is shorter than Little John.*

"Leave her alone," Wilmot said, "you bloody Sawney." He grinned.

"Ach," the Scotsman said with an answering smirk, "I'm

146

just introducing meself. Bugger off." He turned back to Alys. "Name's Graham."

"Nice to meet you," Alys said through clenched teeth. Her mother would chide her for offering such an unwelcoming response to a man. Marian would never address a man so, but Alys's leg hurt, and offering a curtsy was the last thing she wanted to do.

"We'll protect you, wee one."

"Oh, you don't have to call me that. I'm not all that keen—"

"He gives everyone a nickname," Wilmot said. "Kind of annoying."

Graham scooped a handful of crispy leaves and tossed them at Wilmot, and both men laughed.

"I'm fine being called Alys. On account of it being my name, you understand."

Graham nodded. "Welcome, wee one."

Alys opened her mouth to protest the nickname but there was something in Graham's eyes that told her it would be in vain. He was going to call her that, anyway. She decided, as he took her other arm to help her up a small hill and over a ridge, to disabuse him of the idea by refusing to answer to it.

They paused at the crest of the ridge. Beyond was a small valley, with a cave nestled in its trough. "Is that—"

"Where we sleep? Eat? Aye, that's our camp, wee one."

That it was so close to the road and neither the sheriff nor Sir Guy had ever found it surprised Alys, though she supposed it was easier to rob nobles if one's camp wasn't too far away from where they passed through the wood. *Maybe they have not looked for the camp yet.*

"At least," Graham said, "for now. We've moved when we've had to."

147

I hope I can finish this spying business before it's time to set up camp somewhere else. The easiest way to appease the sheriff would be to tell him where the outlaws slept. She worked her way down the ridge, but slowed as they neared the cave.

"Is your leg hurting you too much, wee one?"

Alys didn't answer, but stared at the darkness of the mouth of the cave. She didn't want to enter that cave. Alys knew she would be trapped, that once there the Merry Many might discover her true purpose. A rabbit trapped in a hole, foxes and hounds with their snapping teeth waiting at its mouth. If they found out she was a spy, she doubted she'd ever come out of that cave alive. At least there was no way for them to figure that out yet.

Inside the cave, piles of embers glowed every so many feet down the center. On one side lay beds: an endless line of blankets and little piles of brush from the forest. On the other side of the cave were weapons, crates heaped with food, and small chests and boxes with coin and jewels that cascaded to the ground.

Alys felt a sudden yearning for the castle. She had a proper bed there, off the ground, away from bugs, mice, and other creatures that crawled in the night.

"Where should I…" she asked Little John, but he said nothing as he and Graham deposited her on a tree stump near the mouth of the cave.

Robin approached, holding a small leather satchel, and crouched beside her. He withdrew a roll of bandages and wrapped some around the cut on her leg. "You've got to keep this clean or it will fester, and you will take a fever and maybe die."

Alys knew this already. It was impossible to learn to craft

arrows without an occasional break of the skin. She could have wound the bandage herself, but she needed to build more trust between her and Robin.

"Rest your leg." Robin flipped the flap of the satchel closed and stood. "Get food and drink. Tomorrow you work with us."

"What are we doing tomorrow?" Alys asked. She tried to sound innocent and curious and tilted her head to one shoulder.

"Tomorrow is tax day. The sheriff's men will collect taxes from the people. They'll pay from the money we give them, and then we'll collect the taxes from the sheriff's men."

Alys smiled. Too bad she didn't have a way to get word to Nottingham more quickly. But there would always be another tax day. Tomorrow she would observe and take part in their illegal activities, and then she could tell the sheriff how Robin got away with these robberies.

This spying business would have to be like a long-distance volley. If she wanted to hit a target far away, she'd shoot up into the air. *Sometimes you have to feel you're going off course or taking too long.* As long as she found the bull's eye in the end, that was all that mattered.

When Robin finished, Alys settled into the cave near its mouth. The forest floor darkened as the storm clouds rolled in. By the time the skies opened, the Merry Many had filed into the cave and sat together, telling stories and singing songs.

18

Alms for the Poor

Take me my gold again, said the abbot,
Sir justice, that I took thee.
Not a penny, said the justice,
By God, that died on a tree.
-Translated from *A Lytell Geste of Robyn Hode*

Alys woke to the clang of metal. The cave echoed with men preparing swords, bows, and arrows. One man squatted next to her bed and said that Robin summoned them all outside, armed. Alys rubbed the sleep from her eyes and got to her feet, trying to ignore the dull pain in her leg. The last thing she wanted to do was fight today, but she took her sword and sheathed it on her belt, anyway. She shouldered her bow and grabbed her quiver before trudging out of the cave.

Caves turned out to be suitable places to sleep, at least until everyone else woke and moved about. Several of the Merry Many snored, and the rhythmic sawing echoed off the cave walls and drowned out sounds of the green wood that permeated the dark tunnel. They slept in rounds, but because it was her first night and she'd been injured, Alys didn't need to fulfill overnight guard duty last night.

Outside, spears of sunlight pierced the clouds and the canopy to spotlight the forest floor. Robin stood in the center of the clearing, one foot on the stump, and his elbow propped on his knee.

"Good morrow, friends," he greeted.

Alys mumbled a good morrow and gathered around him in a circle with the others. Farming, seeing to Marian's needs, or training with Guy—none of it ever compelled her to enjoy waking up early. Running about with outlaws proved no exception.

"Today is tax day," Robin said. "But no peasant shall be arrested or evicted." He straightened his back and squared his shoulders. "None shall feel the cold damp of the sheriff's dungeon. Not while we yet draw breath." A smile spread across Robin's face. "And not while we have the wealth of several bishops and other nobles to distribute. Time to make good of our takings, boys."

Does that mean I'm one of the boys? Most of them are men, old enough to have families. What did they give up to live as outlaws in the forest?

Robin continued to explain their plan. They would distribute coin to those peasants who couldn't pay, and then follow the tax collector to steal it back. They'd start in Locksley, since of all the villages in the shire, it was closest to Town and first on the tax collector's rounds.

Alys and each of the Merry Many took several pouches full of farthings, ha'pennies, and pence. A peasant who presented larger coinage, like a shilling, would fall under suspicion. With the plan and outlaws ready, and the sun rising, they walked together to the main road that cut north to south through the forest, and then on to the village.

"Are you ready for your first day at outlawry, wee one?" Graham asked. He walked with one hand on the hilt of his sword and a long stride, which he slowed to match hers, so he looked like he floated from one step to the next.

"Who says it's my first?" Alys asked. She cringed. She'd planned not to answer him when he called her *wee one*. Now he'd think it was permissible to call her that.

"I meant no offense, wee one. Your leg bothering you?"

"Only a little." Alys told the truth but then she wasn't running or fighting right now.

"Well, you best tamp that down. I doubt we'll get through the day wi'out a fight, wee one. Though… we've not had to kill anyone yet."

Alys blanched. "Kill? That doesn't seem wise." *Or moral.* It wasn't part of her deal with the sheriff, and she didn't think he'd thank her for participating in such violence against those he sent to collect taxes. The old sheriff had always collected moneys that were due to the shire and the crown himself—this one, Alys noticed, liked to delegate.

"I hope we never have to. The sheriff—he has a way of making men go against their character, regardless of the wisdom."

She never labored under the impression that the sheriff was a nice man or even a good man, but Graham made it sound like he was the devil, tempting souls down evil paths. Someone had to keep law and order in the shire, and Alys didn't think thieves were up to the task. Alys didn't say as

152

much though; she doubted such a stance would be welcome among the Merry Many. Silence settled between them, and she increased her pace so she wasn't walking right next to Graham.

Once in Locksley, Alys set her mind to handing out coins to peasants. If the Merry Many had been doing this work when her family lost their farm, would they have accepted? Alys suspected that her parents and Grandda might have, but it would have burned. *Just because these people are poor doesn't mean they have no pride.* She saw it in the peasants' faces, too, as they received coin: the tightening of their smile, the slight flare of their nostrils, the narrowing of eyes as though to keep tears locked in.

Her next stop was at the door of a chicken farmer named Mack. Mack was a nice man who'd always shown kindness to Alys and her brother when they came around to trade grain for eggs. To trade between market days was discouraged, but everyone did because it was the only way to avoid the bloated market taxes. She stood with Little John and Wilmot while the other Merry Many visited other homes to give coin. Alys knocked on the door.

From the other side, Alys heard a shuffle and tap. Shuffle and tap, and then again. The door opened, and there stood Mack, hunched over a crutch. One side of his face drooped, and a thread of drool dangled from his lip. Alys wanted to ask what happened, but she bit her tongue.

"Alys," Mack greeted. "When you get outlawed?" His speech slurred, but his eyes were as sharp as ever, even though one eyelid sagged. It looked like half of his face was sliding off his head. Alys felt a pang, like she should have known. If her family still lived in Locksley, she would have given Mack and his wife Meggy free grain after his apoplectic attack.

When Alys answered, her voice cracked. "Two days ago."

"I'm sorry to hear that. Robin'll look after you."

"Thank you, Mack." Alys portioned out some coins.

Mack called for Meggy, who came from the depths of their cottage and wrapped Alys in a warm hug. Alys hugged her back. She wanted to melt into it, disappear into two years ago before everything went wrong. Instead, she pulled back and pressed the money into Meggy's hand.

Meggy thanked them, and then Little John said they had to get going if they were going to help others. Meggy thanked them again, wished them safety, and closed the door.

They strolled away from the house and Little John asked, "Are you all right? It must pain you, Alys, to see your former neighbors like this. As an outlaw."

Alys swiped at her eyes. Her fingers came away with tears. "I'm fine. Sun was in my eyes."

He frowned. "Wasn't in mine."

"Yes, well, it wouldn't be, would it? You're taller. Who's next?" Alys didn't want to give him the chance to point out that the sun was behind Mack's house, or that it made little sense anyway that his being taller would make a difference. Or that the sun in her eyes wouldn't make them tear up.

19

Highway Robbery

Light and listen, gentle men,
All that now be here,
Of Little John, that was the knight's man,
Good mirth you shall hear.
-Translated from *A Lytell Geste of Robyn Hode*

The Merry Many moved through the village in groups as the sun climbed ever higher toward its zenith, when it would mark the arrival of the tax collector. Before his arrival, their group hid throughout the village—behind farmhouses and barns and barrels. Alys waited behind a barn with Graham and Wilmot.

"Good fight yesterday," Wilmot said. "Most of us what won our way into the Merry Many did so with a quick nick, no entertainment. Not like yesterday."

Heart hammering, Alys's first thought was that Wilmot should be quiet lest they be caught but then she decided that might be for the best. Then she wouldn't have to spy. "Yes, well, I'd have preferred a faster fight."

"Just saying," Wilmot said, "I'd rather not fight alongside you. I want to live, not entertain."

Alys smiled. "Auspicious for you, that I'm really an archer."

"Yes, I remember," Wilmot said.

"Here he comes. Both of you quiet now," Graham warned.

"Don't boss me, Sawney," Wilmot said.

Graham shushed him again anyway.

Alys wondered why Graham allowed Wilmot to call him that. That term for a Scotsman was hardly complimentary. But she'd often observed males calling one another offensive names in jest. Still, every time Wilmot said the word, Alys endured a prickle of annoyance. It had nothing to do with Graham's benefit, she assured herself, and everything to do with the fact that her own da had some Scottish blood.

The tax collector looked like he'd been log-rolled in brown leather. He was surrounded by more than ten guards. She ran her fingers over the fletching on one of her arrows. Was this the same man who reported to the sheriff that her da hadn't paid his taxes? Her hand closed around the shaft of an arrow.

"Don't," Graham warned. "We don't rob him in the village. The villagers will be blamed."

One of the guards dismounted from his horse and took from the saddlebag a bell. He waved it to and fro, and he called out between each ring that the tax collector had come to Locksley, and all had to come out and pay. People trickled from their homes onto the green in the center of the village. Sheep trotted out of the way and bleated their displeasure. No one worked the fields on tax day, but the sheep still had to graze.

The villagers queued up. Alys recalled going with her family when she was too young to stay in the house by herself. It'd been a different tax collector all those years ago, but she remembered waiting in line with them and, when they got to the front, the sight of her da kneeling at the man's feet to beg for another month. That man had agreed so long as her da paid a portion of what was due. That old tax collector had kind eyes. They were warm and understanding.

This tax collector's expression held no such warmth. He looked like his stare could freeze the sheep and the people, like he could turn them into stone if they displeased him.

She pulled an arrow from her quiver, but Graham reached out and stayed her hand.

"Not yet," Graham said through clenched teeth. "We wait and follow. Knock out the guards, rob the tax collector. Patience, wee one."

Alys replaced the arrow in her quiver. One by one, the villagers stepped up and handed over the coin demanded of them. A ha'penny per child. A farthing for the house. A penny for a farm, two for the mill, and another ha'penny for each cow, horse, sheep, or goat. Chickens were two for a farthing. If someone owned an odd number of chickens, they had to pay a full farthing for the single remaining chicken.

By the time the tax collection was finished, midday had come and gone, and the sun began its descent to hide beneath the horizon until the next day. Alys wondered where it went and how it came back up on the other side of the sky. She'd let her mind wander as the collection had worn on, and now Wilmot was elbowing her side to say it was time to form up and attack the tax collector's guards.

The Merry Many formed a semi-circle around the road beyond the village. They emerged around the tax collector and his guards, some of whom had adopted the role of porters. Graham stood in front of her, his sword drawn. Little John was at her side with a staff taller than her. Alys was ready with her bow and a nocked arrow, the bowstring pulled back to her chin. Robin, Alan, and Friar Tuck placed themselves on the other side of the semi-circle. Wilmot stepped forward, a dagger in each hand. He rolled his wrists; the beveled blades glimmered when they caught the afternoon sun.

"This," Robin said, "is a robbery."

"You don't say," the tax collector said with a drawl. "And if we don't comply with your wishes?"

"Then we fight and take it anyway," Wilmot said, rolling one shoulder like they'd just been asked how to cook pottage.

The porter-guards put down the chest full of taxes. Some guards drew swords; others drew bows. One of them shot an arrow that almost hit Alys's boot. She let out a breath and opened her hand. Her bowstring twanged, and the arrow flew so close to Graham that it would have stuck in the side of his neck if he'd flinched. Instead, it stuck in one of the guard's arms—a bowman. His bow clattered to the ground.

Arrows volleyed from both sides. Between shots, the other men met in the middle, swords clashing more times than Alys counted.

She fired arrow after arrow, never kill shots. Alys aimed for feet. For arms. For anything that would make it easier for Robin and the others to overpower the tax collector and his guards. When a guard broke through the line and came at her, she dropped her bow and went for her sword.

Alys brought the blade up just in time to defend. The guard kicked out; she dodged and returned with a kick of her own, which landed right between his legs. His face scrunched, and he looked like he'd held his breath too long. The guard's sword slipped from his hand and he held his groin, falling to both knees. Alys held her sword at his throat.

Alys bellowed. "Let us have the chest."

The tax collector, who crouched over the chest and waved a small knife from side to side each time any of the Merry Many had approached, straightened and gulped. "N—no. The sheriff will have his taxes. They go to the king, to fight the war in the Holy Land. This—this is treason! High treason, and you shall all be hanged for it."

"Let us have the taxes, or this man will die." Alys didn't want to kill anyone. She fixed her face into as many hard planes and lines as possible to make her bluff more convincing. She looked down at the guard's face. The pain had left his expression, melted out of his eyes and mouth and nostrils. He was steeling himself again.

"I'm sorry," she said to the guard. "I'm sorry the sheriff loves money more than people's lives. I'm sorry the tax collector values his hide over yours."

The guard glowered up at her. What happened next happened so fast that Alys could hardly track it. He pushed her arm away and lunged. He yanked her legs out from under her. Her back and head hit the ground. Alys raised her arms to cover her face, sword still in hand. The guard lunged again and fell onto her blade. He sucked in a short, desperate breath. Blood poured from the wound onto her dress.

Alys let go of her sword. She lay still on the ground, eyes wide. She met the gaze of the guard. A heartbeat—or two—passed. Then the world came back. The copper odor of blood. The warmth of it seeping through her dress. The weight of the guard's body. The pebbles pressing into her back.

"No," she said, her voice a thin whisper. Her vision blurred with tears. "I didn't—you weren't supposed to—it was a bluff."

The guard's eyes widened until Alys saw the white all the way around. He gave a wheezing gasp and his lips moved around words, but no sound came out. His breathing stopped. His jaw slackened and his face stilled. His full weight pressed her to the ground so she couldn't budge.

In the distance—what seemed like a great distance—Robin, Wilmot, Alan, and Friar Tuck gave thanks to the tax collector. The chests, full of coin, jangled like cracked bells. Little John and Graham lifted the guard off of her.

Alys couldn't move. She stared at the sky. Was God watching? Judging? What would she tell St. Peter if she died? Was she wounded? The world flipped as Little John hoisted her over one shoulder and told Graham to grab her sword. Everything was upside down and bouncing as Little John made for the cover of the trees.

* * *

Once under the shade of Sherwood Forest, Little John stopped and put Alys down. She sat back against a tree. "Am I dying?"

Little John prodded her abdomen. "No. You weren't cut, Alys."

Sobs erupted like the guard's blood, unheeded and unbidden. Tears streamed from her eyes, and her chest hurt. Her face hurt. The cut on her leg hurt as though it were fresh. She buried her face between her knees, drawing them close to make herself as small as possible.

Little John's meaty hand lighted on her shoulder. "It wasn't your fault, Alys. He fell on your sword."

Alys's sobs wracked her. "If I hadn't—if I'd—"

"None of us want to kill. Sometimes it happens."

She pressed the heels of her hands into her eyes until the pressure was too much, until it felt like she might blind herself if she pressed harder. *I deserve no less.* Even so, she couldn't do it. Alys didn't imagine her family would forgive her if they knew she blinded herself; it was bad enough her father's sight had faded. Nor did she imagine they would forgive her for killing a man. It was one thing for Hob to kill, for a soldier to kill. But in her family's eyes, she was a girl and shouldn't wish to be a fighter.

She should be doing things like brushing Maid Marian's hair and hoping for a husband someday. She should be weaving tapestries and studying a Book of Hours and praying and brushing her own hair. *What is wrong with me that I never wanted that? I must have been born broken.* She'd never countenanced Ma talking to her about suitors and marriage and keeping house. She'd always been envious of Hob, and Da, and Grandda because they didn't have to wear skirts and stay in the kitchen all day or feed the pigs or worry about a man asking for their hand. No one told them beauty required pain or that it was a pity their noses were too big for their faces, even though they all had prominent noses.

Little John sat next to her. His upper arm touched her shoulder. At first she stiffened, but then her body relaxed. Not like she had a choice—after the fight, the idea of moving her body seemed impossible.

"First time I killed a man was in France," Little John said. "I was there with the army, but it wasn't during a battle. We were marching through a village and my line was bringing up the rear of the column. He came at me from an alley way, see.

Him and a bunch of other Frenchies. I turn and we fight, me with my spear, him with his sword."

Alys didn't want to him to go on with his tale. She knew Little John was trying to comfort her from the tone of his voice, like he was trying to calm a skittish horse. But she didn't want to hear more about killing and death. She tried to cover her ears, but her arms didn't want to move.

"We exchanged blows for a few minutes. Felt like hours. Felt like no one else was there, just me and him, see. He was my size. He gets me on my heels, see, and then slashes at me. I fall. My spear snaps in two. He comes at me and trips and falls onto the broken spear. Impales himself, see."

Sobs bubbled up again. It was too similar. Too close.

"Even though he was my enemy, I was sick after. Lost my breakfast, all down my tunic."

Alys wrinkled her nose.

"So way I figure is, if you ain't losing your breakfast, you're going to be okay."

For a moment, Alys sat in the silence that followed. She couldn't hear anyone else around and wondered where they'd run to. All she could hear was the surrounding forest. "I didn't eat breakfast today."

"Ah," Little John said. "Well, all the better." He smiled, and kindness infused his face. At first glance, Little John looked how she imagined a Viking. Massive, golden-haired, imposing. But right now, Alys could picture him as a gentle father, soothing a scraped-up or nightmare-haunted child.

"I don't want to go back to the cave yet," Alys said.

"That's fine. I'll sit here with you until you do."

Alys leaned to the side and rested her head against his shoulder.

20

Absolution

God thee save, good Robin Hood,
And all this company.
Welcome be you, gentle knight,
And right welcome to me.
-Translated from *A Lytell Geste of Robyn Hode*

B y the time Alys and Little John returned to camp, the blood on her dress had dried. The front of her gown was stiff, and the guard's blood crusted on her own skin beneath. She knew if she had eaten breakfast, she would have lost it from that alone. Alys thanked Little John and asked where she might clean up.

Friar Tuck looked up from separating and stacking coins. "I can show you." He stood and Alys followed him through the trees, her gaze trained on the sway of the friar's woolen robe hem as he negotiated his way down a hillside riddled with roots. At the bottom of a small ravine was a stream about a foot deep and a couple feet across.

The friar balanced one hand on his belly and wiped sweat from his brow with his other sleeve. "Here you are, young Alys. I'll turn away, but wait until you're finished."

Alys waited until he faced away and began unlacing her gown at the sides. She remembered going to pray with Marian. Alys often confessed to such sins as enough exhaustion at day's end so she did not want to leave bed the next morning, and wishing she could return to her family. The priests and friars who came to serve at the castle always told her these were not sins, but she should learn to show more gratitude for her lot. They would utter those three words that were supposed to unburden her soul: Ego te absolvo. But she always felt the same.

Now, Alys wished exhaustion and missing her family were the biggest things weighing her down. Every movement took extra effort. Like there was blood all over her body, but especially on her hands. In her imagination, it oozed over her knuckles, to her wrists, up her arms, and over all of her until it bathed her. She looked down at her shaking hands. *If I floated away on the stream and never returned, would that be so bad?* Like she could send her soul to purgatory, to await judgment, to await an eternity's sentence in Heaven or Hell. Accident or murder?

Lies. Betrayal. Murder. How quickly her sins had added up. What would a priest say now? She peeked over her shoulder at Friar Tuck. "Will you hear my confession?"

Tuck didn't turn, but Alys saw him nod, saw the late-day sun reflect off the bare patch of scalp encircled by a ring of hair. "I will."

Alys chewed her lip. Even though he'd been there, saw what she did, saying the words was harder than she thought it'd be.

Her voice hid from her and at first, all that came out was a choked gurgle.

"God forgives those who confess with genuine contrition in their hearts," the Friar said.

"I—I have killed—" Alys swallowed. "I have killed a—" *Man. Say it.* Alys closed her hands into fists around the fabric of her gown. "I have killed a man." She fell to her knees on the bank of the stream.

"We sometimes commit horrors," Friar Tuck said, "in the name of justice. In the name of defending God's chosen king, in the name of protecting others."

Where is my absolution? The sheriff will not secure it when I took his man's life. Alys didn't want reasons or excuses. She chewed the inside of her cheek, tasted blood—her own—and winced.

"Are there other sins that burden your soul?"

Her gaze snapped up to the friar; his back was still turned. *I am false.* The words were on her tongue. *I have betrayed trust.* Even if Friar Tuck kept her sins to himself, would his loyalty to Robin lead him to find another way to unmask her? Alys decided not to risk it. If she died tomorrow before she had the chance to see another priest, how long would God condemn her soul to purgatory? Would St. Peter and God cast her into Hell? Alys shook her head. She looked down the stream, the way the water flowed over and between rocks and pebbles. "No. It is bad enough, what I have done."

"For your penance, you must continue to serve Robin in his cause."

Alys's breath whooshed out in one gust.

"Ego te absolvo." Friar Tuck turned, his eyes shut, and made the sign of the cross before giving her privacy once again.

"No prayer?"

"Well, always pray. I hear the fear in your voice that continuing on this course will lead you to kill again. And it may. However, your skill with the bow and the sword... you might do great work for God and for his people."

"You sentence me to risk my soul again."

"A penance is not a sentence." He looked up. "The day grows long—best wash your gown."

Alys removed her dress and washed it in the stream. At first, nothing changed, but then as the water soaked into the fabric, it pulled the blood away. The stream streaked crimson. She lay in the water, and it churned over her ears, her shoulders, her arms, her hands, her fingers. Dappled shadow and light played on her eyelids. Alys confessed her other sins, her unspoken sins, her secret sins, to God. She climbed out of the water, onto the mossy bank, wrung out the fabric, and dressed again. "I have finished."

Friar Tuck faced her. "A penance is a choice. As is coming to God, confessing to God. Prayer is a choice. Staying with Robin will be a choice, one you make each day."

"Is it one you make each day?" Alys searched the lines around the friar's eyes and mouth like God might have etched answers into Tuck's skin.

"It is. Do you not imagine it hurts my soul to harm another? We are not sinners or saints, child. We are men. We sin; it is in our nature. We may make the choice to come back to God afterward. We may aspire to and hold sacred the lives, actions, and relics of saints."

"Saints were human."

"And they were fallible when they lived; saints are not God. But their miracles, their love, guided them to a higher calling.

166

Trust me, God does not intend you to be a saint with the fighting skills you possess." He smiled. "Come. Let us return to camp."

Alys nodded and fell into step beside him. "How did you know you were meant to be a friar?"

"God told me. Not all at once, and not in so many words. God does not need to speak the tongues of man. He speaks here." Tuck tapped his chest over his heart. "We may choose to follow His guidance."

Alys had never felt such stirrings; others' machinations directed her life. She wouldn't have come to live in the woods, spy on Robin, serve the sheriff, serve Marian, move to Nottingham Town, say farewell to her brother. She wanted everything to go back to the way it was before Robin led Hob away from home. Alys wished Guy had never come that night to tell her parents he could help her find a husband.

"It is unfortunate," Tuck said, "that you had to kill so soon into your time with us—or at all. God compelled you to join us. Remember that what we do, we do for the people. For the true king, Richard. And for the Almighty."

"Is that not something men say to justify their violence?"

Tuck's smile turned sad. "I believe it can be, as with the Crusade. I cannot direct a king's actions. I do what I can to help those in need here and pray for the king's swift return."

"You want me to do the same."

"Yes, but so too does God. He placed you here, with us, on this path, and each day, you must choose." He sniffed the air. The sound of the others' voices surrounded them. "Now, I smell some rabbit on the fire. I daresay we are all hungry."

Around the fire, no one remarked on her kill. No one remarked on the fact that she was dripping wet. Wilmot handed her a stick with some charred meat on it. Alys sat between him and Robin and gripped the stick with both hands. She took the biggest possible bite. It tasted like chicken and smoke and earth.

Alys thought of the penance Tuck asked her to accept. Stay and help. Fight injustice. Protect the people from tyranny. It all seemed romantic and a simple choice until she thought of her family hanging in the balance. Could she trade the lives of Robin and the Merry Many to save her family? Could she trade her soul?

After she ate and her clothes were dry, Alys retired to the cave to sleep. Before she closed her eyes, she prayed to God to make her choice for her. As she thought the words, she knew He would not. To stay or go—to fight with Robin or spy against him—was a choice only she could make.

21

A Roll of the Dice

Also they took the good pence,
Three hundred pound and three;
And did them straight to Robin Hood,
Under the green wood tree.
-Translated from *A Lytell Geste of Robyn Hode*

S
omeone plopped down next to Alys and expelled a belch first thing in the morning. Several birds flapped, frightened, from a nearby bush. Alys glanced out of the corner of her eye to spy Alan. He wore a half smile, almost hidden by a few days' scruff.

"I know what'll cheer you up," he said. Another burp.

"Been into the ale early?" Alys asked.

Alan shook his head. "I ate some depraved berries. Not poison, but not as fresh as they could have been."

Alys felt a twinge of sympathy. "I'm sorry to hear that." She hadn't even gotten to worrying about that aspect of living in the woods yet. *What if I poison myself? What would happen to my family then?*

"'Tis fine, 'tis fine. Nothing like a bit of fun, eh? To draw my mind away from my stomach."

"Perhaps you should rest, instead."

Alan shook his head. "No, I need a distraction. And I've an errand to run for Robin in Town."

"Oh. I was hoping to speak more with Robin today." About Hob. She wanted to put it to him while she had the chance, before the sheriff could arrest him. Where was her brother, exactly? Why did he leave him behind in the Holy Land? Had he been alive when Robin left? These questions burned in Alys like indigestion. Her sympathy for Alan grew, but all she wanted to do was talk to Robin and then have a lie-down.

"Well, that'll have to wait. You're to come with me, into Town."

"What for? I thought you lot all robbed under the canopy of the green wood."

Alan's face split into a full smile. "We do that, too. But right now, the sheriff is entertaining some wealthy visitors. We're to go to Town and see if we can't find some way to lighten their purses."

"I have no skill as a pickpocket."

"I don't believe that. What peasant doesn't know how to pick a pocket? One of the first skills I learned. Besides, there are other ways to get the quality to part with their coin."

Alys clenched her jaw and dug her hands into the dirt on either side of where she sat. "Some of us like to earn what's ours."

Alan's face darkened. "Aye, girl, well, some of us don't have the means for that. If you don't want to steal from anyone, you can be a lookout. Come on. Get your hood up." He stood and smoothed the wrinkles in his tunic and cloak.

Alys didn't budge at first. She doubted news that one of the Merry Many spent his spare time stealing like a common criminal would impress the sheriff. *What could Alan gain from purses? Most people—especially those who had coin—were smart enough not to carry all of it with them.*

Alan nudged her with his boot.

"Didn't you ever learn it's not nice to kick people?" Alys pushed his foot away.

"I didn't kick you. You'd know if I had. Besides, I don't kick women." He paused. "That came out wrong. I don't kick. Not unless I'm being attacked."

With an impatient sigh, Alys got to her feet. "You talk too much, Alan."

* * *

Town was busier than Alys had seen it in a long time. People with tunics and gowns and cloaks of satin with golden embroidery, ladies with wimples that looked light as clouds, men who wore weapons with jeweled hilts. Alys thought she spied Alan salivating at the sight of so much wealth.

"Where do we start?" Alys whispered like even those words would pin targets on their backs.

"Tavern," Alan said.

They wove through the busy streets. Alys felt a pull toward the poorer sections of Town, toward her parents' home. She felt like it'd been a year since she'd seen them, even though it'd only been two months. Guy had promised to look in on them... but did he have the time? Did he remember? How was her da's vision? Did her family have enough coin to get by?

Maybe I can get them some today. No. No—I don't pickpocket.

Compared with the street outside, the tavern was even noisier. Laughter, chatter, and the clink and tink of mugs filled the space and pressed in on Alys's ears.

The plan worked like this, as Alan had explained on their walk to Town: He would lure rich folk into a game of chance. Alys would stand behind him and keep an eye out for any of three things—cheating by the rich folk, suspicion of the tavern keeper, or guards. Any of those three would spell an end to the game. Alan had told her not to worry about how he'd get coin out of the wealthy beyond that.

With all the grace he'd displayed earlier in the morning, Alan dropped into a chair across from a man with a pointed beard and cold, narrow eyes. "All right, sir?"

The man nodded and waved a hand to dismiss Alan. He spared a glance up at Alys, but looked away a moment later. For Alys, fading into the background was nothing new. Given that she had to keep her eyes in three places—the table, the bar, and the door, she didn't mind if the rich man ignored her.

Alan pulled from his pocket a pair of dice. "Fancy a game of chance?"

The other man waved him off again, but Alan leaned closer to whisper something across the table. What he said, Alys couldn't hear, but Alan's words caught the rich man's attention. He nodded and turned to face Alan full on.

Each of them took a turn rolling the pair of dice. Then the rich man scowled and Alan held out his hand. The rich man pressed some coin into his palm.

"Double or nothing?" Alan asked.

The rich man agreed and swiped the dice from Alan's other hand.

So it went with the next few patrons. Soon, there was a crowd around the table so that Alys couldn't see where the tavern keeper was—or the door. A ring of men—rich and poor alike—stood around them, laughing, cheering, and calling out their astonishment as men lost their coin, again and again, to Alan's game.

Alys suspected he'd done something to the dice. They always rolled in his favor. She didn't know the rules of this game, but that the others always had to pay up suggested as much.

When a man in a ragged tunic sat down and asked to play, Alan still won, but leaned forward, and Alys saw him drop some coins into the purse on the man's belt. She smiled. At least Alan hadn't forgotten their job was to help the poor.

So invested was she that Alys didn't see the aproned man press his way through the crowd.

"What's this?" the tavern keeper asked. He had a ring of yellow curly hair around his head, like it needed his ears to hang on or it would all fall out. "No gambling allowed in my tavern." His voice boomed, stretched up between the rafters, and out through the open casement. "I'll have you arrested, I will!" He leaned close, hands splayed on the table, fingers stretched toward a smattering of money. "Unless you're giving me a cut."

Alan didn't bother trying to explain. He stood, swept his winnings off the table, tossed a single coin at the tavern keeper, who looked like he might perish of apoplexy at so small an amount, and grabbed Alys's hand. He cut a path through the onlookers, rich and poor alike. Alys thought she saw him grab the velvet purse off one man's belt along the way.

The pair of them burst through the tavern door, into the street. Alys almost tripped on Alan's heels because he pulled her arm so hard to tow her along. Then he stopped short. When Alys looked up, she saw the reason: Sir Guy of Gisborne and a handful of guards.

"Run!" Alan said, and released her hand to race down the high street.

Alys spared a look for Guy, mouthed the word *later*, and raced after Alan, kicking up hay and dried mud crumbs in her wake. She was certain that, were it not for Guy, the guards would have given chase regardless of whether they recognized her. But a few furtive glances over her shoulder told her she and Alan had escaped.

* * *

Back at camp, Alan slowed to a light run and then a walk. He piled all of his winnings on the tree stump to sort. "Give us a hand," he said, motioning Alys over his shoulder.

Alys knelt before the stump and piled like coins. She picked up a strange silver one. Within a circled wreath of ivy was the imprint of an eagle or hawk. It wasn't English. "What's this one?" Alys held the coin out to Alan.

He took the coin, turned it over a few times, and shrugged. "Don't know. It's silver though, so good enough for us. We can always melt it down. It came out of that purse…" Alan picked up the purse and dumped it, and more of the strange silver coins came out. "Foreigner, likely."

Robin emerged from the mouth of the cave. "Good morning in Town?"

"Aye," Alan said, "but I couldn't discern why any of them were in Nottingham."

So that was the errand: spying on the sheriff's guests. The coin

174

was just something extra.

"Pity," Robin said, and wandered away.

"What are these?" Alys asked, holding up one of the foreign silver coins.

Robin turned back. He pored over both sides of the coin. "This is a pfennig. From Almany, I'd wager." He furrowed his brow. "Nobleman or merchant?"

Alan rolled one shoulder and held up the pouch. "They came out of this."

Robin took the pouch and pressed his lips together. "I would guess nobleman… or a very rich merchant. To have such a fine purse and so much silver on him. But why is he here, in Nottingham?"

"Beats me," Alan said. He returned his focus to coin sorting.

Alys stood. "Robin, may we speak? In private?"

Robin put the pfennig down, his eyebrows knit together into a single dark line across his forehead. "Not right now, Alys. Pressing business… I must talk with Little John. Later we may speak." His face relaxed and he smiled. "Excellent work. Glad you've joined us." He turned and walked away.

Robin left Alys with the same questions she had earlier. Where was Hob? Was he alive? Only now, new queries joined those. Why was the sheriff hosting a foreign nobleman? Would Guy tell her? What would she tell Guy about what happened in the tavern?

"You going to help me or what?" Alan asked.

With a smile, Alys sat down again to sort and count the coins. "How's your stomach?"

"Better, I thank you."

"Good. Not sure which is worse—you talking too much or belching too much." A smile blossomed on her face.

Alan's own grin answered. "A lady, with us, in Sherwood. May we never pass wind again?"

"I'm no lady, but I'll thank you not to all the same," Alys said. "Or at least, have the courtesy to stand further off." She helped with the rest of the coins. Counting was easy. Ignoring the memory of gratitude on the peasant's face after Alan had slipped him money in the tavern was not.

22

A Cup of Ale

And walk up into the Sayles,
And to Watling Street,
And wait after some unknown guest,
Upon chance you may them meet.
-Translated from *A Lytell Geste of Robyn Hode*

The next morning, Alys woke intending to speak with Robin. The fact that Hob wasn't back did not satisfy; even quieting the notion that Robin and Hob had gone to war and that war was unpredictable didn't stem her need to speak with Robin. She emerged from the cave at dawn, to find Wilmot restringing his bow.

"Where's Robin?" she asked.

Wilmot jumped a little and almost lost his grip on the bowstring. "Christ above, Alys. You shouldn't sneak up on a man with a weapon."

"Sorry. But I wasn't worried. It's not even ready to fire."

Wilmot shook his head and returned his focus to his task.

"Robin left this morning."

"Left? Why? I mean—where?"

Wilmot stopped again and glowered. "He has some friends in the north. He and Friar Tuck left to meet with them."

"How far north?"

"Planning to tag along?" Wilmot slipped the string in place and tested his work by drawing the bow. Then he tested with an arrow, shooting it into a nearby tree.

Alys had to admit he had excellent form in archery. "No, I just—I was hoping to talk to him, that's all. When do you think he'll return?"

"Wouldn't know. A few days? A week perhaps? But I know this—you and I are to go into Nottingham Town today. Little John, Graham, and Alan will take the road."

Alys chewed her bottom lip. It was as if Robin could sense she wanted to talk to him about his promise, about her brother, about the war, and made himself unavailable.

"We'll leave after breakfast," Wilmot said. "We've food to deliver. It'll be dangerous, so if you'd rather I ask Little John…"

"No, no—I want to go deliver food." If she stayed in the forest, there'd be no hope of getting word to Guy that Robin had gone north to seek an ally. If she went with Wilmot, there was a chance she could slip away long enough to visit the castle.

"Good. Hurry—we've got a cart to fill."

A cart? If they had to work together to pull a cart, that would make ditching Wilmot for a spell more difficult. Alys's heart sank. There was no backing out now, though. She couldn't tell Wilmot she no longer wished to help him in Town because then she couldn't deliver secret messages to the sheriff. With a sigh, Alys hurried to the stream to wake herself with a splash of cool water.

* * *

By the time Alys and Wilmot left the forest, a chilly silence had settled between them. Packing had been an hour rife with argument as they debated how best to fill the cart while hiding its contents. Alys suggested hay, because it was light. Wilmot wanted to use wood because the day already grew warm and, according to him, heat from a blanket of hay would melt some of the cheese. Alys argued logs would bruise the fruit and crush the bread. Little John had settled their argument with a booming voice that wasn't quite yelling but also brooked no more opposition.

A bed of leaves covered with wood.

As they exited the forest, Alys thought hay still would have been better. Lighter. Sweat dampened her forehead, her neck, and her spine, a small stream of moisture running between her skin and her dress until the fabric touched it and wicked it away.

Then there were their mismatched gaits. "Would you hurry?" Wilmot said.

"My legs are only so long. Maybe next time we could get a horse?"

"From where, Alys? Do you see so many grazing in the forest?"

Alys mumbled her reply. "I bet a villager would have lent us a draught horse."

"What was that?"

"Nothing." Alys clenched her jaw and strained against the

cart to pull it faster and try to keep up with Wilmot.

Once in town, they had to slow down, and Alys no longer had to drag a cart at a canter. The streets were busy, like when she came the day before with Alan. "Do the Merry Many come to Town every day?"

"No," Wilmot said. "Once a week to drop off food to those in need, like we're doing right now."

"And none of the guards have caught you at it."

"There've been some near misses, but the sheriff's men haven't arrested us, if that's what you mean. If they give us trouble, run. Make your way back to Sherwood, to camp."

"What about you?"

He smiled. "I'll be doing the same."

"We wouldn't stick together, help each other…?"

"If we split up, the guards would have a harder time chasing us both. One of us escapes, then they can rally the rest of the Merry Many to mount a rescue."

Alys nodded. She eyed the street, hoping to catch the attention of one of the sheriff's guards. But there weren't any to be found right now.

"Here we are," Wilmot said. He stopped walking.

They—and the cart—stood outside a home that looked much like her family's: tired. Alys longed to see her parents and Grandda. Were they all right? Had they heard again from Hob?

Wilmot knocked on the door. It opened to reveal a woman with a wrinkled face. Her eyes, though, were bright. Alys didn't think she could be that old. Two small children—a boy and a girl, each with straw-colored hair—clung to her legs.

"Eliza," Wilmot greeted. "This is Alys. Newest member of the Merry Many."

Eliza looked over Wilmot's shoulder. "Thank you for your courage, Alys."

A lump grew in Alys's throat. She opened her mouth to speak, but no sound came out. She tried to swallow past it, but the lump wouldn't go away. Courage was not something Alys thought she possessed. Not when she was sneaking around and spying. She was just doing what she had to in order to get her family back.

"You must be thirsty." Eliza looked down at her son. "Robert, fetch a cup of ale each for Wilmot and Alys."

Robert? The boy's name is Robert. Like her own brother. It wasn't an uncommon name, but it made Alys feel as though she might never speak again.

Wilmot pulled some food from the cart. "Are you going to help or not, Alys? Come now, earn your ale." He scowled over an armful of bread, cheese, root vegetables, and a pouch of berries. The juice from the berries seeped through the pouch so it looked like blood.

"Go easy on her, Wilmot," Eliza said, her tone gentle but chiding.

Alys turned and filled her arms with food. Wilmot passed food to Eliza's daughter, and Alys filled Eliza's arms with some of the bounty from the wagon.

"Do you need coin?" Wilmot asked.

Eliza smiled. "No, thank you. Not this week. Bless you both."

Robert returned then with two cups of watered-down ale, the liquid spilling over the rims. Alys accepted hers and emptied it in one gulp. Nothing had ever tasted cleaner or fresher. "Thank you."

"She speaks." Wilmot finished his. "We best go. Other

deliveries to make."

"Nice to meet you, Alys," Eliza said. "Look after her, Wilmot. An outlaw's life cannot be easy for a girl."

Alys passed back her empty cup and thanked Eliza. If she got the Merry Many arrested, Eliza and her children wouldn't have someone to drop off food and coin. Who would look after her? But what, too, of Alys's family?

"Her husband died in the Holy Land," Wilmot said as they pulled the cart down the road again. "And she had an older son, but pestilence took him. Everyone we bring food and coin to needs it—and so much more." There was a softness to Wilmot's voice and expression.

Alys's heart shredded to hear it.

By the time the sun set, they'd delivered food to two dozen families. All of them—like Wilmot said—were in dire straits. The balance of their fates weighed against that of Alys's family. But they too had suffered because of the Holy War. They too had suffered because of Hob's absence. They suffered still, she knew, even though she hadn't seen them in weeks.

* * *

When a guard stopped them near the castle, Alys let her hood fall back enough for him to recognize her. He called for the other guards to help arrest her and Wilmot.

Alys shoved Wilmot toward an empty alleyway. "Go! I'll distract them."

"You're a girl. I can't leave you alone to—"

"Go!" She shoved Wilmot again and let a pair of the guards arrest her.

They did not drag Alys to the dungeon, but to the courtyard.

There, she saw Guy walking toward her, hurrying down from the keep, his spurs chiming on the stone steps.

"I'll take her from here," he said to the guard, and hooked one hand around her elbow.

"I thought all outlaws were to be brought direct to the dungeons, Sir Guy."

"Do I not rank high enough to relinquish this prisoner?"

The guard looked down and released Alys so that Guy could lead her away. Back up the steps, back into the keep. The castle seemed so foreign now, as though she didn't know its corridors, like she needed Guy's guidance.

When he turned a way she'd never walked, Alys looked up at him. A shake of his head told her not to speak yet. He stopped at a door that made her think of the sheriff's, studded with iron, though there was only one door, not two. The keys at his hip jangled until he found the right one, and then he unlocked the door. Guy led her inside and closed the door after them.

"Good to see you're still alive, cousin. Getting yourself arrested was an interesting way to get my attention."

"I had, at first, planned on just sneaking back to the castle alone."

"That would have been simpler. We'll have to orchestrate some sort of pardon, some story to explain your release… without drawing suspicion from those criminals Robin associates with these days."

Alys concocted a plan. "Perhaps softened by Maid Marian's—"

Guy held up a hand. "I'll come up with the plan to get you back out. Don't worry."

"I wasn't worried… I was trying to help."

"What have you come to tell us? That would be the most

help. What have you learned in the week you've been away?"

Was that all it was? A week? "Erm, a few things. First and foremost, Robin isn't in Sherwood or even Nottingham right now. He left early this morning. He went north to find some ally."

"Which ally? What are their plans?"

"I—I don't know."

"You need to find out."

"I'll try."

"Alys, if I bring that and that alone to the sheriff, he's likely to lock you up instead of Robin. That's not enough."

Alys felt like an icy stream of water flowed down her spine. She reached back. Just sweat. "They deliver food and coin once a week here in Town. With a cart. Pulled by hand—no horses. Leaves and wood on top to hide the bounty."

Guy paced the room. Alys looked around. It must be his because he walked through it like he owned it. A four-poster bed sat in the corner under a burgundy canopy. Two enormous wardrobes took up the opposite wall, and on either side of the bed sat a table. One was empty; the other was covered with a candlestick, a pitcher, a plate, and a goblet. A fire burned low in the hearth between the wardrobes. The windows were like sentries over the courtyard.

"If you can tell me when the drop-offs happen—is it the same day each week?"

Alys felt a hot flush. *What a fool I am, not to have found this out.* "I don't know."

"Alys, you've got to give me something."

Panic rose in her. What would happen if the sheriff decided she was a useless spy?

"The guards will include your arrest in their reports. The

sheriff will ask me what news you brought."

"Oh! I could tell you about the tax collector. Robin gives coin to the peasants to pay him off and then steals it back—"

"We know that already. You've got to give me something new." Guy stopped pacing. "The camp. Where is the camp?"

The image of the sheriff, Guy, and guards descending on the little clearing with the cave and the tree stump made her heart pump hard in her chest like it was trying to run away. "I—"

"Yes?"

The stream where Friar Tuck forgave her, the trees where Little John consoled her after she took a life, the cave where she slept alongside all of them, where they trusted her not to take their lives or take the money they'd stolen for the poor, and the clearing where she'd promised to have their backs—and where they'd promised to have hers.

Eliza and her children and everyone else who would have no food or coin if she turned in Robin and the Merry Many.

Her family, in a hovel in Town. Da's milky eyes. Hob fending off waves of Saracen soldiers in the deserts of the Holy Land.

"Alys? Where is the camp?"

I need more time. More time to decide. "I—it changes. It moves," she lied. "That is, Robin moves it. I could tell you, but I believe he will move it again when he gets back. I'd say follow me now, but then you wouldn't have Robin."

Guy sucked his teeth. He scratched at his beard. "That… that won't do. The sheriff and the prince both want Robin. It's likely he'd come if we arrested all his friends… but maybe not."

"That's everything I know so far."

"Stay here. Rest. I will speak with the sheriff."

He left the room, and as Alys followed, she heard the lock click into place. It might not be a dungeon, but Alys knew she was a prisoner.

23

Secrets

Took he there this gentle knight,
With men of arms strong,
And led him home to Nottingham ward,
In bonds both feet and hands.
-Translated from *A Lytell Geste of Robyn Hode*

Night had fallen across the courtyard by the time Guy returned to the room. Alys had lit no candles, but she'd poked at the logs in the grate now and again, so an orange glow flickered across part of the chamber. The door swung open to admit more light before her cousin blocked it out.

"You locked me in," Alys said. She got to her feet, grip tightening on the wrought iron fire poker. She determined from the heft that the blacksmith had been skilled. "Like a prisoner."

"It was for your own protection. If the sheriff had become irate, I didn't want him sending guards to drag you down to the dungeon."

Alys perched her free hand on her hip. "What did he say?"

"Well," Guy walked into the room, closed the door, and approached the fireplace. He lit a long reed and touched it to candle wicks to fill the corners of the room with light. "We will go with the simplest explanation for clemency this time. Your service to Maid Marian, and your connection to me... we will release you. After all, the cart was empty, except for hay and wood. Just because the guards thought they saw you with a known outlaw..."

Alys put down the fire poker. "Thank you, Guy."

He nodded. "But Alys, next time you bring information, it needs to be good. It needs to lead to Robin's arrest. The sheriff won't be so forgiving a second time."

"I'm sure with your influence, you could—"

"No. No, Alys. You have one more chance. So make sure when you come back to us or send word that it's useful." There was urgency in his tone. Earnestness. Like he needed her to believe him more than he'd ever needed anything in the world. A single wrinkle curved into a horseshoe on his forehead.

"Very well, cousin. Next time I bring information, I'll make sure it's more useful."

Guy's face relaxed, back to his mask of cool indifference, of ready obedience to the sheriff. "Good. Remember, do not make me regret what I've done for you."

"Why—why do you serve him, Guy?"

He squared his shoulders. "You are not doubting him, are you?"

"I—no. He is the law. But is he a good man?"

"Alys, you have not spent as much time with the sheriff as I have. I served him in France. He takes care of those who are loyal to him. He—others may think him cruel or ambitious, but you haven't seen all that he's seen. The anarchy of war, the fearful chaos of battle… it makes one appreciate order and authority. Tell me that your time with the outlaws is not making it difficult to do what must be done."

Alys steeled herself. "It is not."

"Good."

"I'm ever grateful for all you've taught me with the sword and bow, as well as with horses—and for securing work for me and the sheriff's forgiveness." *Lay it on thick.* Guy was as kind as a man in his position might be expected, but his pride was bound to his ambition and Alys didn't want to cross him by offending either.

Guy nodded. "You best get on. If you're gone too long, it's likely the outlaws will come for you—and without Robin, they would not be so great a prize."

Alys nodded. "Can I have some food? I left the forest this morning and haven't eaten since."

With a glance around the room, Guy retrieved a hardened crust of bread and a bit of cheese in a waxed rind from the nightstand. "Here. Eat and then you must be on your way."

"Will you give Marian a message for me?"

"It's best not to."

"But—"

"Maid Marian is busy preparing for her upcoming wedding. Best to let her move forward and forget Robin."

And forget me. Alys accepted the food and tried to eat some but a lump grew in her throat when she thought of her friendship with Marian as nothing but a distraction. Now eating seemed impossible. Alys pushed the food into a pouch at her hip. "The guards will let me pass?"

"I'll escort you to the gate."

Moonlight bathed the courtyard in a silver veil, and a chill danced down her spine and arms. The courtyard seemed so quiet, like all the guards were asleep. She heard no guffawing, no bragging, no rattle of dice cups or clink of coin. Guy seemed to notice it too, and pushed Alys just as she heard an arrow cut through the air.

Little John, Graham, and Wilmot all bellowed a battle cry and attacked. Guy drew his sword fast enough to deflect a blow from one of Wilmot's daggers. Then Little John was after him with a staff that looked as large as a young tree. Graham grabbed Alys's arm, a bow in his other hand, and ran for the gate.

Alys tried to wrench free, but Graham would not release her. *Is Guy okay?*

"Alys, what are you—"

"We should make sure Sir Guy is alive."

"What? Alys, he's the sheriff's man. He arrested you. He—"

"If he's killed, it won't help us."

"Wilmot and Little John won't kill him. Come on."

Graham darted through the open portcullis, but Alys lagged to peek into the gatehouse. Several guards were all piled in the center of the flagstone floor. Their chests rose and fell with each breath. Knocked out. Graham pulled her through the gate and into the streets of Town.

"The others will catch up, wee one."

"But—"

"Don't worry. Did you think we would leave you to that scum?"

Alys figured he meant the sheriff, and not her cousin.

Graham led her through a labyrinth of streets and alleyways.

He knew Town well. Alys almost tripped, trying to keep up with him. When the toe of her boot got stuck on a cobble a second time, he stopped to catch her. They were on Tanner Street. The stench of this place told Alys where they were, and the hides hanging in a nearby window confirmed her guess.

"Are you hurt, wee one?"

Alys tried not to grimace at Graham's continued use of that pet name. "I am uninjured."

Graham nodded, and his expression relaxed, then his brow furrowed. "Wait a moment. How did you get Guy of Gisborne to walk you out?"

Robin knew Guy was her cousin, but did the others? Would they lose their trust in her? "Marian. Maid Marian begged for my release. In honor of my past service to her." This was a better lie than the one Guy had cooked up of the sheriff deciding on his own to let her go, though she wished she'd had time to tell Guy to go with this tale instead.

"Aye, I see. You're lucky not to have a rope 'round your neck, wee one."

"I knew I would escape—that is, I calculated that Marian would speak on my behalf. I made Wilmot leave because I didn't think he had such a champion within the castle walls."

"A good thing, too. It's him what fetched us to Town as soon as he found us, to rescue you."

"You three might have been killed."

"You're one of us now, wee one. And a girl."

"I'm a young woman, not a girl." Old enough to be married and a mother several times over, as her own ma liked to remind her. In the wake of Graham's assumption, a mixture of annoyance and a warmth spread from her heart through the rest of her body. The lump was back in her throat.

Little John and Wilmot ran up the street toward them, both grinning ear to ear. "Left him flat on his back staring up at the moon," Wilmot said. He was breathless, either from running, the excitement of defeating Sir Guy of Gisborne, or both.

"Does he live?" Alys asked.

"Yes," Little John said.

"We try not to kill if we can help it," Wilmot said.

The blood drained from Alys's head, and she shivered. *We try not to kill.* She had killed. She had not forgotten, even if Friar Tuck had absolved her. Even if it had been an accident.

Graham unfastened his cloak and draped it over her shoulders, over her own cloak. He pulled the hood up and took her hand.

Alys wanted to pull free because she didn't need a man to mollycoddle her, and she didn't like the way his hand felt around hers. It was too hot, too calloused, too enclosing. Like her hand was a prisoner.

The four of them ran back to Sherwood. Alys thought she'd never be so happy to see the cave again, even in winter. *At least this winter, thus far, is mild.* Wilmot wandered off to get firewood, and Little John muttered something about seeing to the weapons. Graham still held Alys's hand.

She started toward the cave, but he held firm. "I'm tired, Graham."

"I know. But I want to talk to you, wee one."

Alys turned back toward him but something in her expression must have changed his mind, because he released her hand.

"It can wait until tomorrow morning," he said. "Sleep well."

Alys nodded. She thanked him for the rescue and stooped into the cave, following the line of beds, weapons, and small banks of glwoing embers as deep as she could, and lay down on a pile of leaves and pine needles covered in a wool blanket. She covered herself with another blanket and cocooned into its warmth, not because she was cold but because she felt like the wool somehow protected her. *Never let them get you on your heels. The sheriff has me on my heels.* Alys wished for nothing more than solitude. There were too many lies and betrayals to keep track of, and she did not want to speak to anyone or have to hide anything else for the rest of the day and night.

* * *

The next day, Alys collected her bow and quiver. She tiptoed over the others, intent on some early morning practice by herself, near the road. Robin might be back today. When he returned, she could find out what happened to her brother.

Little John was still snoring. Wilmot slept in silence, but fidgeted on his pile of hay and blankets. Graham wasn't in the cave. Alys hoped he was getting firewood or water, or perhaps hunting for breakfast.

But he wasn't. When she stepped into the clearing, she saw Graham sitting on the tree stump. Staring at the cave.

"Good morrow, wee one." He eyed her bow. "Going somewhere so early?"

"Erm, I was just going to practice a bit."

"Can we talk first?"

Alys weighed the decision. If she said yes, she'd have to stay and hear whatever he wanted to say. *What if he suspects me of spying?* If she said no and he didn't suspect her already, he might start to wonder. She ran her fingers along the fletching of one arrow, like it was still on a bird, and she could pet it to soothe her frantic heart. Then she nodded. If he suspected her, she could always try to escape. And she was armed—Graham wasn't.

"Thank you. I would suggest we walk off aways, but Little John won't be right pleased if I gave up my watch."

"Here is fine." She looked anywhere but at Graham. Alys scanned the ground for roots and rocks that might impede her escape. *If only I had a horse.*

"Two years ago, I left my home in Scotland. Had to leave, because I killed a man. With these hands." Out of the corner of her eye, Alys saw Graham hold his hands out, palms up. Then he continued to speak. "He killed my ma and my sister. Protecting them was my job."

Alys wondered when he was going to accuse her of spying, when he was going to say he'd tell Robin if she didn't, and that the others already knew, too.

"I swore to myself that if I ever took a wife, she'd be someone who could protect herself. A man's supposed to protect the women in his life, but I wasn't home when it happened."

A wife? Now, Alys wished Graham would accuse her of spying on Robin and the Merry Many. "Graham, you don't have to—"

"Aye, wee one, I do. I like you. You're strong and you can fight and you aren't afraid to face the sheriff and his men."

"Graham—"

"No, let me speak, wee one. There's no other woman like you in this world. Ever since we met, since you challenged Robin that day, I've been impressed by your courage and strength. I can't stop thinking about it, about you, about us—"

Alys felt as though her head was so hot it might burst into flame. "Graham, I don't plan—"

"I know it's unexpected. But I don't want any of the other lads our age asking you before I could."

Oh God, please tell me Wilmot and Alan don't feel the same! Alys felt like she was going to drop. Like she'd pass out, or perhaps perish on the spot—either would be preferable to this conversation. She'd rather discuss marriage prospects with her ma for days on end. *What would Ma say?* At Alys's age, she would probably tell her to accept Graham, that beggars couldn't choose, and then she'd point out the absence of men lining up to ask for her hand.

"Robin can perform the ceremony, being a lord, with Friar Tuck. We could be wed when they return. I wouldn't demand you stop working with us, with the Merry Many. We could stay here in the forest still. At least, until children—"

Alys didn't remember looking back at Graham. She didn't recall picking up an arrow from her quiver or sense her own hand squeezing it until her knuckles whitened. Alys didn't realize it'd snapped, at least not right away. It was Graham's sudden change of countenance. From hopeful to hurt, like she'd smacked him across his face and knocked his smile into the undergrowth.

"You've another. Wilmot's already asked you, maybe. Is that it, wee one? Are you—"

"No!" Birds and squirrels fled their nests in an exodus of flapping and scuttling, all squawking and squealing their surprise. Behind her, from the cave, Little John snorted, and she feared he might wake and witness Graham's proposal. He snored again, and Alys released the broken arrow. "No other. I—I do not plan to marry, Graham. Thank you, but—but you would do better to seek another woman to marry."

When Graham opened his mouth, all that came out was a

choked gasp.

"I'm sorry," Alys said. "Don't follow me." She took her bow and quiver and ran into the woods, away from the cave, the clearing, the stump, Graham… Robin forgotten, and Graham's proposal? All too simple to recall.

24

Revelations

He did him straight to Bernysdale,
Under the green wood tree,
And he found there Robin Hood,
And all his Merry Many.
-Translated from *A Lytell Geste of Robyn Hode*

A lys spent her entire quiver shooting into a tree about forty yards away. When she found her quiver empty, she hung her bow on her shoulder and followed the path of her shots. Sap dripped like wax over the rough bark from the holes made by her arrows. Closing her hand around the shafts, she pulled them free of the trunk, one after the other. Alys used the hem of her skirt to wipe them clean and dropped them back into her quiver until it was full.

"Your skill rivals Wil's," someone said from somewhere to her left.

Alys swung around, bow at the ready, arrow nocked. "Who goes there? Declare yourself."

Robin emerged from a thicket of saplings and vines, his hands held aloft, palms out. "I mean you no harm, Alys Fletcher." Laughter teased his words.

Alys lowered her bow. "I'm a better archer than Wilmot."

"Maybe we should host our own tournament to decide."

"How did you know I was here?"

"Graham pointed out which way you came. I can guess what you want to talk to me about. I haven't been avoiding you."

"Oh? Is that so?" There was an edge to her voice that never would have been present with Robin in the past, before he and Hob left, when he was her lord. "You might have talked to me when Alan and I got back from Town or the day I joined the Merry Many, while we're at it."

"I am here now, am I not? It is just us. Ask your questions."

Alys clenched her jaw. If he knew what she wanted to talk about, why was he making her ask? She blew out a sigh and felt her shoulders relax. "My brother. Was he alive when you left? Why'd you leave him there? Where was he when you left?"

Robin walked up to the tree and leaned against it, taking care not to press his shoulder against the sap trails. "I was wounded in the Holy Land. An arrow to my back. We were near the gates of Acre when it happened. We were not even engaged in battle when I was shot." He laughed, but there was no humor in it. "Your brother saved my life. The arrow would have killed me if he hadn't pushed me aside."

Alys clutched her bow. In her imagination, she saw Hob pushing Robin to safety and taking an arrow himself. Even though that wasn't how it happened, since Robin was the wounded one, clearing the image from her mind seemed impossible. "Go on."

Robin examined her, expression uncertain.

"Go on," Alys said again.

"It was a small band—an advance guard—that attacked us. When I woke up in a monastery, he and the rest of my men had moved on with the king. The king left orders for me to return and recover, and then bring more men to the Holy Land."

"You should have taken Hob with you."

"Alys, did you not hear what I say to you? He was gone when I woke."

"You made a vow."

"I had orders from the king."

"A vow, Robin."

"I am sorry, Alys. I did not even know where the king led them."

"You could have found out."

"And lost my head in the pursuit of such knowledge. I was lucky to leave with my life, to return home, to be able to tell you that when last I saw your brother, he was hale and hearty." His voice was gentle, and something in his eyes pleaded with her.

Alys didn't want to forgive him but she felt the tension, the anger, and the pain evaporate out of her. The mossy earth came up to meet her knees as her legs buckled. Alys wiped at hot tears, and for a moment, she might as well have been alone in the forest.

Then Robin's hand was on her shoulder. "I wanted to go to your parents. Explain what happened in person. But then the sheriff outlawed me—"

"By your own actions, you were made an outlaw," Alys said through sobs, through tears, through the mucus in her nose.

"I did better by Little John than by your brother and your

199

family. And you have my humblest apologies. Your brother and I—we did what we could to keep one another safe. I did what I could to keep my word to you… but you had to know when we left it was a promise I shouldn't have made."

"Then why did you?" Alys neglected the fact that she, too, had broken a vow to Robin.

Robin offered a sad smile and knelt, facing her. "Perhaps I needed to. Perhaps I wanted to believe I had the ability to keep him safe, keep myself safe, keep all my men safe, return and marry Maid Marian and have the life I always dreamed of. The life my parents dreamed of for me."

Alys wanted to push his hand off of her shoulder, but she didn't have the strength. Robin must have misread her attempt to shoo at him, because he hugged her. At first, Alys froze. What if, realizing a life with Marian was out of the question, he wanted what Graham wanted? But then he pulled away and held her at arm's length. Alys searched his face. She didn't see any traces of longing, but more of a brotherly affection.

"I am desolated that I had to break my word to you. I was not in fighting shape and orders… orders are orders."

"You aren't following them now."

"Well, not yet, no. England is in the clutches of an evil regent. If the king was aware of half of what his brother does in his name, he would not expect me back in the Holy Land. Besides which, I bartered passage on a ship which shortened my travel home. It's bought me some time before failing the king's expectations."

"So you will abandon us, too?"

Robin winced, like a bee had stung him. "No. No, I intend to stay until things are right, or until the people can protect themselves."

200

Alys gave him a look. *He is a dreamer. He thought he would bring Hob back and that life would be the same as it always had been, and now he thinks the people will protect themselves from the likes of Prince John.* Dreamers were dangerous. Alys would have to get reliable information to the sheriff, and fast, before Robin got people killed with his visions of an ideal and equal England.

"I'd like to be alone now," Alys said.

"Right. I understand. Come back to camp before dark. Oh, and Alys—the king was winning when I left. Maybe Hob is alive and well and will return to England soon."

Alys nodded. She wouldn't allow herself to believe in such foolish hopes again. A draught horse might as well have trampled her chest in. She wanted nothing more than to fire off more arrows in solitude.

Robin got to his feet and brushed dirt and bits of leaves off the knees of his hose.

"Before you go, one more question," Alys said, ignoring his offer to help her up off the ground.

"Yes?"

"Where did you go? These last few days?"

Robin hesitated. Chewed his lip. "North. To—to Yorkshire. I have some friends there. It was a matter of state." His expression closed, and he turned and walked away, back toward camp.

* * *

Alys reached into her quiver. *North to Yorkshire. To friends.* What friends did he have there? Other outlaws? Noblemen? What affairs of state? What else, she wondered, might the king have ordered him to do? If she found out, Alys might convince the sheriff to send for Hob even without Robin being captured.

The arrow she selected was one her da had made. She could tell by the craftsmanship. The way the vanes of the fletching were spaced to allow a more perfect flight, truer aim.

"Let's see Wilmot out-shoot this," she said to the forest. Alys nocked, drew, breathed, and loosed the arrow. It burrowed deeper into the tree trunk than any of the others had. She reached for another. And another. Soon, there was sweat on her brow, and her quiver was empty once more.

Alys continued shooting the rest of the day, taking a break to search for some mushrooms and berries, and to drink from the brook. Only when the sun sank below the trees, its last rays of the evening stretching through their trunks like it was trying to hold on above the horizon, did she return to camp.

* * *

The plan was simple: More noblemen were due in Nottingham to meet with the sheriff. Robin wanted the Merry Many on the North Road, which cut through Sherwood, to relieve as many of them of their ready coin as possible. They would wake at first light and take all their weapons. They would harry carriages, stop riders, and steal on threat of life and limb if necessary.

"It is not good for the king, for England, or for us if the sheriff is meeting with all these noblemen. I know not yet what his plans are, but this," he held up a coin, "is a pfennig. A penny from Almany, lads." He turned the coin. "And on this side, the Holy Roman Emperor. What is the sheriff doing meeting with foreign noblemen? The prince is not here. There has been no word of a delegation." He flipped the coin and caught it again. "Friar Tuck and I tried to find answers among the noblemen of Yorkshire, but they had none. So tomorrow, we steal purses and figure out what the sheriff is planning."

So that was why they went north. Alys didn't imagine any of the Merry Many would be welcome among nobles in Nottinghamshire. Whatever the sheriff's motives were, they would remain hidden for now. And Alys was still without a secret to sell for her family's restoration. That's when it occurred to her: Wouldn't the sheriff love to know Robin's plans to ambush nobles?

She could almost feel her family embrace her—Hob, too. Her nose detected the smell of harvest on their Locksley farm, even though it was a memory. Her ears opened to the sound of the babbling stream that flowed south beside their home. Scents and sounds dredged up from years past seemed as real as the present, and Alys thanked God for inspiring her to find a way to restore her kin to their rightful home.

Alys memorized the points where Robin planned to set up ambushes. Then she offered to take the night's watch. Leaving when she was ordered to guard the cave and the sleeping Merry Many would be risky. But she had to get word to Guy. She had to prove herself to the sheriff. If Robin was right, Hob might be on his way soon—but if he was wrong and the king wasn't winning against the Saracens, then Hob might not make it home without her spying. Alys wished the Holy Land was in France or Scotland—some place she could go to find her brother—instead of in some desert thousands of miles away.

She tracked the moon to the top of the sky, listening to the snoring from the cave behind her, which sounded like some great beast growled from within. She imagined a dragon inside, hoarding its wealth, its fiery breath spewing from the mouth of the cave. *What's more dangerous? A dragon or the Crusade? As though there are any more dragons.* Everyone knew they all died out in the days of Arthur and his round table, leaving behind nothing but bones. Alys shook her head at her own childish whimsy.

When it seemed none of the Merry Many would stir, Alys slipped from the clearing into the cover of the canopy, pulling up her hood so that she became a shadow, passing between the trees. She could still make it to Nottingham Castle and back by dawn if she didn't dawdle.

* * *

The castle looked larger in the gloom of night, especially where its walls receded into darkness. Torches on either side of the West gate shone like twin stars. The guards' spears reflected their orange glow so that it looked like fire fairies danced before the portcullis.

Alys opened her arms wide as she approached, to show she had no intent of attacking. Despite her gesture of good will, the guards pointed their spears at her.

"Halt! Who goes there?"

"Alys Fletcher, cousin to Sir Guy of Gisborne."

"State your business."

"That is for Guy's ears." Alys held her chin high and looked down her nose at the guards. "I shall content myself to wait here if one of you will fetch him."

The guards didn't respond at first. She couldn't see their

eyes because of the dark and their helmets. Then one of them barked an order at the gatehouse door. Another guard, without a spear, ran out of the gatehouse and toward the keep. The other two guards kept their spears trained on Alys—at least until Guy arrived. His chin was scruffy, and he rubbed at puffy eyes. His tunic was askew.

Guy walked through the portcullis and took one of the two torches, motioning with his head for Alys to walk with him along the outside of the castle wall. "What news do you bring?" he asked when they'd turned a corner and there were none about to hear them.

"I know where Robin plans to set up ambushes tomorrow. To rob the visiting noblemen."

The torchlight filled Guy's smile. For a moment, Alys thought of him as a dragon. "That," he said, "is useful information. No doubt the sheriff will be pleased. We will arrest Robin and the other outlaws tomorrow. Likely you, too—but worry not, cousin, you shall not share their fate."

A pang of guilt. It knotted her stomach. Then she remembered why she'd agreed to spy in the first place. Revenge, yes—and she didn't feel as strong a pull toward that goal anymore—but also to reunite her family. She shared Robin's plan with Guy.

"Would you like some food? Drink?"

She shook her head. "I best get back before they wake." But her feet seemed stuck on the ground, like roots stretched through the road to grab her boots. "This is the right thing to do, is it not?"

"They are criminals, Alys. And this will restore your family. I would not hesitate to do the same."

She nodded. "How—how is Maid Marian?"

"She gets on well enough with her new serving girl."

Alys's face slackened. *Does she despise me now?* She couldn't ask Guy. What if he said yes? What if he asked Marian if she despised Alys? *Perhaps I can sneak up to her chambers and speak to her.*

"Erm, but not as well as with you, cousin. I can tell she misses you. Whatever you used to whisper to her during meals to make her smile… this other girl cannot compare."

"And she readies soon to marry?"

"You did not know. The wedding is off."

"How come? What will she do?"

"Maid Marian has arranged to take holy orders after the harvest festival."

"Was Sir Edward cross?"

Guy shrugged. "Perhaps. Perhaps not. I have not seen him since she announced her decision."

"And you?"

"She would never have married me, Alys."

Alys placed a hand on Guy's shoulder. "I am sorry for you, cousin. I know you care for her."

Guy cleared his throat and looked away. "You best get back. I—I don't suppose you'd show me the way to the camp? We could take them by surprise at dawn?"

So much for seeking an audience with Marian. As Alys focused on what Guy asked, the idea of the Merry Many being ambushed as they woke made Alys's stomach roll. *The cave where they live? Their home? That would make me no better than the sheriff, evicting peasants from their homes. Peasants like Da.* A swoop of faintness threatened, and she had to adjust her stance to keep herself up. "No—no, that would not do." Alys groped in her mind for a reason. "The way is—ah, the horses

206

wouldn't be able to navigate the path. Best to ambush them on the road in the morning."

Guy gave her an assessing look and a slow nod. Alys wondered if he read her mind, and she willed him to stop, to focus on anything else, anyone else—Marian, even if it bruised his heart to do so.

"Until tomorrow," Alys said before Guy questioned her further. Then she turned and disappeared into the streets of the Town. Alys didn't peek over her shoulder to see if Guy followed or not, but when she reached the clearing between Town and Sherwood, she didn't hear any soldiers behind her or outlaws ahead. *No fight tonight.* She ran back into the woods, back to the cave, and planted herself on the stump as though she'd never left.

25

An Ambush

When she came to the forest,
Under the green wood tree,
Found she there Robin Hood,
And all his fair many.
-Translated from *A Lytell Geste of Robyn Hode*

Alys watched Robin as the men filtered out of the cave the way a bear might after months of winter sleep. He didn't give her any pointed looks, but every time he glanced her way, she wondered if he read her betrayal on her face. Now she did call herself a traitor. Not because he was once her lord, but because these men helped people like her family. It was hard to hate a man who gave of himself and asked nothing in return. The people in Locksley whose taxes they helped pay. The people in Town who took their deliveries of food. Robin giving up land and title and his noble status to save Little John's neck.

She almost opened her mouth to warn the Merry Many

against springing the ambushes today. To suggest they choose another location along the North Road. Hob hung in the balance. Her family and their home. The lives and livelihoods of the peasantry of England—did Robin miss war so much that he sought to muster them into a surrogate army? And, if they won the day in Nottinghamshire, would he lead them out of England to fight half the world away?

Farmers and tradesmen stood no chance against knights, horses, and battle-hardened soldiers. Robin's idealism was dangerous. Alys could only weigh so many consequences.

I only have to get the Merry Many arrested. I can free them after that, somehow. In disguise, or perhaps once her family was safe and word sent to the king to send Hob home. Alys could save the Merry Many, and maybe they could save or protect England from Prince John—at least until the king returned—without turning peasants into warriors. As for Robin, Alys hated to think what would become of him. Guy didn't know about Robin's ambitions, and he said he'd help the sheriff arrest Robin if he wore Alys's boots.

She'd never been so torn, pulled in so many directions, all at once.

Alys had to focus on today. She'd be in Robin's group, and almost protested because she didn't want to see the look on his face when the sheriff's guards turned up instead of the targeted nobleman, Sir Thomas of somewhere she didn't recall.

It wasn't time to leave yet, so Alys stationed herself across from a tree. She nocked an arrow, drew, aimed, and loosed. It thudded into the trunk. Alys grabbed her arrows and backed up five paces. She repeated this process, backing up every time she struck the center of the trunk.

"Think you can fire two at once, wee one? And still hit your target?" Graham sat on the stump in the middle of the camp.

Alys jumped a little; then relief washed over her when he smiled. He didn't seem angry about her refusing his proposal. Nor did he bring it up again.

"I've never tried, but I think I could." She picked up two arrows and nocked them. She drew the bowstring.

"Ah, wait a moment." Graham stood from the stump and walked over to her. "Stay just like that." He stood behind her and wrapped his arms around to cover her hands with his.

Alys felt like she'd run afoul of a gorgon. Powerless to move, what she wanted most was to push Graham away. She wasn't comfortable with him in such proximity when she knew his intentions. When she knew her ma would say at her age, she was lucky to find a suitor—even though he was an outlaw.

"When you're firing with two," he said in her ear, "you want to hold the string thus." He demonstrated, and she moved her fingers so they kept the arrows in place on the bowstring. "Everything else is the same."

Together, they drew the string taut again and brought it to her jaw. They breathed together. On Graham's count, they loosed together. Both arrows launched from the bow and buried themselves into the bark.

Graham released her hands and stepped back.

Alys stared at the two arrows, breathless, like he had taken her breath without permission. She would have preferred his anger to his kindness.

"Well done, wee one. You *are* a natural with a bow." Graham spoke as though it was a fact still contested among the Merry Many and he'd just solved the mystery.

"Thank you." She cleared her throat. "Always good to learn new skills." Alys left Graham to run to the tree and collect her arrows, though a few remained in her quiver, rattling with each step.

When she returned to her shooting spot, Graham had sat down on the stump again. She didn't look at him or speak to him. She just fired single arrow after single arrow, collected them, and started again. After a few rounds, he got up and walked away to do something else—perhaps train himself.

* * *

The Merry Many and Robin of Locksley left the camp early to set up their ambush. Their typical ambush plan: a few of the men would stand in the road to block the way and stop whichever noble they were trying to rob. Then Robin would play his game and if the noble resisted, he would call the rest of the Merry Many out from hiding to threaten the noble into giving up his or her purse.

This time would be different. Robin stationed himself and Little John in the road, with Alys and Wilmot on the ridge. The others were farther north, ready to help or act as a second ambush in case Robin didn't succeed, or in case Sir Thomas rolled onto the North Road from a different path. Alys had fifteen arrows in her quiver, and her bow on one shoulder. When Sir Thomas came into view, she was to nock an arrow. When he and his men stopped, she was to draw. But Alys knew Sir Thomas wouldn't be coming. It'd be the sheriff and his men, with Guy ambushing the others.

Alys hoped no one—on either side—perished. She had killed no one since that guard on tax day she spent with the Merry Many. Looking at Robin was impossible. She focused on the dead and dying leaves in the road, right in front of him. In

211

her mind's eye, Alys saw the guard she'd killed that day, and blinked a few times to clear her sight.

The skies split, and curtains of rain poured down around them, obscuring her vision. Even the point of her arrow disappeared behind sheets of water. Wet fletching feathers didn't bode well either. Arrows didn't soar the same through sheets of water. They'd still fly, but she'd have to account for the weight and movement of the rain and aim to adjust.

The rhythm of the rain filled her ears, too. Her dress hung heavy on her shoulders and the linen underneath clung to her skin.

Between sheets of rain she heard a shout, but the words were dampened. It might have been a command to fall back, return to camp—or it might have been a command to attack. She didn't fire. Instead, she let the bowstring relax and dropped her arrow back into her quiver.

Alys pulled back from her hiding spot and looked for Robin. All she saw was rain. She ran, and her boots squelched in the mud, moss, and macerated leaves. She didn't know how anyone could attack in this weather.

The rain lightened and she could see again. Alys took a deep breath to calm her frantic heart, but the air was so thick she thought she might choke on it. She'd ended up facing south along the ridge, alone. Alys looked back toward where they'd waited for Sir Thomas and wiped water out of her eyes.

Men fought. Swords clashed, and an errant arrow flew by Alys's head. She nocked an arrow and approached, crossing one waterlogged boot over the other until she was close enough to spot Robin, Little John, and Wilmot all fighting back to back against the sheriff's men.

Alys stopped advancing on the fight ahead.

Not one, but two of the sheriff's guards lunged at Robin. They were only supposed to arrest him. Alys nocked a second arrow, parted them on the bowstring and turned her bow sideways so the arrows would go around Robin, then drew and loosed. The arrows hit their feet and they fell onto their backsides.

Robin spun toward her, offered a nod, and moved on to the next guard. They were trying to kill him, right there—no arrest, no trial, no justice—and that wasn't what she'd agreed to. Alys would protect him. She readied another shot, but Robin kept moving in the way.

The sheriff had brought about fifty men with him. It was only a matter of time before the Merry Many were overwhelmed. Robin called for them to retreat, and Alys fled back up to the ridge. She slipped twice on wet leaves and mud, but using roots as hand- and footholds, clambered out of the small valley. She used her last arrow to scare the sheriff's horse. It reared, and he slipped out of the saddle. With an empty quiver, Alys fled north, toward camp.

By the time she reached the mouth of the cave, some of the others had already arrived. Wilmot gathered them all. Alys stood in Little John's shadow and stared at Graham from across the clearing.

"Where's Robin?" Alys said.

John looked like he was squinting into the sun, though clouds still covered the sky. "Don't know. Thought he led the retreat, see. Those bastards must've nabbed him."

Had someone doused her in icy water? Alys's teeth clacked together as a shiver seemed like it might rip her asunder. Was Robin alive? Arrested? She thought this moment would bring relief, but it didn't. Alys wrapped her arms around herself and

213

stared at her boots. She inhaled a deep breath, and smelled the sweetness of the earth mixed with the acrid odor of the storm. *If they killed him, his blood will forever be on my hands, and no priest can cleanse my soul.* Alys couldn't bring herself to look any of the others in the eye. These men had become her friends—family, even. After everything she'd worked for, Alys would give her life to undo her treachery if she could.

26

On the Battlements

Full many a bow there was bent,
And arrows let they glide,
Many a tunic there was rent,
And hurt many a side.
-Translated from *A Lytell Geste of Robyn Hode*

L ittle John told Alys, Graham, and Alan to follow. "Tuck, Wilmot—you stay here in case Robin returns." They worked their way back through the woods and fanned out through the trees.

"Check the fallen," Little John advised. "Hopefully, Robin ain't among them."

Alys wasn't sure whether it'd be better to fall fighting here on the forest floor or executed in Nottingham Castle. But then, if the sheriff had arrested Robin, there was time to save him. Alys still felt torn about Robin leading the common people to rise against the sheriff, but something had passed between her and Robin on the road. Conflicted as she was, she did not want Robin to die—of that, she was certain. So he must be rescued, and if he endangered the people, Alys would worry about that later. If she was still alive. As for Robin, the sheriff couldn't hang him the same day as his arrest because there'd be a trial, even if it was corrupt—Alys reminded herself of this fact again and again.

Weeks ago, Alys found the sheriff frightening, but it was only in working with the Merry Many, in seeing that so many families besides her own suffered, that she began to agree with her ma. Someone had to stand up to the sheriff, and she had to make up for having been his spy.

They reached the road again with no sign of Robin. So many boot- and hoofprints stamped the earth, and where there were no prints, Alys spotted rippled divots from the heavy rain. Where these impressions were interrupted, men lay strewn over the ground, dead or injured; none of them were Robin. Alys reclaimed some of her arrows that were embedded in the mud.

"Alan, help them as best you can," Little John said as he towered over a soldier who whined and moaned and begged for his mother.

"They're the enemy," Alan replied.

"But they don't deserve to perish here, and they're still Englishmen. Go back and get Friar Tuck." Little John motioned for Graham and Alys to follow him. "We'll go to Nottingham and try to spring Robin free."

John led the way, and Graham fell into step beside Alys.

"Strange, isn't it?" Graham asked.

"Hm?" Alys replied.

"The sheriff. Seemed to know we'd be there."

"Well, we were right on the road. And he expected Sir

Thomas, didn't he? Maybe the sheriff wanted to ensure Sir Thomas' safe passage."

"But Sir Thomas didn't even come."

Alys stopped. She felt like there was something stuck in her throat—her heart, maybe. Heat pounded between her ears and for a moment, she thought Sherwood Forest might flip upside down. "What are you—what is it you're suggesting, Graham?"

"I think there may be someone in our group feeding information to the sheriff. He knew just which part of the road on which to find us."

Breathe, Alys reminded herself. *He didn't say it was you. For all he knows, the sheriff might have multiple spies in the Merry Many.* "Let's just focus on finding Robin and then we can worry about how he was caught."

"But what if this is a trap, too? Going to find him?" Graham nodded toward the road. "Wouldn't the sheriff love to present an entire group of executed outlaws to the prince?"

"So… you think we shouldn't look for him?" Alys knew she'd have to contend with her actions somehow, but it was more important to save Robin from an appointment with the executioner.

"No. I think we should be ready, though, and not walk right out on the road."

Little John stopped. "We don't have time for another route, see. We have to get to Town, to the castle, to Robin."

Graham quieted, but his stormy expression suggested he hadn't forgotten the likelihood they were betrayed. Alys hoped he wouldn't guess the truth.

Before they left the forest, she slipped an arrow onto her bowstring and walked with her weapon at the ready, though the arrow pointed at the ground. There was no need to avoid the road now, as there was nowhere to hide between here and Nottingham Town.

The town itself was quiet, and the streets were empty. The wagon ruts and piss puddles were strewn with baskets and boxes, their contents spilled on the ground like animals had gotten into them and rummaged. Where were the crowds? The noblemen? Alys thought it looked like everyone had vanished. The quick close of some shutters over the windows on a house to the right told her people were still in Town, but not in the streets.

"They must have thought their world was ending," Graham said, his words a reverent whisper. "That many soldiers on a march through the streets."

"How many do you reckon the sheriff had?" Alys asked. "One hundred between him and Guy?"

"At least." Graham walked with his hand on his sword hilt.

Alys nodded. She hadn't found out yet how Guy's ambush had gone further down the road, but she guessed not well since he'd taken no prisoners. Robin was the only one missing, and he'd been fighting the sheriff and his men. "Thank you, by the way. For teaching me how to shoot two arrows at once. It came in handy."

"You're welcome, wee one."

They roamed through the rest of Town until they neared the castle. None of them fancied the idea of walking right through the gates, so they circled around and found a wall with some crumbled mortar that would allow them to grab the edges of the stones. Because Alys was lighter than the others, she was the one to climb up to the battlement. Graham watched her from below while Little John stood lookout for guards.

Alys made it to the top unscathed, though her fingers ached from pulling her body weight up the wall in places there weren't footholds within reach. She peered over to find no soldiers, no guards. She pulled herself onto the battlement and looked down on the courtyard below.

No one. The gallows didn't even have a noose. Instead, the courtyard was filled with sacks of grain, casks of ale or cider, crates of root vegetables, weapon racks, firewood, a few saddles and bridles, baskets of coiled rope, and several bushels of red and green apples. *Where is everyone?*

For today, Robin was safe. It wouldn't surprise Alys if the sheriff wanted to invite the prince here for Robin's trial and execution.

Alys leaned over the wall. "Someone's coming. Go back to Sherwood. I'll get some information." Alys ducked away. No one was coming. The sheriff's men had abandoned the battlements, the courtyard below, and the streets beyond the castle walls. But if the other Merry Many escaped to safety, she could rescue Robin herself. It was her fault he'd been taken and locked up; it was her job to free him. *You can't free him alone.* Alys pushed those words away, into some deep, dark corner of her mind: a gaol for unwanted thoughts.

Alys wanted the Merry Many to know the truth. She also wanted their forgiveness, and if she rescued Robin alone, how could they not forgive her? Perhaps it was the friendship she had struck up with them, or it might have been what Robin said about war and him not leaving Hob behind on purpose. But letting the sheriff and Prince John terrorize the people was unacceptable. She would set him free without implicating herself. The sheriff would send for Hob, her family would be restored, and no one would have to hang.

219

Alys slipped into the nearest tower and hurried toward the keep. She continued until she came to a window that overlooked a smaller courtyard where supplies and extra food and ale were often stored. It looked overgrown, but that wasn't what drew Alys's attention.

All the stored items had been cleared out; this courtyard was full of guards. They stood in neat rows and columns, all transfixed upon a single man: the sheriff.

"We meet here," the sheriff said, "in case any of Locksley's men come to save him. I want them to think the castle is unprotected. Now that we have the outlaw in my gaol—"

Someone grabbed Alys's arm. She turned and came face-to-face with Maid Marian.

"You," Marian whispered between clenched teeth. She was alone. No lady's maid or protective guard. "What are you doing here? I spoke to Robin. He told me he thinks there's a spy in the Merry Many. I can't believe you of all people would do this, Alys. That it could be you." Marian pushed Alys back against the battlement. "Robin told me the sheriff's man—or in this case, woman—would probably come to collect their reward for their treason."

The rough edge of the stone scraped against Alys's back. She considered lying to Marian, but for the friendship they'd shared, she couldn't form the words. And Alys was so tired of lying, and couldn't stomach lying to the one true friend she'd ever had. *What do I have to lose? She already believes I am the spy. She already hates me.* "I didn't have a choice."

Marian's eyes narrowed, and she dug her nails into Alys's shoulder.

Alys couldn't tell Marian about her desire for revenge. About growing to hate Robin for the troubles her family faced.

220

They were hers and hers alone, and besides, if Marian didn't find them reason enough to become a spy, then Alys couldn't bear that disapproval.

"You could have come to me. I would have helped you. I would have found a way. For over a year, you convinced me I should wait for Robin. For what—for you to have him arrested? Executed?"

"You can't understand. You don't know what it's like for your family to be torn apart, to—"

"Oh, no, of course not. I only watched my mother die. Attended my father's funeral when we did not have a body to bury because his corpse never returned to England. I do not know what it is like to lose one's family." The sarcasm wrapped around her like a cloak, and beneath it, Marian's words were clothed in anguish.

Alys winced as Marian's manicured nails bit harder into her arm. "I'm sorry. I'm here to rescue him, though. To set him free. I don't want to be the sheriff's spy any longer. I don't have to. The deal was to get Robin arrested, and now the sheriff has arrested him."

"And why should I trust you? It would be so easy, you know, for me to tell the Merry Many what you've done, who you are."

"Because you are Robin's lover? Does he still come into your chambers at night?"

"No," Marian said. She gave Alys a look that asked if she had to say it.

Alys failed to ignore the chill of realization, and she shivered. "You—you're spying for Robin. You're—"

"Maybe I am… or not. But unlike some," she looked Alys up and down like Alys was decorated in refuse, "I do not need a pass to come and go from the castle."

Alys narrowed her eyes. "Nor do I. Not anymore."

"All it would take would be a word in Robin's ear, and he would never let you back into the Merry Many. He couldn't. It would be so easy, Alys. I could say I overheard Sir Guy and the sheriff..."

"You would lie to Robin about what you heard."

"Does the source matter if the information is true?"

Alys narrowed her eyes. Was Marian angry enough at her to steal Alys's opportunity to confess her own sins? "I will rescue Robin, and I will tell him the truth. Please, do not take the chance to do what's right from me."

Marian sighed. "Listen—you get Robin out, and I will not tell him what I know."

"How can I trust you?"

"As you say, you wish to do the right thing. For all that we were to one another, as sisters, I will not breathe a word of it so long as you do free him and confess. If that does not convince you to trust me, how about this? You do not have a choice, Alys Fletcher." Marian looked down at the guards in the courtyard, and then back at Alys. She released Alys and perched one hand on her hip. "I could scream. Alert the guards and the sheriff that you are here. Or you can agree. Get Robin to freedom and I shall not reveal to anyone that you are the sheriff's spy."

Alys started to nod. "Wait—if you're a secret member of the Merry Many, why not free Robin yourself?"

"Change your mind already?"

"No, but I'm curious."

Marian sighed. "I went down to the dungeon. To see Robin, to free him. He said it had to be the group. He would not

222

come with me—then we heard the guard coming to and…"

"Wait, you knocked out a guard?"

Marian hushed her. "The guard did not see it was me."

"Maid Marian, knocking out guards? I suppose it must be love." Graham walked through the archway behind Maid Marian.

Alys glared at Graham. She wanted to ask Marian why she was offering to keep Alys's secret, but she couldn't do that with him here.

Marian turned to face Graham and released Alys. She shushed him.

"How did you get in?" Alys asked Graham.

"Little John said to follow and check on you. You aren't the only one who knows how to climb."

Alys felt a cold shiver rush down her spine. Had Graham heard the part about her being a spy? He wasn't acting like he'd heard, but Alys wasn't sure if he was trying to lure her into a false sense of security before he turned her in to the Merry Many.

Maid Marian looked between them again. "You two should leave. You will need all the Merry Many to rescue Robin. They will not execute him, not yet. They want to use him to lure the rest of you."

"So we should play into their plans?" Alys asked.

"You don't have another choice," Marian said.

"You," Alys said, "were going to rescue Robin alone."

Marian glanced over her shoulder at the courtyard where the inspection was still taking place. "It would not have worked. That was the other reason Robin would not come with me. His rescue will take more people. It is likely…"

"What?" Graham asked.

"It is likely that not all of you will survive. But you must rescue Robin, for the people if not for his own sake."

Graham looked down at the guards in the courtyard. The sheriff moved from row to row, examining their weapons, their posture, their armor. Graham clenched his jaw and his fist. "We will return to free Robin." He swept past Marian and clasped Alys's hand too tight for her to break free.

Alys lunged after Graham and then looked back at where Marian had stood but she'd already left. She and Graham ran back toward the battlement and the wall with the crumbling mortar and stopped at the edge. At least Graham ran, and Alys tried to keep up, so he'd not be dragging her.

Graham's chest heaved as he caught his breath. "Perhaps we should use the gate, since the sheriff and all his men are in the other courtyard."

"And what if he's got one man in the gatehouse? Even if we escaped, we'd never get back in to free Robin."

"A good point." He leaned forward enough to peer down the height of the wall. "I don't know whether to go down first in case you fall or send you down first to ensure your escape."

They couldn't both climb down next to one another. There weren't enough protruding rocks for hand- and footholds for both of them at the same time. Alys wrenched her hand free and swung her leg over the battlement. "Neither of us will get out of here in time to come back for Robin if you stand there forever and perseverate." She climbed down, and Graham followed right behind her.

A wary weight settled on Alys's shoulders, which made climbing slow and stiff. Perhaps Marian was waiting until Robin was free to unmask Alys's secret. Alys decided she couldn't think on that right now. Like Adam and Eve, Marian had sampled from the Tree of Knowledge, and Alys couldn't take that knowledge back, no matter how hard she prayed.

Once they both reached the ground, Graham took her hand again, and they ran through Town with Little John. The streets were coming to life again after the march of the soldiers, so they had to dodge a few carts and pairs or trios of people as well as the waste puddles in the holes and ditches. They ran too fast to talk, and they didn't slow after they left Town, but bolted for the treeline of Sherwood Forest. Alys wished Graham would let go of her hand, or relinquish his hold enough that she could pull free. She didn't enjoy holding hands with him. His hand felt clammy and made her want to scrub hers in the stream near camp. Graham sent Little John ahead to ready the others.

The whole time they ran, Alys prayed Graham didn't hear her entire conversation with Marian. She prayed that if he did, the Merry Many would forgive her. She prayed Graham wasn't leading her to her death.

27

Rescuing Robin

Nay, for God, said Robin,
Sir knight, that thank I thee;
What man that helps a good yeoman,
His friend then will I be.
-Translated from *A Lytell Geste of Robyn Hode*

Alys and Graham stopped under the shade of the leafy canopy to catch their breath. "How are we going to free Robin? If the sheriff plans to spring a trap, and he has all those soldiers…"

"You should have just shot him, wee one."

"Killing someone isn't something to take lightly."

"I don't take it lightly. I have killed."

"So have I." The memory of the guard dying on her flashed to mind and for a moment, Alys found it hard to breathe. His weight crushed her chest, even though she was standing in the forest with Graham.

"Not on purpose."

"It doesn't matter whether—"

"Aye, it does. What you did is not the same as what I did. I don't take killing lightly. But you had a clear shot."

"So did you."

"You had the bow, wee one."

"Oh, and you couldn't have asked to borrow it?"

Graham shrugged.

"I'm not just going to kill the sheriff when he—" She stopped herself and pressed her lips together. Alys had almost revealed that the sheriff had promised to restore her family, whole, to Locksley. If Graham hadn't heard Marian accuse her of spying, he would know if she said that.

"When he what?"

"When he—" Alys begged her mind to come up with a less suspicious answer, "when he has Robin prisoner. Who knows what would happen to Robin then? The idea of trapping us might go right out the window. What if they killed Robin on the spot?"

Graham shifted his weight from one foot to the other. Somewhere in the distance, an owl hooted. "You make a fair point, wee one."

"We'd better get back and form a plan to get Robin out of Nottingham Castle." Alys started toward the cave, toward the rest of the Merry Many.

For a moment, she walked alone. Then Graham trotted to catch up to her before he matched her pace. Upon reaching the clearing they called home, Alys stood at the mouth of the cave.

"It's me and Graham," she said. "We need a plan. A plan to get Robin out of there, because the sheriff has at least one hundred guards hiding and waiting to arrest us when we try to free him."

Little John, Friar Tuck, Alan, and Wilmot all shuffled out of the cave. Discussion of how to free Robin dominated their small clearing. Some wanted to save him, others thought it best to let the sheriff think they weren't coming for their leader. The arguments grew into a cacophony. Alys climbed onto the stump in the center and yelled for the Merry Many to stop and listen, but they didn't, at least not until Little John bellowed for them to "shut their gobs" because arguing wouldn't free Robin.

Ideas had ranged from distraction to bursting into the castle. But Alys knew that she'd gotten Robin into this mess. It was up to her to get him out. Regret filled her, but she tamped it down; there was no time for that now. Now was a time for action. *I hope when they find out I betrayed them they don't take my life if I risk it now for Robin's.* She felt free from the sheriff's deal now that he'd arrested Robin, but not yet free from the imaginary axe that hovered above her.

"I know the castle well," she said. "I can get us in undetected. They won't have the chance to spring their trap. We'll go in through a servant's entrance. There's one outside of Town, to bring game into the kitchen. The kitchen isn't far from the dungeon. We might even get Robin out that way."

"What about the kitchen staff?" Alan asked.

"If we go at night, they'll be asleep; if we're quiet, we might get in unheard."

"What about getting out?" Wilmot asked.

Alys looked from face to face. She didn't hold tender feelings for any of them—not in the way her ma did for her da. But they were all her friends. She'd betrayed them, but she'd agreed to the sheriff's deal before she knew them. She'd continued to spy because of her family. But the idea of the Merry Many not making it out of Nottingham Castle made her throat tighten. She cleared it and then said, "We do our best. We knock out the guards in the dungeon if we can. We avoid killing if we can."

"But we do what we must," Little John said.

Alys nodded. "Like soldiers."

Friar Tuck looked down at the ground and then up again. "I will not kill."

"If," Alys said, "I may confess my sins to you afterward, if we both survive this night, then you won't have to. I will watch out for you. I would... I would shed or lose blood for any of you. You are all the least selfish men I have ever known. You... you gave up everything to help the poor. To fight against injustice. You've all always known who you are and... and that is admirable as well."

"Alys," Wilmot said with a half smile, "you're one of us. You must count yourself in this regard."

Tears made everything blurry. Alys wiped them away. The others all smiled up at her, except for Graham who looked disappointed.

Maybe he still hoped I would marry him. Alys felt for him, but she could not be someone's wife. She'd never wanted to be. She didn't even enjoy holding Graham's hand. All she wanted now was to free Robin so she could undo some of the damage of her treachery. Alys longed to stand for justice and help people, like the Merry Many did.

They waited in tense quiet for the day to wear on. Wilmot honed his knives. Little John checked the traps he'd set around the camp for rabbits or squirrels. Friar Tuck prayed, his mouth moving in relentless but silent supplication, eyes closed and hands clasped around the rough-hewn cross he wore. Alan and Graham played dice, betting acorns, twigs, and pebbles. Alys restrung her bow and examined her arrows.

* * *

When the light of the afternoon began to fade into twilight, Alys packed her quiver full of arrows. They'd have to go through Town to get to the other side of the castle. As they neared the road, they split into smaller and smaller groups, fanning out, until they were in pairs by the time they reached the open field nestled between the green wood and the streets of Nottingham.

Alys stopped for a moment. Graham stood with her. "I think we should pray," she said. "We will need God's help tonight." She felt Graham take her hand, and even though she didn't enjoy holding his, she didn't pull away. *Dear God,* she thought, *safeguard the Merry Many and Robin. I was wrong to want him gone from this earth, and I was wrong to help the sheriff. If I die tonight, safeguard my family and friends.* "Amen."

Graham released her hand. "What did you pray for, wee one?"

"My friends and family. You?"

Graham hesitated. "The same."

Alys didn't believe him, but there wasn't time to stand around and talk about it. They crossed the open land on the way to Town.

"Whatever happens, Graham, I am glad to be your friend."

He smiled and thanked her, and Alys wished his tone wasn't threaded with defeat. He sounded like he dragged a stomped-on hope for something more. Something Alys could not give.

After he found out about her betrayal, Alys didn't think Graham would want to marry her, anyway. She would tell him now, come clean, if not for the need to rescue Robin. But Alys knew she'd have to confess. She dreaded carrying her treachery to her grave, to the shining gates of Heaven or the bland hall of Purgatory. *Now is not the time. Rescue Robin, then confess.*

"Are you coming? Or did you change your mind about saving Robin?" Graham stopped to stare at her, and it wasn't until then Alys realized she'd slowed to a halt.

"I—I'm coming." Alys fell into step beside him. "Do you miss it?"

"Miss what?"

"Scotland."

"Oh, aye, wee one. I do. But I feel… freer here. And indeed I am. If I'd stayed in Scotland, I'd have likely been caught and hanged for what I did."

She recalled it was a soldier Graham had killed before leaving Scotland. "Surely they wouldn't have hanged you. You were defending your family."

Graham scoffed. "My reasons would not have mattered, wee one."

Alys wrinkled her nose when the pungent odors of Town surrounded them. They made their way through the winding streets, and no one stopped or bothered them. What guard—not that she saw one—would bother to interrogate a pair of people when he expected a larger group?

They wended their way through Nottingham Town, to meet up with the other Merry Many outside the tunnel that led to the kitchen. The door was locked, but Wilmot picked the lock with his knives, and then they all slithered inside.

We're coming, Robin. You'll be free by dawn. I swear on my life.

The only light in the kitchen came from the embers banked in the hearths on either side of the room and the door, left ajar, behind them. Alys motioned to Graham that the Merry Many should all follow. In the dim light, she saw Graham turn to motion to the next to do the same, and so on down the line. Alys pulled an arrow from her quiver and nocked it, just in case.

Alys heard them behind her: their footsteps, their breaths, and she could have sworn she could even hear their beating hearts. They sounded too loud, but no call of alarm rent the quiet that packed the kitchen. No soldiers or guards burst through a door to ambush them. They were halfway across the kitchen when a pot clattered to the stone floor. Alys froze, and then she turned.

Friar Tuck apologized. Though he whispered, even his words seemed too loud.

Alys shushed the line. Her heart hammered in her chest. It beat throughout her entire body. All was quiet and still, but she waited for the sound of footsteps from beyond the door leading to the corridor, from above, from anywhere.

Then she tiptoed forward again. Alys eased open the door; it whined on the hinges, but another moment to stop and listen proved they were yet undiscovered. The corridor was long and narrow, unadorned save a bracketed torch every ten feet. One step at a time. One foot over the other. Eyes trained on the far end of the corridor, where the dungeon waited. Even if soldiers didn't descend on them, Alys knew they'd have to contend with guards inside the gaol. She halted a few paces from the door.

"Alan, you stay out here and stand guard," Alys said, her

voice a hoarse whisper. "Graham, Little John, Wilmot, Friar Tuck and I will go in. We'll take care of the guards—knock them unconscious—and get Robin."

Alan asked, "Why do I have to wait out here?"

"Because you're the last in line," Alys said. "Because this was my plan. Because I said so, and because we don't have time to argue about it. Besides, if any guards escape, it'll be your job to make sure they don't raise the alarm."

Alan opened his mouth, but a scowl from Little John silenced him.

Little John led the way into the dungeon, followed by Alys next. The moment she entered, she remembered the way the air clung to the inside of her chest, the way it weighed on her shoulders and sat there, unmoving and unrelenting. She felt her throat close against the fetid odors of urine, feces, and bodies—living and perhaps dead, too. She could smell and taste that sweet-sick odor that clawed its way into her nostrils and wrapped around her tongue.

With his quarterstaff, Little John knocked out a guard. The man went down so fast and so loud that the other five guards turned. One guard—he must have been the man in charge because he was the only one with a helmet—yelled to attack and the others obeyed.

In the same instant the guards sprang into action, Alys fired an arrow and missed, hitting the stone wall instead. *Too many people, not enough space to shoot.* She drew her sword and clashed it against one of the guard's pikes.

The guard disarmed Alys. He thrusted. Little John shoved her out of the way, and she knocked into Graham, who caught her around her waist. When she looked back, she saw the guard with the pike in his hands. In the gloom, Alys couldn't tell if Little John had been stabbed or if he had caught the weapon.

No one moved, not even the guards. It seemed in one breath, they were all trying to see whether the legendary Little John would be felled.

Little John's brow furrowed, his nostrils flared, and a sheen of sweat glistened on his face. He grunted.

Don't die. Little John couldn't die; he was too strong. Little John was Robin's second in command. He had been there for Alys when she'd taken a life.

Wilmot screamed and charged, blade held high, and attacked the guard who tried to stab Little John. The melee commenced.

Alys pulled away from Graham and hit a guard with her bow. She shot another in the foot before Friar Tuck punched him, knocking him out cold.

When Little John swept a guard's feet out from under him with the spear that'd almost run him through, and then hit him on the head with his quarterstaff, Alys realized he'd not been stabbed, and a rush of relief swept through her. Little John was like a windmill of weapons, and somehow, in the tight quarters, he managed to fight. *It must be his soldier's training.* Together, the Merry Many fought the remaining guards until all five lay sprawled on the floor, battered but alive.

Alys breathed deep the thick stink, which now included the coppery bite of blood. Alys gagged on it but her lungs hungered for air, so she took another deep breath. Chains rattled against bars, and Alys realized the prisoners must have been clamoring about and yelling during the whole fight.

"Robin?" she asked. "Robin of Locksley, we are here to free you."

"I'm Robin," an old man called from the left. Alys could tell he was old because his voice shook with age. Another man claimed to be Robin, but his voice sounded too high.

Alys followed the silence. At the far end of the gaol, in a cell by himself, knelt Robin of Locksley, leader of the Merry Many, lips pressed together. He didn't bang on the bars or rattle his chains. He didn't even wear chains.

"The guard with the helmet has the keys," Robin said. He said it like he'd expected them all along. "And we take everyone in here with us. We free them all."

"But Robin," Wilmot said while Graham backtracked to collect the keys, "we don't have the time to free everyone."

"We liberate everyone," Robin said, "or I stay."

This must be why he wouldn't leave with Marian. There was no way that Robin could protect all the prisoners by himself—even with Marian's help, there were too many.

"I have the keys," Graham said, and then ran up to the barred door. He slid the key into the lock and turned, and metal clanged. The hinge squealed as Robin pushed open the door to his cell.

"Free the others," Robin said, "and help me take their weapons." He nodded toward the guards.

Alys, Wilmot, Friar Tuck, and Little John helped Robin collect spears, daggers, and Alys's sword.

"How did you get in?" Robin asked.

"Kitchen," Little John said. "There's a servant's entrance there." A proud smile spread across his face. "Alys led us."

"Well done, Alys," Robin said. "But I don't doubt someone heard this fight. We should hurry."

Alys thought they could make it out faster if they didn't have to get all the other prisoners out. But then, Robin wouldn't be

Robin if he left them here to rot for being unable to pay taxes, for speaking out against injustice, or for stealing when they had no food to fill their bellies.

28

Sanctuary

Still stood the proud sheriff,
A sorry man was he:
Woe worth thee, Raynolde Greenleaf!
Thou hast now betrayed me.
-Translated from *A Lytell Geste of Robyn Hode*

R obin and a half-dozen prisoners in tow, the Merry Many led the way out of the dungeons and through the kitchen. It wasn't until they ran out of the kitchen into the night that the sheriff sprung his trap. Robin, Alys, and the others stopped on a farthing to find a semi-circle of soldiers, Guy at the center, facing the kitchen door. For a moment, no one said or did anything. Then Robin gave the call to break through the line.

"Rendezvous in Sherwood!" Code for camp.

Alys nocked, drew, aimed, and fired. Out of the corner of her eye, she spotted Wilmot do the same. They were the only two with bows right now. "We'll cover you," she said to Robin.

"Go."

Arrow after arrow. It was hard to aim for hands and feet, for areas of the body that would not lead to an instant death or a slow one later. Alys didn't want to kill, but hands and feet were small and moved with more rapidity than a torso. Robin broke through the line of soldiers right before she reached for another arrow, only to find an empty quiver. "I'm out!"

"Go," Wilmot said. "I have a few more."

Alys drew her sword and ran after the Merry Many and freed prisoners, some of whom were fighting—or trying to fight—with the spears they'd taken off the guards in the gaol. Alys's arms and legs felt as though lead weighed them down. She pushed exhaustion back and with a battle cry, launched to the defense of one of the older prisoners.

Everything was confusion and the repeated clash of swords and spears and armor. Alys wasn't sure how she made it through, but soon she was running, alone, through Town.

Alys imagined herself far away and out of the castle, out of Town, out of the shire. Nottingham Town looked different when fleeing alone for her freedom and life. Streets whirred by in her peripheral vision like arrows, from Tanner Street to Hosier Street to Shielding Street. Slight movements of shadows and flickers of torch- and candlelight, and small sounds made her heart pump against her insides. Alys didn't even pay attention to the puddles of waste, or that urine from those puddles wicked up the hem of her skirt. By the time she reached her parents' home, she could smell the sharp odor wafting from her boots with every step.

Alys slammed her fist and palm into their door. She heard a muffled voice from inside—her da. In an instant, she recalled his warm eyes, his warm hugs, and the warm sun on their faces while he fletched arrows outside their farm home. For an instant, Alys was back there, back then, a little girl who never spied or lied.

Then the door opened. Da's eyes looked cool, like someone had poured milk in them. He asked who called at their door at such an hour.

Alys's voice caught in her throat, but she pushed the words out in a raspy gust of breath. "It is I, your daughter."

* * *

Da slid to the side and opened the door wider. She saw half his face in the glow from the cooking fire. More lines around his mouth and a new fold between his eyebrows. The crinkles around his eyes no longer looked like lines of mirth but made him appear care worn. His hands grasped the air near her and then landed on her shoulder and her head. Da pulled her into one of his hugs, and Alys felt like he rearranged her bones in that one embrace.

"Can't… air…" She gasped.

No sooner had he released her than her ma wrapped her arms around Alys's middle. She hugged her almost as tight. "Where have you been?" she asked.

"I don't have time to explain. It's—I'm so glad to see you both again. Where is Grandda?" She realized how she might not have seen them again if the sheriff won, and then, with no use for a spy, had sent his army after her. What would the sheriff's retaliation for Robin's rescue be?

"Your grandfather's gone on a pilgrimage to Canterbury. Your cheek…" Ma led her into the heart of the kitchen.

Alys reached up to touch her face. When she noticed blood

239

on her fingertips, she sensed the sting of a cut she didn't know she'd received.

Da closed the door. Ma released Alys and then turned away. Alys heard Ma grinding something in a mortar and pestle. "We were so worried about you, Alys. Where have you been?"

"I can't—I can't say." Alys glanced again at her da. "Da, how long…?"

Although he was blind, or close to blind, it was like he could see what was wrong. Alys wore a tapestry of her transgressions. The guard she killed. Betraying Robin. Lying to them. Refusing an offer of marriage. Spying.

Tears stung the slice on her face, and the sobs that followed soon after shook her entire body. Once more, her parents held her. They held her tight, but not so tight that she couldn't draw breath to support those sobs. Alys knew they didn't know the actual reasons she cried, and she also knew they could never learn of them—but she welcomed their comfort.

Alys embraced them both until Da spoke.

"So you received our ill news, too?"

Alys's arms fell limp at her sides.

"What ill news?" Alys wriggled free to look from Da's face to Ma's. Maybe they meant his eyesight.

"We—we received word—" Now, Ma was the one who shook with sobs. "I cannot."

"The king is coming home, but your brother," Da said, "died in the Holy War."

Alys was certain everything collapsed around her. The wattle and daub walls, the rafters, the patched and thatched roof. She was awash in it all, like the house had come apart and all its pieces flew around her in a foul wind. Her chest ached. Her face stung. God was trying to squeeze the life out of her, to beckon her to Heaven or cast her to Hell.

Alys crumpled to the floor and curled on her side. She grasped her skirt and drew it over her body, swaddling herself in the sweat- and urine-soaked wool. A strangled cry tore from her throat, ululating until she ran out of breath. Her lungs ached. Her body ached. Alys didn't even notice her parents' gentle palms on her head, cheek, or shoulder. She was impervious to consolation. Everything she'd done was for naught.

29

Confessions

Christ have mercy on his soul,
That died on the road!
For he was a good outlaw,
And did poor men much good.
-Translated from *A Lytell Geste of Robyn Hode*

The fire from the hearth cast a weak flicker onto the beams above. Alys turned onto her other side; somehow, the flagstone floor was even harder than the cave floor. She missed the tufts of moss she used to soften her bedding at the camp. Alys brushed some strewing herbs under her head, but the leaves and stems were dry and poked her scalp, so she rolled onto her stomach and rested her head on crossed arms. She wasn't sure how much time had passed since the quiet numbness set in.

"When I was a girl," Ma's voice sounded from the other side of the cramped kitchen, "I lost my favorite cousin."

"I thought Guy was your favorite cousin," Alys said.

"No." She heard Ma's scrunched face in that one word: the nasal quality of it, the way she drew it out. "His sister was my favorite cousin. We were the same age, she and I, and we used to play often. Guy was much younger than us, and didn't want to play with girls, anyway."

Alys didn't think Guy had a problem playing with girls, but then, Alys enjoyed playing soldier and hero. *Guy always came to play with me and Hob. Hob. Gone.* Alys turned over again, so her back faced her mother. "I'm sorry she perished, but it's not like Hob dying. Thousands of miles away, without us nearby."

"She was like a sister to me. Then, after she died, my parents tried to arrange for me to marry her intended. He didn't like me and made it plain, and besides, I'd already fallen in love with your father."

That is when you ran off with him and most of your family never spoke to you again. Alys didn't begrudge Ma marrying beneath her. Alys wouldn't exist if not for both her parents, and beyond that, she loved her da. But it had cost them. Alys never met her ma's parents. A chill wrapped around her. Alys rolled onto her side again, toward the hearth, and felt the stone press back against her shoulder and hip. She drew swirls in the dust on the floor with her fingertip and remembered learning to read with Ma.

Lessons were always in the weeks after harvest. Hob and Alys would follow their ma outside and draw in the dirt or, when it rained, they'd make their letters on the floor of the house. When they knew their letters well enough, Ma would ask them to read from her book of hours. It was the only book the Fletcher family owned, and Alys spotted it on the mantel, its spine split and repaired with dark veins of pitch or golden trails of honey.

Right now, Alys couldn't think of a single passage from that book that offered her comfort. She both wanted her ma's comfort and needed to push it away, and Alys tried to close her eyes and let the rhythm of Da's snores from across the room lull her into sleep, or at least into a daze. It didn't work. Her mind conjured images of Hob's death, violent in every imagined scenario. Each grim vision ended with Hob's face streaked with blood, his eyes fixed on the heavens though he could no longer see. No one stooped to slide his eyelids shut and place a penny to hold them closed or cross his hands over his heart. In her mind's eye, he was one of hundreds scattered in the sands in the shadow of Jerusalem. There his body would rot and wait for his spirit's ascension.

Ma's hand interrupted those visions when it slipped into Alys's and squeezed. "I want you to stay here. You know how to make arrows. You could take over for your da. And I—I cannot have both my children gone."

"If I were married, I would be gone. You used to want me to marry." Alys only saw part of Ma's face, but the glow from the embers illuminated enough to prove the older woman's smile by the crinkled crows' feet at the corner of her eyes.

"I want you to marry. To experience love, to have children. But I don't want you to leave. We can want more than one thing sometimes, even when those things are opposite."

Warmth at her mother's wanting her to stay and bitter regret warred for dominance over Alys's heart. She wanted to stay. But she also wanted to go to the forest, to confess what she'd done—not just to Friar Tuck, but to Robin. Even if it cost her life. *Then I would see Hob again. But then, I would not go to Heaven, for my sins are too many.* Everything pulled her in a different direction. She felt like she was being quartered, but not torn limb from limb. Rather, she felt her soul was thinner than it once was, about to snap like a bowstring stretched too far too many times.

She wished she'd known the right course of action from the start. She wished she'd never agreed to spy for the sheriff. True, her family would remain separated and in this wretched place, but now Hob wouldn't come home, anyway. At least her soul would have been pure if she'd known her own mind. *Maybe the actual sins, the ones that send you to Hell, weren't killing and the like, but not standing for what's right.* "How did you choose Da?"

Another eye-crinkle. "I followed my heart."

Alys turned onto her stomach again so she could face her ma. "How did you trust what your heart said? How did you know it wasn't your head?"

Ma allowed a quiet laugh to escape, but it sounded wrong, mirthless in the wake of Hob's death. "To marry below my station wasn't smart, Alys. I lost almost everything. I sneaked out of my father's house with an extra gown, a single book, and a few coins. Most of my family refused to talk to me. Many still refuse, and I was not even told my parents died until months later when Sir Guy returned to England from France. But I love your da and would choose him again and again. Even with our difficulties."

Alys clenched her teeth and let out a low growl. "How am I supposed to tell the difference, then? Between what my head and my heart say?" She wasn't sure how she could determine what the right choice was in any situation if she was supposed to follow her heart, but she didn't know how to heed it.

Ma's answer seemed to take months. "Whichever choice

feels right in the morning when you wake and at night before you go to sleep. That is when your heart speaks."

Alys pulled her hand free. "That's when I have my most conflicted thoughts." Ma's advice wasn't helpful at all. She stared at the embers. Their glow pulsed like a heartbeat, and Alys tried to figure out if her own heart was talking to her. Stay in Town with your family, Alys, it said. Go to the forest and confess, Alys, it told her with the next beat. She wished she could silence it and squeezed her eyes shut as though that would quiet the pangs of her heart. These opposing desires filled her mind until the thoughts melted into an incomprehensible mess.

Alys focused on Hob instead. The last thing she remembered before she fell asleep was a memory with her brother, playing hide and seek in the rye on their farm: the sweet aroma of warm earth mixed with wildflowers that grew nearby, birds singing, the soft rye under her palms as she ran through the crops to find rye grass tall enough to hide behind, the press of her toes into the soil, the rush of panted breaths, and the pump of her heart louder each time Hob called out a higher number.

* * *

Alys woke before her parents. She rubbed the sleep from her eyes and scrounged around for a quill, but found none. Instead, she took a feather from a basket of feathers that were waiting to become part of an arrow. With beet juice as ink, she left a message in the book of hours to tell her parents she loved them, but was not sure if they would ever meet again. She left the book open so they would find the message, grabbed as many arrows as would fit in her quiver, and tiptoed out of the house.

She had to make things right; she'd freed Robin, but she had to come clean. If she died with this secret in her heart, she'd spend eternity in Hell. *Better to suffer now, in this life, than for eternity.* With a deep breath and a final glance at her parents' home, she whispered an apology and ran toward the edge of Town, the clearing beyond, and the trees of Sherwood Forest.

When she returned to camp, only one of the Merry Many seemed to be awake. Robin. He sat on the stump before the mouth of the cave. When she approached, he smiled. Alys wished he wouldn't smile at her.

"You survived," he said. "We worried. I can wake up Friar Tuck to look at that cut." Robin stood from the stump and turned toward the cave's entrance.

"No."

He half-turned. "You saved me and will not allow me to see to your well-being?"

"You won't want to, Robin. We—we need to talk."

Brow furrowed, he turned toward her, his shoulders squared to hers. "What must we talk about?" There was an uncertain edge to his voice.

"We—that is—you have to know I—I thought you abandoned Hob in the Holy Land when I agreed, and he—the sheriff—promised to bring him home."

All traces of friendliness and care melted off of Robin's face. "What have you done?"

"I want to tell you. I want to confess. Because it's the right thing to do—but you must hear me first, Robin. You must hear all my words. You must swear." She bit back tears.

Robin sat again on the tree stump. "I swear."

247

Alys took a shuddering breath, then launched into an explanation, telling Robin of her anger at him for returning without Hob. She told him about the sheriff's deal. How she tried, at first, to provide information that would only hinder Robin's efforts. That Guy said the sheriff needed information that would lead to Robin's arrest. The only part she left out was how Marian discovered the truth. Robin and Marian couldn't be together now, with him an outlaw and Marian pledged to take holy orders, but Alys wouldn't make Marian a liar or traitor in Robin's heart. When she finished, she sunk to her knees in the dirt before Robin.

"My lord," she said, hands clasped together, "I throw myself on your mercy. Please. Please forgive me."

Robin clenched his jaw. True to his word, he'd listened to everything she'd said. "You betrayed me, Alys. I need—I need time to think."

She nodded. "Of course."

"This is going to hurt."

"What?"

Robin pulled his dagger. For a moment, Alys worried he would kill her. Instead, he brought the hilt down on her temple so hard that all the world turned black.

30

Truth & Freedom

And when they had drunken well,
Their troths together they did plight,
That they would be with Robin
That ilk same day at night.
-Translated from *A Lytell Geste of Robyn Hode*

When Alys woke again, she realized her feet were bare. Did the Merry Many think she wouldn't flee barefoot? Her head ached too, and it hurt to open her eyes. Had demons crawled in through her ears and smashed their little horned heads into the inside of her skull all night? She took a deep breath. Rope bound her to something solid and scratchy. She smelled evergreen. Evergreen and bodies. Live sweaty bodies. Men. Someone nudged her foot.

"I say we kill her," Wilmot said. "Can't trust her not to betray us again."

Alys wriggled against the ropes binding her to the tree stump, but they were tight enough to restrict movement. Her

249

ankles were bound, and above them a crude tripod. A tent of logs and kindling waited under the tripod. Did they intend to burn her feet? Icy fear crystalized in her core, its reach spreading and chilling her limbs. "Please don't torture me." *I'd rather they take my life.* Torture was not something she thought them capable of. In every scenario that played out in her head following her confession, this never factored in. Alys sought Friar Tuck. He averted his gaze. Robin looked troubled. It hadn't been his idea. "Robin, please."

An angry murmur circled her. Wilmot and Alan looked the most livid. Graham seemed confused, and Little John looked as though she'd carved his heart out.

"Please, Robin. You know why I did what I did. And I've nothing else to tell you, so why—don't let them do this."

Robin pinched the bridge of his nose. "They don't want to do this, Alys. I set it up."

Her breath caught, and she struggled against the rope. "Why? This is—I never dreamed you would—"

"And I never dreamed you would betray us. But I have to know. I have to be sure. Did you—does the sheriff know Marian—"

"Spied for you? No! I wouldn't do that to her. I only did what I had to."

Graham stepped forward and crouched next to her. For a moment, Alys thought he'd be a voice of reason, of gentleness. Instead, he wrapped her hair around his fist and pulled her head back against the tree stump, so it forced her to look at him. "Is that what you claim, Alys? That you had no choice?"

His use of her real name hurt more than the strain on her scalp. "No," she said. "I had a choice and made the wrong one. I should have—I should have realized that no man can promise to bring another back from war. Fear clouded my judgment, the need for vengeance. Against Robin. And the need to have my family back. Then it was too late. I—" Sobs cut her off. *Hob is dead. Hob is never coming home.*

"Don't let her tears sway you, Robin," Alan said.

Graham released her hair and turned away with a snarl.

"Please," Alys begged again. "Please, Robin. Banish me if you must. But do not torture me or take my life. Ask of me any favor, but do not kill me. I am not ready yet, to face St. Peter's ruling." *If he banishes me, perhaps I will go on a pilgrimage, like Grandda.*

Robin looked over to the side. "John? Tuck? You've said nothing of the fate of our spy."

"She's just a girl," Little John said. "Young enough to be my daughter, Robin. Would a man have been able to withstand the sheriff's request?"

"So she can spy because she's a girl?" Graham sounded desperate.

"No," Little John said. "But Robin… what if it'd been Marian? Or Graham, what if it'd been your sister? Any of our sisters, daughters…" His eyes met Alys's and he offered a sad smile. "Alys has done a lot of remarkable things. But that doesn't mean she was raised with the same sense of honor that a man must uphold, see."

"I have honor," Alys protested. "Robin, tell them how I wanted to take my—my broth—my brother's place! Tell them."

"I thought you had honor, Alys." Robin sighed and scratched at the scruff on his cheek. "Tuck, what say you?"

"I will never advocate for torture or the taking of life, Robin. Every soul should be given every chance at redemption." He looked at Alys, then at the tripod and logs. "This is wrong,

251

and you know that. No matter what she did, this will blacken your soul."

Robin looked up at the trees. "The thing of it is, though… so long as the sheriff lives, I cannot trust you, Alys."

"So it's her or the sheriff," Little John said.

"Robin, Little John, I—" Friar Tuck started, but stopped when Robin held his hand up.

"We do not need to kill the sheriff. But Alys must come clean, in public. Yes, I think that is the way forward, with the least bloodshed. Alys, you will accompany us to Nottingham Town. You will tell the people—in the company of the sheriff and his men—what you did, and I will confirm that I am giving you a chance at redemption."

The blood drained from Alys's face. "I—please, Robin, banishment would be better—I will go on pilgrimage, I will—"

"This is not enough," Wilmot said. "She betrayed us, Robin. How do you know she won't just spout some pretty words and betray us again?"

"We need to make her pay," Alan added. "If someone is caught thieving, they lose a hand. Consequences exist for a reason."

"And," Robin said, his voice loud but not high, "we have fought against such brutality at the sheriff's hands." Robin massaged his temples. "Tuck, does not the Bible say something about truth and freedom?"

"The truth," Friar Tuck stepped forward, "shall set you free."

"Untie her," Robin said to Wilmot and Graham. "Give her back her boots. We go to Town."

"This is too risky," Alan said.

Robin smirked. "Everything in our lives is risky. Alys will condemn the sheriff and all his unjust acts. She will become

252

one of us, for real this time. What will you choose, Alys?"

She wondered if the whole torture setup was a ruse to earn her obedience, but she wasn't eager to test the theory. "I will do it."

* * *

Alys wished she could fall asleep and perhaps this entire episode could pass her over, like a bad dream, and she would wake the next day to find that the deed was already done. To go into Nottingham Town right now was madness. Defying the sheriff in the middle of Town was lunacy. For Robin to not take her life, though she was grateful for it, was absurdity. Alys wore that gratitude like armor against the sneers and glowers that Wilmot, Alan, and even Graham shot her way as they left behind the protection of the forest.

Robin carried her bow on one shoulder. Alys still wore her quiver full of her father's arrows, but the Merry Many had confiscated her sword. She looked down at the arrows. Most of them were fletched with gray and brown feathers. But one arrow stuck out with a single crimson vane. She ran her fingers over it and tried to imagine herself sitting in Locksley, winding gut string around an arrow shaft to bind the fletching in place.

This may be insanity, but I'm finally doing what's right. Alys looked up to find Tuck watching her. "Does the truth always hurt so much?"

He smiled. "No, not always. But sometimes it is like pulling free a splinter from your foot."

"Or from your heart."

"You will heal from this, Alys. When you first came to the

green wood with us, you seemed… nervous and angry. After the tax collection fight, I could tell you stood at a crossroads. Today you choose your path. You will feel better for it, knowing it to be the path of truth and justice."

Alys half smiled. "I still say pilgrimage would have been easier."

"Many pilgrims walk barefoot for thirty, sometimes forty miles a day. They face marauders. Disease. Starvation. Thirst. Assault. It would not have been easier." Tuck's voice constricted.

"I am sorry. You have known those hardships?"

"I have. And I have seen what happens to pilgrims who fall by the wayside. It will take time to earn everyone's trust again, but this will be easier than a pilgrimage. Than banishment."

"I hope you're right. About earning their trust again. Will I earn yours again?"

"You never lost it, Alys. I knew you had the capacity to do good in this world when you showed such remorse over the death of the tax collector's guard."

Alys laughed. "Wish you'd told me what you knew."

Friar Tuck smiled. "But then it would not be your journey, would it? Come on now, let's not fall behind."

"Thank you, for what you said at the camp."

Tuck set his jaw. "You need not thank me for that. Men are often driven to violence when their blood boils, but there are some acts which I cannot abide."

Robin led them through the streets, their hoods up, until they stood right outside the east gate of the castle. "Send for the sheriff," he told the guards. "Tell him Robin of Locksley wishes to have a word."

Little John jammed the portcullis with his quarterstaff so

the guards couldn't raise the gate. The castle sprang to life, with guards running toward the gate and some back toward the keep. Archers formed a line in the courtyard. Robin called out a warning and the Merry Many scattered to the side.

After a few moments, the sound of so many boot scuffles, and threats from guards and soldiers to the Merry Many, the sheriff's voice boomed in the courtyard.

"Robin of Locksley! Too frightened to talk to me face-to-face?"

"Not at all, sheriff. But I'm not the one with something to say. Call off your archers, and you'll find out why we're here."

Please don't. If you don't call off the archers, maybe I won't have to say it.

But after a moment, Alys heard Guy's voice ordering the archers to stand down. From across the ramp leading up to the gate, Robin nodded at her. She looked over at Tuck, who offered a smile. Alys stepped in front of the gate. Before she turned to face the curious townspeople she hadn't realized had gathered, she saw the surprise on the faces of the sheriff, Guy—and Marian, who was exiting the keep. The lady's gaze chilled when she spotted Alys.

As Alys turned her back to the castle courtyard, she remembered walking through the streets with Wilmot, distributing food and coin to those in need. This was for the people of Nottingham, not her. She needed to regain their trust to help them. Because even if the king was coming home, it would be months before he arrived, and the journey was perilous. The Merry Many were still needed.

She took a deep breath, but before she spoke, she saw both her parents in the crowd. Ma looked worried, but Da kept an arm around her shoulders, his unseeing eyes almost on Alys.

She opened her mouth, but at first, no sound came out. How could she say this with her parents there?

The truth shall set me free. I am no longer about revenge. I would give everything for these people. Even my life. Alys took another deep breath, during which all the world seemed to stop. The people looked like a sea of statues. Even the trees stilled as the warm breeze died down.

"People of Nottingham. I once lived in this castle and served the noble Maid Marian. After Robin of Locksley returned from the Holy Land, I became angry because I expected my brother to return, too. I know many of you have lost husbands, fathers, and brothers in those wars. After Robin was outlawed, the sheriff asked me to spy on him."

Behind her, she heard the sheriff call to get the portcullis open. Little John doubled his efforts to keep it jammed. On the other side, guards tried to lift against him.

"I agreed. I agreed because I wanted my brother home. The sheriff offered to bring him home and give my family back their farm." Alys looked everywhere but at her parents' faces.

Behind her, she heard the sheriff send the archers up to the battlements.

Her heart beat loud and hard in her chest. "It was because of me that Robin was arrested. It was also because of me he was freed, because I realized how wrong it was for me to betray him. To betray you. Robin is giving me a chance at redemption, and I will not waste—"

Behind her, wood snapped. Little John called a warning. The portcullis lifted. Alys searched now for her parents, but couldn't spot either of them. People screamed as guards and soldiers poured from the courtyard into the street. Robin thrust Alys's bow into her hand just as another hand grabbed her upper arm and yanked her from the path of the guards.

"Sherwood!" Robin called.

Everyone tried to disperse, but there were too many people in the street. Alys didn't even have space to nock an arrow. She tried to see who was leading her away. Friend or foe?

It wasn't until they broke away from the crowd that she realized it was Graham. He ran with her down an alley, then a wider street, then another alley. A chestnut bay with a white starburst on its face stood in a small pen, eating hay.

"Can you ride without a saddle?" Graham asked.

"I have before, but it was a pony."

"Good enough." Graham lifted Alys and put her on the horse's back. He climbed on behind her and wound one arm around her waist. Alys spared an instant to feel like she wanted him to move his arm away, but they didn't have time to argue about his tender feelings or her lack of them. Graham held onto the horse's mane with his free hand. "Cover us if you can." Then he kicked.

The horse bolted forward, splintering the fence.

Alys nocked a gray-fletched arrow. She drew the bowstring, ready to fire. They had to ride back to the high street since they'd found the horse on a dead end. Alys fired arrows to keep the guards back. Her arrows bounced off the road, but it slowed them. She wasn't aiming to kill.

By the time they reached the clearing between Town and the forest, Alys had one arrow left. When she looked down, it was the one with the red fletch.

31

The Red Fletch

These bishops, and these archbishops,
You shall them beat and bind;
The high sheriff of Nottingham,
Him hold in your mind.
-Translated from *A Lytell Geste of Robyn Hode*

Everything seemed to happen at once: A volley of arrows arced from the hidden archers in the trees; they cascaded like water over the ridge and swept away the first row of guards that pursued Alys and Graham. She didn't need to see the faces of the Merry Many to know the band of outlaws would not abandon them, even if some still had not forgiven her. Graham turned the horse and drew his sword.

She imagined this clearing was a desert, that she was fighting alongside Hob. Not for the first time, she imagined what it might be like—dying in battle. Alys pictured her spirit floating up above the canopy of leaves, through the clouds, to the gates of Heaven. In her mind, they were wrought of gold, brighter than the sun, and covered in cloisonne clusters of every gemstone she could think of. In front of them stood St. Peter with his book; he asked for her name, and Alys couldn't keep it from him. The words flew from her mouth like startled birds. Then he flipped through the pages until his finger landed on her name. He saw the man she killed. Her betrayal was marked there as well. St. Peter's placid face contorted into rage, and the clouds split beneath her feet. Alys plummeted through the sky, past the earth's patchwork of farms, mountains, and waters—into a pit of fire.

She bit back a scream as Graham swung his blade down on the shoulder of a soldier who rode up beside them.

Around them, men screamed; horses stamped their feet and whinnied. Alys nocked her one arrow, the one Da told her was fletched red for war. She might not be in the Holy Land, but this was war—if not for Nottinghamshire and England, then for her soul. Alys knew now the sheriff had enticed her to evil, and she had to defend Graham, Robin, and all the Merry Many. She no longer believed the sheriff would have ever brought Hob home.

Stop the sheriff, stop the fight. An arrow to the shoulder ought to do it.

She drew her bowstring. Two white fletching feathers and one red.

Alys took aim and thought of Hob lying somewhere in the desert, arms and legs spread and eyes open to the sky and vultures circling above. She adjusted her grip on the bowstring. She pictured her da, too blind to fletch another arrow, to make another tool of sport, of hunting, of death and art like this one ever again. Alys blew out a breath, slow and steady despite the jittery horse between her legs, the swings of

Graham's sword to each side, and the surrounding cacophony of shouts and cries. She pictured her family's farm, rye stalks straight like the arrow's shaft and tall. She imagined Robin and Marian marrying, happy, living not among walls of trees but in a manor house. A smile tugged at one corner of her lips.

She released.

The fletching swished by her skin, grazing the cut on her cheek.

Straight toward the sheriff on his draught horse it flew. Red for Hob, for her da, for her ma, for her grandda. For Robin, for Marian, for herself, and for all of Nottingham. One strike to make up for the wrongs she'd committed, to halt injustice, to give the Merry Many a chance to escape. To earn the trust of Wilmot, Alan, and Graham. Robin, Friar Tuck, and Little John already seemed to believe that this time she was really one of them, but Alys wanted to strengthen that trust, especially with Little John, who stood up for her even when she had no right to expect it of him.

For the first time since she learned archery, Alys's aim was off. Or the sheriff moved. Perhaps in her heart she didn't intend to aim for his shoulder at all. The pointed iron tip pierced the sheriff's neck and blood sprayed onto his ermine collar. Red stained the white fur in splotches and streaks. The shaft of the arrow, with its single red fletch, stuck up out of his neck like a banner once he slumped over the neck of his horse. The sheriff's blood drained onto the horse's mane, dyeing that tawny hair red, too.

Guy called out someone had hit the sheriff. Not killed, hit—but Alys could tell the sheriff was dead. He didn't move despite his horse dancing in circles, like it knew how close it came to danger, though Alys would never have fired at the horse. Like most of Nottingham's residents, the creature had no say over how the sheriff used it.

One soldier galloped toward Alys and Graham, his spear leveled. The metal tip flashed in a ray of sunshine that broke through the clouds. The spear would have skewered Graham if Alys did nothing, but escape to the forest wasn't possible without trampling several men. *If one of us is going to get hit, it will not be Graham.* With one hand, she jerked their horse toward the attacking soldier and his spear.

"What are you—" Graham asked.

Alys didn't respond. The spear stabbed into her right side. The pain was blinding, and the force of the blow knocked her from the horse. When she fell to the ground, she heard something snap under her body.

If I go to St. Peter, let my sacrifice for Graham secure my chance to see Hob.

Under Guy's command, the soldiers organized around the sheriff's horse. Guy grabbed the reins. "You win, Robin," he called. "Let us take his body back to the castle, where it belongs. This battle is yours."

From somewhere on the ridge, Robin said, "My quarrel isn't with you today, Guy. Return to Nottingham; Sherwood is ours!"

The Merry Many took up the claim and chanted "Sherwood is ours!" again and again until Guy, the remaining soldiers, and the dead sheriff's horse had ridden away.

Alys groaned. Her breathing was shallow and short. She stared at the sun beams above; they looked like God's fingers reaching down to the soil. If one of them touched her, maybe she would die and go to Heaven. No purgatorial wait. Would

God forgive her for taking the sheriff's life? Since she offered her own?

Someone pressed the wound on her side, and Alys winced and groaned again. Graham.

"You'll be okay, wee one."

Alys shut her eyes and basked in the warmth of her renewed friendship with Graham.

* * *

Alys woke to muffled voices around her. Her eyes were still closed, but Alys couldn't see the golden blush of the sun beyond her eyelids anymore. *I must be dead.*

She peeled her eyes open to see darkness. *Have I been sent to Hell after all? Perhaps it is not endless fire, but endless darkness. Are those voices the Devil's demons arguing over who may torture me first?* The absence of fear at such a notion surprised her. She closed her eyes. They didn't want to open again, so Alys fell back to sleep. She figured the demons would wake her if they needed her.

The next time Alys opened her eyes, they weren't as sticky. Her side stung and ached, and the skin there felt tight. She tried to move her arm on that side of her body to touch the flesh around the wound, but it took too much effort. A groan bubbled from the back of her throat, and the muffled voices drew closer, as did the glow of a torch.

"Try not to move," Graham said.

"Am I not dead?"

She could hear his smile when he answered. "No, wee one, though you tried."

Half her mouth tipped into a smile before slumber pulled at

her again.

She couldn't tell when time passed. Sometimes it was dark when she woke, and other times there was some pale light at the edge of her vision. Sometimes voices were muted and far away, and other times they were near and clear.

She overheard the Merry Many talk about the sheriff's funeral and Prince John's anger. The prince would travel north, they said, to swear in a new sheriff.

Great. Another man to squeeze the people. Another man to fight against. Alys imagined the prince demanding the head of the sheriff's murderer. She had never seen the prince, but in her mind, he was a shadow, and he wore a black crown and gray robes.

She imagined standing on the gallows, the scratch of the noose around her neck, the suffocation of the hood over her face on a hot day, and how it filled her mouth when she tried to cry out. It didn't matter that it was not summer; her hanging would be on a hot, stuffy, sticky day in her mind. She pictured her parents at the base of the gallows. She imagined them forgiving her and laying flowers at her feet.

"Alys," a voice said. Graham's voice.

She forced her eyes open and waited until they adjusted to the dim, gray light. Graham's face, or at least the highlights and shadows of it, sharpened into view.

"You saved my life. That spear would have been the end of me," he said. "It was almost the end of you. You took a fever, and we thought you would perish."

"I didn't want you to die. I didn't want anyone to die. Not even the sheriff—"

"I know. I thought you were taking us away to freedom. My eyes were on the sheriff and your shot. I didn't notice the other soldier riding at us in time."

"I know." He studied his hands. Graham crouched at her side."

"Yes, well, it's a little hard to ride to freedom when you have a new hole in your body. Besides, I didn't admit what I'd done just to flee Nottinghamshire. What of my parents if I'd left?" Fear froze her like she'd swallowed a bucketful of snow. "My parents—Robin has to get them to safety. T-too many people saw me kill the sheriff. The prince will punish them if he cannot punish me." She tried to sit up, but Graham dropped to a knee and pressed her shoulders down, forcing her to stay flat on the pallet of leaves and sack cloth.

"Don't. You can't go running around yet. Besides, there's a price on your head. But don't worry about your parents. We've already moved them."

Alys's head spun with relief. She closed her eyes for a moment. "Thanks be to God."

"Thanks be to Robin, in this case."

"Where are they?"

Graham released her shoulders. "I don't know. Only Robin knows." When Alys tried to sit up again, he held up a hand. "But he will not tell you, not until you're well."

"How long has it been?"

"Almost a week. They will inter the sheriff tonight. Robin wants a bunch of us to steal from the nobles who will gather there."

"Don't. What if you all get caught?"

He smiled. "I'll stay with you. That way if they get caught, we can rescue them. Besides, someone has to stay and make sure you rest." His voice cracked. "You almost didn't make it, wee one." Graham wrung his hands. "Do you remember when I asked you to marry me?"

"Yes, but—"

"Let me just say this. Even with a price on your head, I want to be with you."

Alys shook her head. "Thank you, Graham, but I do not plan to marry. Just as Maid Marian is devoting herself to God, I plan to devote myself to Nottinghamshire and England. I—I didn't want to marry before and I don't plan to. I'm sorry, but never have I harbored those tender feelings... for anyone."

He closed his eyes. "Very well, wee one. The people are lucky, to have one so brave as you devoted to them."

"And you. We are still friends, are we not?"

Graham stood and beamed down at her. "Aye. We are. You best heal, Alys Fletcher."

"I'm doing my best."

Robin called for Graham at the mouth of the cave. Alys told him to go ahead—they could talk more later; and besides, she needed more sleep. Graham watched her for a moment, and she watched him, silhouetted against the afternoon sun. The beams wrapped around him on their way into the cave and warmed Alys's body. She imagined the sunlight reaching in and healing the wound on her side.

32

Emperors and Kings

Welcome be you, gentle knight,
Welcome are you to me.
-Translated from *A Lytell Geste of Robyn Hode*

A lys didn't track how long her wound took to heal. Her parents were safe, so at least she could rest. There was a price on her head now—fifty whole pounds—so hiding in the cave felt like a good idea. The price on Robin's head was sixty pounds, which meant the prince assumed she was almost as much a threat as Robin.

I'm flattered, in a way.

Graham visited her several times a day. Sometimes she would wake to find him shaving sticks to make arrows. He'd fill her in on how things were going in Locksley and all of Nottinghamshire. The prince had arrived and would stay for a month. The harvest had been a good one, with many hands and dry weather. Marian had gone to Yorkshire to take orders. Wilmot and Alan had forgiven her since she destroyed the sheriff and almost died to save Graham.

"I want to talk to Robin today," she said. "Is he here?"

"Tired of me already, wee one?"

Alys smiled. "No. I want to figure out how we're going to get rid of the bounty. Being outlawed is one thing... having a price on my head is another, and I'm ready to move about."

Graham rubbed his hands on his knees. "Are you sure? There's a sort of peace to be found in taking time to heal."

The last several weeks might have been peaceful if not for the pain in her side, though it'd ebbed away to a light throb by now. Graham sat with his back to the cave wall, and when the sun came in, she saw the furrow in his brow.

"I will be all right," she said. "Don't worry."

"You'll leave. Bounties don't go away on their own."

"Is Robin going to banish me?"

"No, that's not what I—"

"Then talking to him will not mean leaving. He has a bounty on his head, too, and I doubt he plans to abandon Nottinghamshire. I can't live my entire life in a cave, Graham. Safe or not. Even with your friendship, I need to shoot arrows again. I need to see my parents. I need to live a life, have a purpose. You know... although spying on all of you was the wrong thing to do, having a purpose made me forget sometimes how poor my family is. Not forget, not really—that's not what I meant," she said when Graham's jaw dropped open. "But I felt I was helping them. If I spied and did what the sheriff wanted, he'd get my brother home. I hoped he would. I expected my family could work on a farm again."

"You had faith."

Alys nodded.

"With us there's none?"

267

"No; I have faith in all of us, but I can't stay hidden away forever. It will start to feel like a dungeon, and then for all your safeguarding, I'll resent you. Perhaps even hate you."

Graham's jaw clenched and unclenched. "It's possible to be too honest. I'll go get Robin." He stood, but Alys stopped him by grabbing the sleeve of his tunic. "Sorry, wee one. That you don't wish to marry doesn't anger me, but I don't want to imagine you hating me."

"I was teasing; I wouldn't hate you."

A smile flickered across Graham's face. "I'll go get Robin."

Alys released his cuff. She sat back against the cave wall and tried to imagine her parents in a new village. She pictured a small home, perhaps even the size of the house they'd had in Nottingham Town, but cleaner, lighter, where the sun's rays reflected off waves of rye and brightened the house. This new home for them would be bathed in perpetual golden light, even though the harvest had come and gone for the year and the days were getting shorter.

* * *

"Alys Fletcher," Robin said as he entered the cave and approached. "I did not expect you to kill the sheriff."

"I—"

Robin shook his head. "He was a corrupt man."

"It was an accident."

Robin smirked, but it didn't linger on his face. "Well, he's gone, but our work is far from over. The prince didn't take long to put in place another sheriff, one of his own creatures. Your cousin."

Alys sighed and brushed her fingertips over her wool

blanket. "His ambition. But perhaps he'll remove the bounty on my head."

Robin shook his head. "Afraid not. Word is, the prince insisted Sir Guy hunt you down—and me. They've even given us new last names. Hood."

"Oh, that's charming," Alys said, letting the sarcasm seep into the words. "Just like at an execution?"

"Mm hmm. It also binds us." He leaned forward. "I won't let you be caught and executed, Alys Hood."

"So help me, if you try to kiss me, I'm running away."

He pretended to gag, and Alys laughed.

"What are we going to do?" she asked. "If Guy won't lift the bounty, and we can't rely on the prince to—"

"There is one man. One who can free us both from this shadow... and I think he'd be more than glad to."

Alys sat up straighter. "Great! Where is he?"

Robin chewed his lip. "That's the problem. The only man who can overrule the prince is the king. While he left the Holy Land, he's been captured for ransom."

Her jaw hung open. "Captured? So he will not return."

"It's not likely the prince will pay the ransom soon. He covets the throne for himself, as king—not regent. I was considering sending someone to free the king."

"Where is he?"

"Emperor Henry VI holds him captive."

"The pfennigs!"

Robin nodded. "I expect the old sheriff—on behalf of the prince—conspired with Henry to capture Richard, in the event the crusade should end and Richard survive."

Some knot of muscle between Alys's shoulder blades eased. If the sheriff had acted against the king in this way, it wasn't such a bad thing he was gone… though Alys conceded it was wrong that he hadn't been tried for his crimes. Guy might be ambitious, but he would never commit treason. "How will we recover the king from the Holy Roman Emperor?"

"Short of raising one-hundred fifty thousand marks, we will have to orchestrate a daring escape. Can you think of anyone who's led such an escape lately?" There was a gleam in his eye.

"Me? You want me to go to Almany and rescue the King of England? I'm just a peasant, a—"

"Can't trust anyone outside our group—they might work for your cousin, or worse—the prince. I believe in your ability, Alys. Besides, you are no mere peasant. You are Alys Hood. My kin now, by name if not by blood. Noble blood runs through your veins. And, you're a member of the Merry Many."

"I don't know…"

"I'm sure he would lift the bounties for your securing his freedom and bringing him home. And then we could intercede for the others. Well, except Friar Tuck; he was never outlawed."

That the friar spent so much time with them, helped them, even though he was not an outlaw, raised Alys's esteem of him even higher. "But—shouldn't it be you to go since you know the king?"

"Perhaps. But I am known here. Even if I wanted to leave England…"

"I'm not sure I can do this, Robin."

"Alys. You can ride, you can shoot, you can fight."

"Are you saying I'd make an able soldier?"

"Soldier, spy, savior of the people. I should not have been so dismissive of you when I went to the Holy Land.

Perhaps—perhaps Hob would have come home if I'd let you join in our ranks. To me, back then, you were nothing more than a farm girl. I knew not that you had the heart—and skill—of a fighter." Robin cleared his throat and looked up at the top of the cave. "I was—I was wrong."

Alys smiled. "Savior of the people." *Robin may not wish to call me that should I fail. But I must try, for Robin, for myself, for England. But what of my parents? And Grandda?* Alys decided she owed it to them to earn a pardon before risking visiting her family. "Well then. I suppose I can't say no, can I?"

"You could, but if you did, you wouldn't be the person you've become." Robin settled a hand on her shoulder. "You have your honor now. I will send one of the Merry Many with you, so you'll be with a friend you can trust."

Alys nodded, and Robin left the cave, but not before pressing a pfennig into her hand. She pulled her knees to her chest, which stretched and pinched her scar from the spear thrust, so she loosened her hold on her legs. Alys tried to imagine herself leaving not only Nottinghamshire but also England. Here in Nottinghamshire, Alys felt as though she recognized every tree, every hedgerow, every farm. To go some place she couldn't picture was an undertaking that stole her breath.

England needed its king. Even if Guy was kinder than the previous sheriff, the prince would, through him, continue to squeeze the people. Their suffering would see no end if that tyrant became King John.

Alys opened her hand and looked at the coin. The Holy Roman Emperor. The sheriff's army would seem like toy soldiers compared with the forces the emperor commanded. She and Graham were going to a land they didn't know, to elude a massive force they didn't understand, to free—Alys did not doubt—the emperor's most valued prisoner. She blew out a breath and turned the coin over and over in her hand, memorizing the profile of Henry VI.

Graham returned after a little while.

"Did Robin tell you his plan?" Alys asked.

He sat beside her, one ankle crossed over the other. "He did."

"What do you think?"

"Well, wee one, I think the question is… what do you think?"

Alys pressed her lips together. "I think I have to go, but I would rather you come with me."

"So talking with Robin did mean you're leaving."

"Well, yes… but for good reason. And I am choosing to take this on, not succumbing to force or manipulation. Will you join me?"

Graham scratched at his beard. "I'll have to think on it."

"Don't jest."

He laughed. "Of course I'll go with you. It's not like I have any family here anymore and if Robin doesn't mind—I swore my sword was his."

Alys wondered at the ease with which Graham agreed. It would be a long, arduous journey with little chance of success. Despite this, his decision and friendship warmed her, and Alys felt her gratitude swell to form a protective barrier, so nothing could harm her. "Good. Because we're going to need your sword and my bow… and possibly an army of our own to rescue the king." She tossed the pfennig to Graham.

He caught the coin and held it up to examine it in the light. "Ever think you'd meet an emperor?"

A derisive laugh escaped Alys. "I was a mess when I met the sheriff."

"Maybe we ought to practice on the way. Can't have you falling to pieces at the mere sight of a crown."

"How about you?"

"The Holy Roman Emperor? No. But I've seen Prince John before. Mind, he wasn't all that close, but he was close enough for me to see a lot of jewels on his crown."

"That one man should have so much while most people have so little…"

Graham flipped the pfennig back to Alys. "That's why we do what we do."

The coin was warm from his hand. She nodded. "That's why we do what we do."

33

Forest Farewell

With a careful cheer,
The tears out of his eyes ran,
And fell down by his linen.
-Translated from *A Lytell Geste of Robyn Hode*

Another week passed before Alys was strong enough to travel. She could eat anything she wanted now without stomach pains, and she spent her mornings firing arrows and practicing with her sword. At first, her practice was slow, deliberate, gentle. But over the course of the week, she started working harder, pushing her muscles to burn a little by sundown.

She learned how to skin a hare, how to debone a fish, how to dress a wound so it was less likely to fester. Alys took whatever knowledge the Merry Many would give her. She already knew how to build and bank a fire from her days serving Maid Marian. She had some hunting skills from her childhood with Da and Hob, when they would go into the green wood with the other villagers after the harvest to kill wild pigs for their tables. It was illegal in most parts, but back then the sheriff of Nottingham had been a different man, a kinder man, and had gotten dispensation from the king based on centuries of precedent dating back to before William the Conqueror landed on English soil. Back then, Grandda had always said, peasants had more rights and were not burdened by a tax on every piece of straw. But Alys had never prepared the animals after they were hunted. She didn't want to make her or Graham sick, because their journey would be an important one. They might be the ones to bring the king home and end the tyranny in England.

Alys sat, skinning a squirrel one afternoon. *The cruel sheriff may be dead, but the prince is alive and well.* He was just as ruthless as the sheriff—maybe worse. And Guy was too ambitious to put the people first, even if he wasn't outright wicked. The war in the Holy Land had ended; it was time for the king to return. Only then would the work of the Merry Many be complete. Only then could life return to normal.

On the day they'd picked to leave, Alys first made her way over to where Robin sat on the stump. He was tying a long leather lace with a feather and some charms on it.

"This," he said, "is for you. It's the fletching from one of your father's arrows... the last batch he made for me. With a charm for protection."

Alys smiled and accepted the necklace. "Thank you. I didn't realize that my da was supplying you with arrows." *Da. My family. I might never see them again.* Once more, Alys resolved herself to wait to visit them until it was safe to do so.

"Good. That means the secret stayed a secret. Your father would be proud of you."

"Oh, I don't know. Both my parents wished I would have married, had a family, lived nearby…"

"Not everyone is meant for that life. For those who seek it…" His voice sounded pained. Robin cleared his throat and stood. "Trust me. Your parents would both be proud. You're fighting now to make England a better place."

"I'm sorry, Robin. That you and Marian couldn't marry."

He looked away, into the distance. "At least I am certain she is safe."

Alys nodded and thanked him again for the necklace, then slipped it on. She wondered if the Merry Many would be camped somewhere else by the time she and Graham returned—if they lived through this quest. Alys looked back and smiled. The cave was a place of refuge, a place of healing, a place of friendship for her.

She walked to the edge of the clearing. The Merry Many had packed provisions and furs into the saddlebags of the horse Alys and Graham had taken when they rode toward the wood, pursued by the sheriff and his men. Alys ran her hand along the horse's face, right between his eyes.

"I'm not sure if you have a name already," she said, "but I'm going to call you Barnaby. My brother always wanted to name a horse Barnaby, and he was kind and brave, and so too shall you be. You can have his last name, too. Barnaby Fletcher. It's going to be a long journey; I'm glad you're accompanying us." The horse nuzzled her hand, and Alys regretted she didn't have a treat for him. She promised to get him something nice once they were out of England.

Wilmot approached. "I made you something. In honor of when we first met, Alys Hood."

"You—you did? You didn't have to do that."

Wilmot held out a bow. It wasn't a longbow, but short, with a double curved shape. She accepted it and traced the lines, brow furrowed.

"It's called a recurve bow. Robin saw them in the Holy Land and we've been working on this one since he returned and came out to live in Sherwood. We've tested it to make sure it works. It's smaller, lighter, but just as powerful as a long bow. And it's made of yew. We thought since yours broke when you fell on it after killing the sheriff..."

Alys ran her hands along it again. "Thank you, Wil. It's perfect." She pulled the bow over her shoulder.

"You're welcome. There's also a quiver full of arrows—the finest Nottinghamshire has to offer. I expect you'll recognize the craftsmanship."

With a smile, Alys rounded Barnaby and saw a quiver full of her da's arrows. She ran her fingers over the fletching feathers. "I couldn't ask for any better, Wilmot." A lump formed in her throat. Her da couldn't craft arrows anymore. But he was safe now, cared for now, somewhere. Alys was desperate to learn where, but perhaps it was best not to delay her journey to the king any longer. What if visiting them led to my arrest? Or trouble for them?

Wilmot dipped his head and walked away, and Alys took the bow off her shoulder to examine it some more. The draw was perfect; she could feel her muscles at work, but it wasn't so powerful that she couldn't fire off more than a handful of arrows if needed. She eased the bowstring and then fastened the bow to the saddle. It'd be within easy reach, but she hoped she wouldn't need it in battle. Alys had no wish to kill anyone ever again, and hoped to only use it for hunting.

"We made it back in time," Little John said with a smile. Alan and Friar Tuck were with him. "We have some provisions for you."

Alan held out a cloth sack. "In here you'll find some salted pork, a bag of salt, water skeins, and a half wheel of cheese."

"And…" Little John said.

"Oh," Alan said, "and apples."

"Thank you." Alys accepted the bag and fastened it to the saddle. Barnaby pawed the ground. "Too heavy?" The horse, whether or not he understood, shook his head and chuffed. Alys smiled and patted his neck.

Little John patted Barnaby, too. "He's a fine horse."

"Any last words of advice?"

"Don't kill unless you have to… but you already know that." Little John smiled. "Oh, and do whatever you must in order to come back. Now that you're one of us, we'd rather like to see you again."

Friar Tuck held something else out for her. Another necklace, this one a simple wooden cross. "We made that for you, too. To protect you. To remind you that you can have forgiveness, that God loves you, child."

Alys accepted the gift with a smile of gratitude and pulled it over the necklace Robin had given her. "I—no matter what happens, I won't forget any of you. Even if we don't see one another until the next life. Keep each other alive and safe." After a moment's hesitation, Alys hugged Little John, then Friar Tuck, and then Alan. "Give Wilmot a hug for me."

"I'm not hugging Wilmot," Alan said. "But I'll tell him."

Then it was just her and Barnaby. Graham was readying his supplies and weapons. She patted the horse and pressed her forehead to the side of his neck and inhaled his scent. He smelled of the forest and of animal. She combed her fingers through his mane. "Last chance to back out."

The horse nudged her.

"I'm not backing out, either."

Barnaby pricked his ears. They turned toward the sound of footsteps in the brush.

"You didn't think I'd send you thousands of miles away without saying goodbye, did you?" Robin asked from behind her.

Alys whirled and smiled. "I thought we already said goodbye."

"That wasn't goodbye. Besides, I drew you a rough map." Robin held it out and Alys reached for it, but he didn't release it yet. "It will help you find the king and then find your way home. Come back to us, Alys."

Heat and pressure increased behind her eyes; she blinked to keep the tears away. "I plan to."

"Take care of yourself. We are like siblings now, yes?"

"Yes. The Hood siblings."

Robin grinned. "And when you return—"

"If, you mean."

"No, I mean when. When you return, we will welcome you back into the Merry Many as family. As one of us."

Map forgotten for a moment, Alys launched herself forward and hugged Robin. At first, he only leaned back to absorb her momentum, but then his arms closed around her. She released him and stepped back.

"Anything else I should know before I go?"

"Much. Too much to tell you in a day, a week, a month even. I'm afraid you'll have to learn a lot for yourself. You and Graham should take time to train every day, even if it makes your journey take longer. You never know when it may save your life."

Alys felt heavier after Robin's advice. She tried—and failed—to swallow three times before she gulped the tightness in her throat away. "We'll look after one another," she vowed.

"I do not doubt it," Robin said.

Graham walked over with more weapons than she'd ever seen on him. He wore a sword on his hip, a dagger on the other hip, and a battle axe on his back. She could see the handle of a knife sticking out of one boot. Alys's eyes widened.

"Where'd you get all that?" she asked.

"The soldiers dropped some of it a few weeks back. The axe has a small nick in it, but it could still be useful."

"If nothing but as a deterrent. No one is going to want to attack you with such a weapon," Alys said. "But that's good."

Alys unfolded the map and looked at it. Robin had drawn a trail that went from England to Venice, then on to Austria and Almany. An alternate route by land through France was also marked. She paled.

"It seems a long way," Robin said, "and it is. But you will avoid most of the mountains traveling along this path." He traced the line that moved around so much of Europe to Venice. "And there is much to see along the way which will make the journey enjoyable. I've marked some places I found most fascinating on the map," he said. "Oh, and there's money for passage by sea in one of the saddlebags."

Graham thanked Robin because Alys couldn't find her voice.

Alys tucked the map into the purse at her belt. The Merry Many gathered to say farewell, and she took Barnaby's lead. Graham took his place beside her, and they walked away from the camp after giving everyone else a wave. Alys's arm was stiff, resistant to the goodbye.

"It's best if we avoid the roads in England," Graham said.

Alys agreed. "Wouldn't do to be caught and hanged before we can even reach the coast."

Graham smiled. "Aye, wee one."

Alys basked in the nickname he'd given her. She had a family in the Merry Many, as well as her parents and Grandda. Losing Hob would always leave a hole in her heart, a scar, but as with the wound to her side, the Merry Many would keep it from claiming her life.

For the first time in a long time, she felt hopeful. Scared, but hopeful, and that hope wasn't tainted by amoral actions. At least she wasn't alone. Together they would find the king, secure his release and pardon, bring him home, and England would be safe from tyranny. They would enjoy a normal life without threat of arrest or execution.

Alys had always known she was destined for adventure, but she never dreamed it would fall to her to save England and the lionhearted king.

Author's Note

The Robin Hood legend has always been a favorite of mine. When I first conceptualized Alys's story, I came into it having seen more renditions of this legend than I could count on two hands. I'd even volunteered at a Robin Hood-themed Renaissance faire so I could step into something closer to this Medieval legend (though I learned that Renaissance faires, while fun, are chock-full of anachronisms like Robin and Queen Elizabeth I hosting a jousting tournament together). I wanted something more.

I read the original ballads that represent the first written tradition of the Robin Hood legend (if you like the challenge of reading Middle English, I recommend them). The Robin I met in those pages was somewhat different from the Robin Hood of so many more recent representations. I didn't want my Robin to be quite so harsh as I found him to be in some of the ballads, but I did want to make him more flawed, more human. His band of merry thieves were also often referred to as the Merry Many, which I used in this book. After all, there have often been females in the group, so to call them the Merry Men feels wrong.

I also didn't want Robin to be the star of this retelling, even though it's retelling *his* legend. I believe that all of us can strive to encapsulate some of his generous spirit in providing for our fellow humans. We don't need bows and arrows to be heroic; we just need to care for others.

While I tried to imbue as much historical accuracy as possible in this story, it is a work of fiction that seeks to pull together inspiration from a number of representations of a legend that are not always in agreement. For the sake of familiarity, I chose to place my story during the Third Crusade, even though some aspects of the traditional Robin Hood legend suggest he may have lived much earlier—perhaps even before the Norman Conquest of 1066. The legend of Robin Hood as it is commonly known today is rife with historical inaccuracy. For example, a famous character—Friar Tuck—would not have been possible during the 1190s, since the pope did not create the position of friar until early in the 13th century. I took a lot of liberties with the character of the sheriff; there was indeed a real sheriff of Nottingham in the late 12th century, but my sheriff is more based on the legend with some changes for the sake of this story. This book should be read with the understanding that I, as an author of a fictional work, may have taken certain liberties with the past in order to craft this tale.

A note on time: There are some time cues in this novel, but I purposefully kept them to a bare minimum. Someone raised as a peasant as Alys was would not have concerned herself with the abstract reckoning of time we use today (hours, days, weeks, months, etc.). To a peasant of the 12th century, seasonal time was more important. Alys would have cared more about when to sow and reap crops than what the time of year was actually called. Religious feast days drove the reckoning of time more than anything else, but as Alys isn't as religious as most of her contemporaries, I did not want to pull in too many mentions of feast days, either.

A note on weather: Could Alys and the Merry Many live in a cave during the winter? The short answer is yes. There were periods of warmth and though the temperature records for the UK extend as far back as the 17th century (before going into eras such as the ice age), there were periods of excessive warmth that led to wintertime lows around 60 degrees F in the middle of Britain.

A note about language: For a story that took place in England during the 12th century, court proceedings would likely have been conducted in Old French. Thanks to the Norman Invasion of 1066 (referenced as the arrival of William the Conqueror in my book), Middle English was not used in an official, legal capacity. Similarly, Modern English didn't even exist yet. Had I written the novel in Middle English, it would have been inaccessible to most readers. To this end, I even modernized the language of the snippets from the original Robin Hood ballads. While I tried to avoid anachronistic diction wherever possible, I had to weigh that against readability. I always put my reader first as much as I could. I did craft certain characters to have a different voice—for example, Marian tends to speak in a formal voice and the sheriff speaks in passive voice much of the time (especially when he's making decrees). Alys's ma tries to speak like Marian, but when she's angry she reverts to a more informal pattern of speech; she is trying to keep her noble roots front and center, but fails when her emotions overwhelm her. This was all intentionally done to add a historical feeling to the text without making it unreadable.

I tried my best to honor how I think it would feel to live in the Medieval era. Alys bucks against a difficult choice, since adult women who were not wives, nuns, or prostitutes were rare (read: not impossible). The village itself was an important unit in Medieval society, and I hope that Alys's longing for her family to be restored in Locksley captures this. While there are other villages in Nottinghamshire, Locksley is the only one mentioned by name in this book on purpose—it is *that* important to Alys.

A note on the derivation of the name Hood: In my research, I discovered many possible meanings of this last name. Most of my research pointed to the idea that this was not Robin's legal name, but one given to him either by the people, the sheriff, or ambiguous translation work. I chose for it to come from the execution hood, but other sources suggest it might be related to the Wood, indicating Sherwood Forest. It could also be a reference to *rood*, a Middle English word indicating the cross on which Jesus Christ was sacrificed, and therefore be a religious metaphor comparing Robin's sacrifice of his nobility and wealth for the people to Christ's. The reason I made the choice to pull it from the execution hood is that in the latter portion of this novel, Alys often worries about the consequences of her choices, and Robin sharing this name from her with the derivation I chose allows her to subvert the crooked justice that the sheriff represented.

Where Alys's asexuality is concerned, I drew from my own experiences—in that some are accepting of asexuality while others fear it, do not understand it, and use other societal norms and fears to try to pressure asexual persons into acting against their asexuality. I wanted Graham to ultimately accept her asexuality, even though he doesn't understand it, to allow Alys to truly love him as a friend and ally. Alys happens to be both asexual and aromantic, and the story within these pages is specific to her—asexuality represents a wide range of orientations and experiences, and no one character can possibly represent them all. To learn more about ace orientations, visit The Asexuality Visibility and Education Network at asexuality.org.

Acknowledgments

Even when a book is independently published, it takes a village. I'd like to grasp this opportunity to thank the village of people without whom this story would never have seen the light of day.

To Rachel McNellis, Lisa Landa, Rebecca Cubells, Laurelann Easton, Joe Winkler, Deborah Lucas, Elli Comeau, Sarah Kuchta-Humphrey, Diane Kuchta-Humprhey, Storm Kuchta, & Morgan Green, thank you for beta reading, for questioning what didn't work and for inspiring me to shape this story until it did.

Special thanks to Rachel McNellis, my mom, for listening to me read the original Robin Hood ballads in Middle English & give her a guided tour of my own version of Locksley Village. It takes true unconditional love to listen to someone try to translate Middle English to Modern English on the fly or squint at a little map of a Medieval village and try to find the little drawings of anatomically incorrect pigs.

Special thanks to Rebecca Cubells for asking me the tough questions about indie publishing, which helped me realize, along with Author Accelerator's Navigating the Path to Publishing course, that this was the journey I wished to take for this book.

Thank you to Tabitha Wintermute, for always listening to me go on about this story, for receiving every text with excitement equal to my own, and for inspiring me to continue the work of writing stories from the past.

Thank you to Susanne Dunlap, who not only has my admiration as a fellow book coach, but especially as an author of historical fiction. You have my eternal gratitude for inviting me to host a joint-launch party with you and devoting your time to this story. Thank you for welcoming me on your podcast, It's Just Historical.

Thank you to Stuart Luca-Wakefield, both for your excitement for my book launch, and for welcoming me on your podcast, Write-Hearted.

Thank you to Jo Knowles, who not only inspired me to write a story for young adult readers, but always showed up with kindness, authenticity, and integrity.

To Rachel B. Glaser, thank you both for your insights and for keeping me on track during the 2020 pandemic. My summer would have been a fallow one—and perhaps this book might not have seen the light of day—without you.

Thank you to Mitch Wieland, who helped me develop a stronger understanding of crafting a character's interior journey. This book would have been fun, but not as meaningful, without the lessons I learned from you.

Thank you to Robin Wasserman, who helped me discover my style. Both my prose and characters found their voice because of the work we did together.

Thank you to Lydia Peelle, who helped me learn how to play in writing. Without that mindset, this story would never have made it past the first draft.

To Rachel Means, a fellow book coach, who helped me bring Alys into her own with a thoughtful alpha read, thank you. Alys jumps off the page because of your honest editing work as someone far more likable than she once was.

To Travis Bevis and Phil Lemos, who helped me feel like I could and should write characters who identified as ace, who helped me live authentically, thank you from the bottom of my heart.

To Jennie Nash and all of Author Accelerator, thank you for the skills to understand story on yet another level, guiding me in choosing the indie publisher path, and giving me the confidence to set a publication date.

To Fiona Duncan and The Magickal Path School, thank you for the guidance that helped me bolster my confidence to bring this book to fruition.

Thank you to the Henry Carter Hull Library Creative Writing Group, who heard the first draft of chapter one and gave me excellent feedback.

To these named individuals and so many more friends, family, fellow book coaches, and faculty mentors who offered support, open ears, and willingly traveled back in time with me almost 1,000 years while I talked and thought about Alys's story, thank you. You helped me breathe new life into one of my favorite legends of all time.

Finally, to you, my reader, thank you. Without you, Alys and her story would live in the confines of my mind, and nowhere else.

Stay tuned for Alys's next adventure in OUTLAWED.

About the Author

Margaret holds a B.A. in Art History, an M.A. in English & Creative Writing, an MFA in Fiction, and she also has a graduate certificate in the teaching of composition.

Margaret writes primarily historical/herstorical fiction for adults and young adults.

She has over a decade of professional freelance writing and editing experience, and a few years' experience teaching and tutoring in English. She now works as a book coach and author. Margaret is a member of the Historical Novel Society, JASNA, and SCBWI.

You can connect with me on:

- https://www.mcnelliswrites.com
- https://www.goodreads.com/mcnelliswrites

Made in the USA
Middletown, DE
09 September 2021

47251173R00177